T0208939

On her seventeenth birthday, Megan of Chaumont discovers she'll be sold as a bride to the brutish Volodane family—within hours. Her father grants only that she may choose which one of the ruthless, grasping lord's three sons she weds:

~ Rolf, the eldest: stern, ambitious, and loyal?

~ Sebastian, the second son: sympathetic, sly, and rebellious?

~ Or Kai, the youngest: bitter, brooding, and proud?

As shy, horrified Megan flees the welcome dinner for her in-laws-to-be, she finds an enchanted mirror that will display how her life unrolls with each man, as if she were living it out in a breath. But there is no smooth "happily ever after" in her choices.

Deaths and honors, joys and agonies, intrigues and escapes await her in a remote, ramshackle keep, where these rough but complex men reveal one side and then another of their jagged characters—and bring forth new aspects of Megan, too. But the decisions of one teenaged marriage-pawn reverberate much further than any of them have guessed . . .

THROUGH A DARK GLASS

New York Times bestselling author Barb Hendee spins a tale of castles and assassins, ambition and envy, toil and desire, as one woman lives out three very different lives . . .

Visit us at www.kensingtonbooks.com

Through a Dark Glass

Barb Hendee

REBEL BASE BOOKS
Kensington Publishing Corp.
www.kensingtonbooks.com

Prologue

Late in my life, at a gathering of friends, I heard a story that caused me to sit down and tremble.

It meant nothing to the others who were listening, but it meant something to me. I simply couldn't remember what.

The story went like this . . .

Long ago, a vain lord enslaved a young witch so that he might force her to use her powers to keep himself handsome and youthful. His most prized possession was an ornate three-paneled mirror via which he could see himself from several angles. He loved to gaze in its panels and admire his own beauty.

Seeking revenge on him, the young witch began secretly imbuing this mirror with power, planning to trap him in the reflection of the three panels where he would view different outcomes of his useless life over and over. He would see himself growing old and unwanted and alone.

Though the young witch had once been kind and generous, her thirst for vengeance began to twist her nature into something else.

Unknown to her, as she continued to cast power into the mirror, it came to gain a will and awareness of its own.

One night, the lord caught her as she worked her magic, and he realized she was attempting to enchant his beloved mirror. In a rage, he drew a dagger and killed her. But her spirit fled into the mirror, seeking escape, and there she was once again enslaved . . . this time by the mirror itself.

It whispered to her that it would protect her and use the power she'd given it for tasks more important than punishing a petty, vain lord. Together they would seek out those facing difficult decisions and show them outcomes to their choices.

"Wait!" she cried, inside the mirror. "What does that mean?"
The mirror then vanished from the lord's room.
Where would it appear again?

Chapter 1

I was trapped, and I knew it. Worse, it came as a shock on my seventeenth birthday, the same day my elder sister died.

Daughters of the nobility are mere tools for their families, so in truth, what transpired shouldn't have come as such a surprise, but I'd been trained and honed as a different type of tool than my sister, Helena.

She was beautiful, tall and well figured with ivory skin, green eyes, and a mass of silken red hair. She was quick-witted and skilled in the art of conversation. When she walked into a room, all heads turned. She expected everything in life to come to her just as she wished, and as a result, it usually did. Our father had always intended to profit from her by way of a great marriage to improve our family's fortune.

In contrast, I was small and slight, with light brown eyes and dark blond hair. Although I was much better read than Helena, my prowess in circles of social conversation normally amounted to nodding and appearing attentive to those more proficient than myself.

Helena was the shining star of our family.

Yet, on my seventeenth birthday, I stood over her bed, wringing my hands as she lay dying. Her once ivory face had gone sickly white, and her green eyes were closed as she struggled to breathe, each attempt resulting in a gasp followed by a rattle.

My mother stood beside me, looking down at the bed, her face unreadable.

"She may yet recover," I said by way of attempted comfort. "She has always been strong."

I shouldn't have bothered.

My mother glanced at me in contempt. Like Helena, she was tall with red hair, and she had no patience for offers of false comfort.

Only three days ago, Helena had complained of feeling warm at our midday meal. Shortly after, she'd been helped to her bed by several of the household servants, and within hours, the fever had taken hold. In a panic, my father had called upon our physician, who had done what he could—which in my opinion hadn't been much. The illness settled quickly into Helena's lungs.

Although I had been allowed inside her room, I'd not been allowed to touch her.

As Mother and I stood over her, my sister fought for one last breath. The following rattle was loud, and then all sounds vanished from the room as Helena went still. Looking down, I didn't know what to feel. We had not been close, but she was still my sister.

As if summoned, my father walked in, dressed in a blue silk tunic and black pants. He was of medium height with broad shoulders and a thick head of light brown hair. He shaved his face twice a day.

"Well?" he asked.

"She's gone," my mother answered. "Just now."

Father frowned, but that was all. His initial panic at the prospect of losing a valuable tool like Helena had passed yesterday—for he was ever a realist.

Walking over to the bed, he didn't even look at his eldest daughter. Instead, he looked at me, and I couldn't help noting the disappointment in his eyes. "Megan," he said. "The Volodanes arrive this afternoon. You'll have to take Helena's place."

I blinked several times, not certain I'd heard him correctly.

"Take her place? What does that . . .?"

"You know what it means," he said coldly. Then he turned to my mother. "Make sure she's presentable."

I took a step backward as the awful truth set in.

The Volodanes were arriving afternoon.

And I was to take Helena's place.

* * * *

Less than hour later, I found myself seated at the dressing table in my own room, wearing a muslin dress of sunflower yellow—that had been hanging in my closet for over a year—and staring at my own reflection as my maid, Miriam, tried to do something with my hair.

Her mouth was tightly set, and she was not any happier about the situation. Miriam was pretty with dark hair, and only five years older than myself. She'd been hired by my mother when I was fifteen and Mother had deemed it necessary that I should have a "lady's maid." I'd resisted at first but not for long. Miriam had soon become devoted to me, and I welcomed her friendship.

The turn of events today had taken her by surprise.

"Your father was very clear," she said, holding handfuls of thick hair. While the color might not be enticing, at least it was abundant. "I may have to cut a few pieces in the front."

"Do what you must," I answered quietly.

Normally, I had Miriam weave my hair into a single thick braid, as no one cared too much about my appearance. All my life, I'd been told that I would never marry, that I'd remain here in my family's manor serving as a shadow advisor to my father, for I possessed a unique . . . skill that was of use to him.

He was the head of our great family, the house of Chaumont, and he held a seat on the Council of Nobles that met four times a year in the capital city of Partheney.

The power and prestige of our name reached back over eight hundred years, and every family for five hundred leagues envied us our name, our bloodlines, and our political power. Unfortunately, noble bloodlines don't always correlate into wise financial management, and my grandfather had nearly run our reserves of wealth into the ground. He drank. He gambled. To pay debts, he'd sold off our more lucrative investments such as the family's silver mines, which decreased our income.

Though my father possessed greater wisdom, upon inheriting the family title, he'd fought to make a good show of things, to try and prove we were not paupers. This had meant quietly borrowing large sums of money, and now several of those debts were being called in.

To his great relief, Helena had proven herself everything he'd hoped for, and in recent months, he'd made an arrangement to solve all his immediate financial woes.

Another family, the Volodanes—of noble birth so low they were scorned by the better families—had made my father an unprecedented offer.

When a young woman married, a part of her worth was determined by the size of her dowry. Lord Jarrod, the head of the house of Volodane, had offered a small fortune in exchange for Helena marrying one of his three sons. For while the Volodanes might suffer snubs for their painfully low birth, in recent years, they'd become one of the wealthiest families in the nation. They had money in silver, in cattle, in wheat, and in wine. They also ruled their own territories in the north without mercy and taxed their peasants nearly dry. Now, they wanted to use this wealth to link their name to the name of a great family.

Jarrod offered to forgo a cash dowry and pay my father a great deal of money for Helena. She in turn would bring certain furnishings from Chaumont Manor to make it appear as a dowry. In this way, the secret could be kept.

My father had jumped at the bargain.

At first, my mother and Helena had not. They'd both been appalled at the thought of regal Helena tied forever to some brute who most likely had no idea how to dine at a proper table. But instead of ordering Helena to obey, our father had cajoled her, and then he'd promised that of the three brothers, she would be allowed to meet them and choose one for herself. Then he'd appealed to her sense of family honor and obligation.

In the end, he got his way . . . and this afternoon, the Volodanes would arrive so that Helena might spend time in conversation with the young men, allowing her to make her choice.

But my sister was dead.

Staring at myself in the small mirror of my dressing table, I wondered what a slap in the eye I was going to be.

Miriam continued twisting my thick hair and piled it on top my head. She left several strands in the front loose, and before I could follow what she was doing, she took up a pair of scissors and snipped those strands at about the length of my jaw. The strands instantly curled up to frame my face. The result was astonishing. I *did* look a bit more like a lady than I had a few moments before.

She put small silver earrings in my earlobes and then drew something from her pocket. I blanched. It was a diamond pendant.

"That's Helena's," I said.

She glanced away. "You mother wants you to wear it."

Without another word, I let her fasten it around my neck. This was only the beginning. Miriam wasn't even dressing me for dinner yet—but rather to help greet the Volodanes when they rode into the courtyard.

I rose from the dressing table.

"You look lovely, miss," she said. "You should go down."

I didn't feel lovely. I felt a knot growing in my stomach, and I wanted to reach out and grip her hand. In the entire manor, Miriam was the only one who cared for me, and she had no power.

So, I left my room and made my way down the stairs, past the great dining hall, and down the passage to the main front doors. The guard there opened the doors for me, and I stepped outside into the open courtyard.

My father, my mother, and six other manor guards stood waiting.

Turning, my father looked me up and down. Instead of looking at me, my mother looked at him. His eyes focused on my sunflower-yellow gown and my hair. Then he nodded once at my mother in approval. She returned to her vigil of waiting for the Volodanes.

I held back, near the doors. We didn't wait long.

I heard several of our guards down at the front gates calling to each other before I saw anything. Then I heard the grinding of the gates being opened . . . followed by the sounds of hoof beats.

Within moments, an entire retinue pounded into our courtyard, led by four men—one out front and three riding behind. This quartet was followed by at least thirty guards. I wondered where we were going to house them all.

Then my attention focused entirely on the four men at the front.

Although I had never met any of them myself, and neither had Helena, she'd been provided with a good deal of information, and before falling ill, she'd spoken of little else in the last weeks of her life.

It wasn't difficult to note Jarrod, the father, riding at the lead. As he drew closer, my trepidation began to grow. He appeared in his late forties, tall and hawkish. His head was shaved. He wore chain armor over a faded black wool shirt that had seen many washings. My eyes dropped to the sword sheathed on his hip.

My own father never wore a sword.

As Jarrod pulled his frothing horse to a stop, I turned my gaze to the three men behind him. Again, it wasn't difficult for me to name them by gauging their age.

Rolf was the eldest, in his late twenties. Like his father, he wore his head shaved and he wore chain armor, but there the resemblance stopped. There was nothing hawkish about Rolf. He was muscular and wide-shouldered with broad features and a bump at the bridge of his nose. Every inch of him exuded hardness and strength.

I shivered in the summer air.

Next came Sebastian, in his mid twenties. He was smaller than either of his brothers, with neatly cut black hair. Noticing my attention, he flashed me a smile. He was handsome, and the only one not wearing armor. Instead, he wore a sleeveless tunic over a white wool shirt. I had a feeling Sebastian cared about his appearance.

Last came Kai—wearing armor and weapons. He looked only a few years older than me. In many ways, he resembled his father, tall and slender with sharp features. But he wore his brown hair down past his shoulders. His gaze moved to the front of the manor, which was constructed of expensive light-toned stone.

As Kai took in the latticed windows, whitewashed shutters, and climbing ivy vines, his features twisted into what I could only call an expression of resentful anger. If hardness rolled off Rolf and vanity rolled off Sebastian, it was anger that rolled off Kai.

Jarrod jumped down from his horse and strode up to my father.

"Chaumont," he said shortly, not bothering with my father's title or given name.

Both men gauged each other in mild discomfort, and it occurred to me that this was their first meeting. All marriage negotiations had transpired in writing or by proxy. Under normal circumstances, a family as lowborn as the Volodanes would never be invited to Chaumont Manor—and they knew it.

My father nodded and responded in kind. "Volodane."

Then Jarrod's dark eyes swept the courtyard, stopping briefly on me before moving onward, and he frowned.

My father leaned forward, speaking softly. I watched Jarrod's expression flicker in surprise, and to his credit he said, "Oh . . . my condolences."

A few more quiet words were exchanged, and I heard my father say, "daughter, Megan." Jarrod's eyes turned to me again, this time in cold assessment. After all, he had never seen Helena and only heard the tales of her beauty. He had nothing with which to compare her. I struggled to look back and hold his gaze. After a moment, he nodded his assent.

"Good, then," my father agreed, sounding relieved. "You must be tired from your journey. We'll all meet again at dinner." He seemed equally relieved this initial meeting was over and he was now able to extract himself.

But the knot in my stomach tightened at the thought of leaving my home and going with these men, with a warrior for a father and one of his sons for my husband.

Trapped or not, I couldn't do this.

I would refuse.

* * * *

My father and mother both went to the room he used as his study, and without asking permission, I followed them in and closed the door. They were both taken aback by my boldness. This was certainly something Helena might have done, but not me.

"I can't do it," I said instantly. "And I cannot believe you would force me."

Mother's eyes narrowed in caution. I had never spoken to either of them like this. My father's face turned red in anger, but my mother held up one hand to stop his tongue.

"Megan," she began slowly. "Of course I understand your reticence. It is beneath us to even have them in the house, but this must be done, and the middle son . . . Sebastian? He looks less savage than the others. Could you not consider him?"

I stared at her. "Less savage? You would have me in his bed merely because he seems less savage than his brothers?"

She flinched at the indelicacy of my question and then drew herself to full height. "And would you have our situation exposed? Our debts known publicly? Would you have bailiffs in the manor taking our paintings and tapestries and furniture? Would you have your father disgraced from his seat on the Council of Nobles?"

Feeling myself begin to deflate, I shook my head. "Of course not."

The anger left my father's face, and he stepped toward me. "Jarrod has already agreed to my provision that Helena choose from among his sons. He doesn't care which of them marries into the house of Chaumont. He wants only the prestige of the connection and grandsons who carry our blood. You'll have the same provision as your sister. You can choose."

"And if I don't?"

His eyes hardened. "Then I will pick one myself, drag you to the magistrate, and use my power as your father to answer and sign for you."

Breathing grew difficult as I realized he meant it. He would sell me off like a brood mare rather than face public humiliation and lose his seat on the council.

In desperation, I played one last card. "But, Father, what will you do without me? In meetings with the other nobles, how will you know who's honest and who is not?"

This was something we rarely spoke of openly. I could do something no one else could, something that made me of great use to my father. Would he throw it away so easily?

His expression flickered once and then steeled again.

"Do you choose one for yourself, or do I?" he challenged.

The room was silent for a long moment.

I somehow managed to answer. "I'll choose for myself."

What else could I do?

* * * *

A scant few hours later, I found myself seated at our table in the dining hall.

Miriam put a great deal of effort into dressing me for dinner. The result was both awkward for me and a triumph for my parents.

I looked nothing like myself. Miriam had arranged my hair even more elaborately and used a small round iron on the curls around my face. Then she'd put touches of black kohl at the corners of my eyes. I wore an amber silk gown with a low, square-cut neckline that showed the tops of my breasts.

I don't know where she'd found the gown. It wasn't mine, and it was much too small to have fit Helena. I supposed my mother must have had it made at some point while anticipating its need.

However, at the sight of me, my father beamed. I couldn't meet his eyes.

Seating at dinner was equally awkward with my father at the head of the table, my mother and I seated on one side, and all four of the Volodanes seated on the other—so I had no choice but to look at one of them when I raised my eyes from my plate of roasted pheasant.

None of them had changed for dinner, and with the exception of Sebastian, they all wore armor and swords. Jarrod hadn't bothered to shave his face and sported a dark stubble. I could almost feel my mother's discomfort, but she smiled and made attempts at polite conversation.

Only Sebastian responded to her questions about weather and wild flowers in the northern provinces. Rolf spoke only to his father or mine. Occasionally, he glanced at me as if I already belonged to him.

I wasn't listening to any of them. My heart pounded too loudly in my ears. But then I did hear Rolf say something about heading back north as soon as he and I were married.

A long pause followed, and for the first time, I paid attention.

"It is not settled yet that she will marry you," my father finally responded. "Per our agreement, Megan will choose for herself."

Rolf's face clouded. "I never agreed to that. I am the eldest. She will join with me."

Jarrod turned in his chair. "You'll do as I tell you! Nothing less and nothing more!"

Mother, Father, and I all flinched at his tone and his unthinkable manner at the table. Rolf's face went red, and Sebastian leaned back his chair, smiling. Something about him was beginning to strike me as sly. He clearly enjoyed his older brother's chastisement and discomfort.

"Now, now," he said, dryly. "We mustn't seem uncouth."

Kai ignored all this. He ignored everything but his surroundings. His eyes were light brown like mine, and they moved from the opulent tapestries on our walls to the peach roses in silver vases on the table to the porcelain plates and pewter goblets.

Then for the first time, he looked directly at me.

"I fear you'll find the furnishings at Volodane Hall somewhat lacking," he said.

His voice dripped with resentment, and I knew I'd not been wrong in my first assessment. He was angry.

His tone was not lost on my mother, who answered him with a strained smile. "Of course, we'll be sending some household things with her, and Megan will give your hall a woman's touch."

These words made me wonder what had happened to Kai's mother. I'd never asked and no one had mentioned this, but it seemed I would be the lady of their house. The very thought ensured I would not manage to eat another bite of dinner.

Kai studied my mother evenly and breathed out through his teeth. "Our hall won't be good enough for her. Nothing of us or ours will be good enough."

Then I realized the source of his anger. He resented the need for this bargain as much as we did. He knew that we—and most of the noble houses—looked down upon the Volodanes, and the last thing he probably wanted was a permanent reminder in his home of their lowly state in comparison to ours.

"Quit!" Jarrod ordered him, pounding one hand on the table.

In obedience, Kai stopped talking and withdrew back inside himself, ignoring everyone again.

Sebastian looked at me and raised one eyebrow in amusement. I glanced away.

Somehow—and I never quite knew how—we made it through the rest of dinner.

By the time my mother rose, signifying the meal was over, my heart pounded in my ears again. I felt the edge of my self-control slipping away and knew that I had to gain a few moments to myself or I might possibly do or say something I'd later regret.

"Please make my excuses," I said quietly to Mother. "I will return quickly."

She frowned briefly, but then her face smoothed in annoyed understanding, and I realized she most likely thought I needed to relieve myself.

I didn't care what she thought.

Turning, I fled the dining hall as fast as I could without running. Upon reaching the passage that led toward the kitchens, I couldn't stop myself and broke into a run, racing in my heavy silk skirts until I reached an open

archway in one side of the passage, just a few doors from the entrance
to our kitchens.

There, I took refuge in an old, familiar hiding place.

As a child, I'd come to this storage room whenever I didn't wish to be
found. It was filled with crates, casks, and places to hide. No one ever
entered except servants from the kitchens, and none of them ever noticed
me secreted away behind a stack of crates.

I hadn't come here in years, but now, I breathed in relief at the respite
of solitude and the illusion of safety.

Slowly, I sank to my knees.

As we were expecting a delivery of goods any day now, the storage room
was nearly half-empty. I didn't even attempt to hide behind crates or casks,
as I knew I'd have to return to the hall long before anyone came looking me.

A dismal prospect.

What was I going to do? I couldn't face the thought of my life married
to any of those men. Until this afternoon, I'd never faced the prospect of
marriage at all . . . but to one of *them*? I was not a weeper. My parents had
never allowed such an indulgence, and I honestly wasn't aware I knew
how to cry, but tears came to my eyes and one dripped down my cheek.

The water in my eyes made the following moment even more uncertain
than it might have been.

The air in the storage room appeared to waver. Alarmed, I wiped away
my tears, but the motion of the wavering air grew more rapid, and then...
something solid began taking shape.

Jumping up to my feet, I gasped.

There, near the far wall across the storage room, a great three-paneled
mirror now stood where there had been only empty air an instant before.
The thick frames around each panel were of solid pewter, engraved in
the image of climbing ivy vines. The glass of the panels was smooth and
perfect, and yet I didn't see myself looking back.

Instead, I found myself staring into the eyes of a lovely dark-haired
woman in a black dress. Her face was pale and narrow, and she bore no
expression at all. But there she was, *inside* the right panel gazing out me.

Was I going mad? Had my parents driven me mad?

"There is nothing to fear," the woman said in a hollow voice.

I doubted that statement. I feared for my sanity, but as yet, I'd not found
my voice to answer her.

"You are at a crossroad," she continued, "with three paths." As she
raised her arms, material from her long black sleeves hung down. "I am
bidden to give you a gift."

Here, sadness leaked into her voice, especially at the word "bidden," and my mind began to race. Was this truly happening?

"You will live out three outcomes . . . to three different choices," she said. "Lives with men . . . connected by blood. Then you will have the knowledge to know . . . to choose."

I shook my head. "Wait! What are you saying?"

Lowering both hands to her sides, she said, "The first choice."

Before I could speak again, the storage room vanished. Wild fear coursed through me as the world went black for the span of a breath, and then suddenly I found myself back in my family's dining hall, only everything was different.

Chairs had been set up in rows, and guests were seated in them. I wore a gown of pale ivory and held my father's arm as he walked me past the guests toward the far end of the hall.

Flowers in tall vases graced that same end, and a local magistrate stood there with a book in his hands.

Beside the magistrate stood Rolf, wearing his armor and his sword.

Turning, he looked at me in grim determination.

He was waiting.

The First Choice
Rolf

Chapter 2

The first time I laid eyes upon Volodane Hall, I was wet, damp, and struggling not to give way to misery.

Within hours of the conclusion of my wedding at Chaumont, I'd been lifted onto the back of a horse. The journey north took two days, and I rode quietly along with my new husband, his father, both his brothers, and their retinue of guards. My one comfort was that I'd been allowed to bring Miriam with me. Though it had seemed unfair to ask her to leave our comfortable home, I did ask.

She'd not hesitated to pack her belongings.

Another blessing to this arrangement was that as Jarrod paid for rooms at inns along the way, Miriam and I were given a room to ourselves, so as of yet, I'd not been expected to share a bed with Rolf.

I was poignantly aware that state of affairs wouldn't last long.

The farther north we traveled, the thicker grew the trees and the darker grew the sky, even in the afternoons. Though it was early summer, a cold drizzle began to fall, soaking through my cloak. None of the men seemed to notice, but Miriam and I both shivered.

Near dusk of the second day, we passed through a village. I saw few people, as most of them ran for dwellings at our approach or took other cover. The sight of this did nothing to ease my trepidation.

Jarrod glanced down at me from his tall horse and pointed ahead. "The hall is just up there, beyond that rise."

These were among the few words he'd spoken since the wedding, but I knew he hadn't purchased me for conversation.

I nodded to him in polite response. After all, he was my new father.

Rolf and Jarrod led the way, and I somehow fell into place riding beside Sebastian. I still thought him vain and sly, but he was also given to occasional acts of kindness and had forced several stops along the way so I could rest.

"Brace yourself," he said. "It's not a pretty sight."

As we came over the rise, the sun—what could be seen of it through the thick clouds—was setting, and I gained my first view in the fading light. My hands tensed on the reins, and I heard Miriam's soft breath of dismay from behind me.

Though Jarrod had called the place "a hall," this wasn't a term I'd have chosen. In my mind, I'd imagined something like a large two-story hunting lodge with a barracks, surrounded by a tall fence. Though I had been warned my new home was in need of improvement, I'd been visualizing a place that *could* be improved.

Instead, a squat keep upon a second rise loomed out of the surrounding forest. Even at a distance, its dark profile looked worn and ill kept. Its upper rim was uneven, perhaps with broken stones, leaving gaps like missing teeth. A single tower stretched into the darkening sky.

I kept my eyes upon the dwelling as we drew closer.

It was simple, barely a fortification, and more than a bit worn with age. Moss grew between lichen-spotted stones on its lower half. To one side was an undersized stable while the other held a mid-sized barracks with a clay chimney. Around all the grounds was an intact but decaying stone wall. The wooden front gate appeared solid—and was currently closed.

Sebastian glanced at me, but I offered no comment. I was lost for words. I could only imagine the inside.

Jarrod urged his mount into a canter, rode up to the gates, and called out. A moment later, a loud grinding sounded, like timber creaking across timber, and then the gates opened.

We rode inside to a small, muddy courtyard, and the flurry of activity that followed kept me from taking in much more. We had several wagons of goods sent by my parents, along with my luggage. Guards from all around me began dismounting as their captain, a man named Marcel who had traveled with us, began calling out orders for proper unpacking and storage. Large, growling wolfhounds stalked between the horses.

Jarrod jumped to the wet ground and called back toward us, "Kai! Get the women and take them inside."

Before I knew what was happening, two strong hands gripped my waist, and I felt myself lifted off my horse. In spite of my misery, I managed to say, "Put me down!"

In mid-air, I found myself looking into Kai's surprised face.

"I can dismount a horse!" I told him.

His surprise shifted to resentment. "Suit yourself."

He dropped my feet to the ground and turned away from me to help Miriam. She was so utterly exhausted, she let him lift her down and even leaned on him for a moment to steady herself. Poor Miriam. What had I dragged her into?

Without delay, we were taken inside the front doors of the keep . . . and I was home.

The foyer and first passage were both dim, but then Sebastian was suddenly with us, and he slipped past to lead the way.

"Bring them along, Kai," he called over one shoulder, hurrying ahead. "I'll make sure the fire is stoked in the hall, and I'll order some food."

There was that word again: hall.

At the end of the passage, we emerged indeed to a great hall with a fireplace large enough that I could have stood inside. The sight of burning logs and the emanation of warmth filled me with relief.

In addition, half a dozen dogs came running toward us, wriggling and whining for attention. These were not guardian wolfhounds, but smaller friendly spaniels, and one of them leaped up into Kai's chest. He caught the dog with both arms and smiled.

"Lacey, stop that. You know better."

It was the first time I'd seen him smile. He held her for a moment and let her lick his face before putting her down. She was a pretty thing with long soft ears and a smattering of red-brown spots over white fur. Down at his feet, she continued wriggling for his attention.

Miriam grasped my hand and pointed to the hearth. "My lady?"

Nodding, I let her lead me to the warmth of the blaze. We both removed our cloaks and laid them near the hearth to dry—after looking for a clean spot. The walls were bare of any ornament or tapestry, and the floor was filthy.

Behind me, I could hear Sebastian giving orders to servants when heavy footsteps sounded, and I turned to see Jarrod and Rolf walk in. I supposed they had been seeing to the proper distribution of luggage. Rolf didn't even glance my direction. So far, of my new family, I had exchanged the fewest words with him. Even sullen Kai had spoken to me more.

It was not an auspicious beginning to a marriage.

Two serving women hurried in carrying trays, and Jarrod waved me toward the table. "Over here."

Miriam and I both moved to join him and Rolf, and I realized I wouldn't be allowed to see my room and change for dinner. While I didn't exactly wish to dine in a damp dress with my tangled hair hanging about my face, I was hungry and hoped fervently for a mug of tea.

In truth, anything warm would have sufficed.

I waited for Jarrod to take his seat so the rest of us could follow suit. He did not. To my shock, he stood beside the table and poured himself a mug of what looked to be ale. Then he poured another and held it out to me. I didn't care for ale.

Of course, though, I nodded and took it, and he gestured down to a tray on the table. "Help yourself."

The only items on the tray were two loaves of hardened bread and a half wheel of cheese with mold on the rind.

Sebastian had the good grace to look slightly abashed. He stepped in to begin cutting cheese and bread.

Kai watched my face carefully, and his resentment was unmistakable. He thought me a snob who viewed them all as far beneath myself, who viewed this place as far beneath myself. Perhaps he was not wrong.

"With your help," he said slowly, "we can dine properly tomorrow."

Without noticing his youngest son's biting tone, Jarrod nodded at me. "The kitchen women have grown lazy. It's your place to shake them into minding their tasks. You'll see to it." He paused. "I want to have guests here soon and not be ashamed."

I was hungry enough to eat the chunk of cheese and sip at the ale to wash it down, but my mind reeled. These men expected me to take this bleak, decaying place and turn it into a home suitable for entertaining?

Could Helena even have managed that?

Maybe she could. I only felt daunted. No one had trained me to run a household. I'd been honed for other things—for watching and listening and helping my father to know whom he could trust and whom he could not. What did I know of organizing the kitchen staff?

After a few bites, I felt too exhausted to eat and set down my mug.

Taking note of this, Jarrod waved to one of the serving women. "Show your new lady to her room. You know which one." He looked back to me, and his eyes were hard. "Rolf will be up later."

Somehow, I met his gaze and nodded.

Then Miriam and I followed the serving woman out.

* * * *

Thankfully, the room I was given, on the second floor of the single tower, was not entirely awful.

It was—or had been—a woman's room. I'd wondered if the Volodanes would abide by noble customs that the lady of the house should have a room to herself, where her husband might visit when he pleased. Apparently, they did, as there was nothing in this room to suggest Rolf had ever slept here.

The furniture was old, faded, and in need of a polish, but the four-poster bed was large, with a thick, eyelet comforter. The dressing table was well crafted from rich-toned mahogany. A matching wardrobe stood beside it. A moth-eaten tapestry covered one wall. There was no fireplace, but two candles burned on a bed stand, providing sufficient light.

Walking to the dressing table, I gazed into the mirror and cringed, as I was more bedraggled than I'd realized. I looked like a drenched peasant girl.

Miriam stood in the center of the room, taking in the furnishings. There was a second small table on the far side of the bed sporting a basin and chipped pitcher. I briefly wondered if there was water in the pitcher, but then I saw Miriam's face. She was pale and stricken.

"Oh, my lady," she breathed. "Your mother couldn't possibly have known."

"Yes, she did," I answered shortly. "Or she didn't care." I sighed. There was no use for either of us to stand there feeling sorry for ourselves. This was our home, and we had to make the best of it. One of my chests had been carried and set at the end of the bed. "See if I have a clean nightgown in there. I must get out of these damp clothes."

She needed out of her damp clothes too, but one thing at a time.

Taking action of any kind took my mind off the impending outcome of this night. Miriam peeled off my dress and my shift and then helped me into a long white nightgown. I sat down at the dressing table and she used an extra blanket to rub my hair nearly dry before brushing it out. Soon, it sprang in its usual curls around my face.

Looking at her reflection in the mirror, I couldn't help saying, "I'm sorry I begged you to come. I was a coward, fearing to be alone here."

She continued brushing my hair. "I'd never leave you, my lady."

Her devotion did not assuage my guilt.

Before I could speak again, the door opened, and Rolf stepped inside. He hadn't bothered knocking. Though I didn't turn, I could see in the mirror that he'd at least removed his armor and sword.

"You'd best go," I told Miriam quietly, and then it occurred to me I had no idea to where she was supposed to go.

As if reading my face, Rolf said, "A small room's been readied. One of the servants can show her."

With a reluctant nod, Miriam hesitated for a breath and then fled, closing the door as she left.

I rose from my chair and turned. As opposed to looking at me, Rolf looked about the room in obvious discomfort. He was dressed only in a wool shirt and dark pants. Even without his armor, he made an imposing figure. But here in the candlelight of the room, his face was not unpleasant. Though his features were broad, they suited him, even to the bump at the bridge of his nose.

"Whose room was this?" I asked.

His eyes flashed to me, and his discomfort grew. "My mother's."

Finally, someone had made reference to her. I had no intention of letting this pass. "How did she die?" For I was certain she must be dead.

"In childbirth. With Kai."

"Oh . . ." The ramifications of that began to set in. "So this place has had no lady for twenty years?"

He shook his head. It was indeed a house of men.

"Poor Kai," I said without thinking.

His eyes were still on my face. "Why?"

"To grow up without any mother at all. No wonder he's so angry."

Rolf hard face softened slightly. "Sometimes, I think he blames himself, but none of us do."

I realized then that Rolf cared for Kai, and this changed my opinion of him. At least he cared for someone.

As we fell silent once more, the tension in the room became palpable, and I realized something else. Rolf had no more desire to be placed in this situation than I did. Oh, he'd wanted me to choose him well enough. He thought it his due as the eldest brother. He'd wanted the connection to the house of Chaumont and all that went along with such a connection.

But maybe that was all he'd wanted, and now he was faced with the stark reality of a wife. His father most certainly expected the marriage to be consummated and for grandsons to follow soon.

Rolf wasn't stupid though, and as these thoughts ran through my mind, he watched my face.

His own face hardened again, and he pointed to the bed.

A measure of fear settled in my stomach. While I knew I could not refuse him, I wasn't entirely certain what was about to happen. My mother never spoke of such things. Still, there was nothing to stop it now, so I walked over and crawled under the comforter on the bed.

Rolf pulled his shirt over his head and got in beside me. I'd never seen a man without a shirt. His arms reminded me of tree branches.

For few moments, he did nothing and almost seemed to expect me to do something. If that were the case, he would be sorely disappointed. Finally, he sighed and leaned over and touched his mouth to mine. It was not unpleasant. It simply felt as if he was acting out a duty. I tried to respond, but wasn't quite certain how.

Then I felt his hands on my sides, pulling up my nightdress.

Apparently, he did know what to do.

What followed was both invasive and uncomfortable, but it didn't last long, and I had the distinct impression it wasn't any more pleasant for him.

Once again, this was not an auspicious beginning to a marriage.

* * * *

The next morning, I was relieved to awaken and find Rolf already gone.

Miriam brought me water for washing, and then she pulled the yellow muslin gown from a chest.

"No," I said quickly. "I'll wear my old blue wool. It's warmer and I want to look like myself again."

Though she hesitated and seemed on the verge of argument, she held back and fetched my favorite dress. It was a simple gown of blue-gray that had probably been washed too many times. It fit me well and laced up the front.

Once I was dressed, I had her weave my hair into its usual thick braid and I pushed the new shorter strands behind my ears. If I was the "lady of the house," I should be allowed to dress as I pleased. Rolf probably wouldn't care one way or another, and I had a good deal to accomplish today.

"I'm going down," I told Miriam. "Would you mind sorting through these chests and putting my gowns in the wardrobe?"

I wasn't entirely sure what the chests held as my mother had packed for me, but I'd managed to stash my blue wool when she hadn't been looking.

"Of course, my lady," Miriam answered, pushing up her sleeves.

And so, with that, I headed out of the room, down the passage, and down the curving stairs of the tower. I had an aging keep to try and put in order, and it seemed only sensible to begin in the filthy main hall.

The first things I saw upon entering were Sebastian and Kai, standing by the table, eating the rest of the cheese from the previous night. The pack of cheerful spaniels wriggled at their feet.

"Where is Rolf?" I asked.

"He and Father are out checking the wheat fields," Kai answered. He took in the sight of my dress and hair and seemed slightly taken aback, but not displeased.

Sebastian, on the other hand, frowned in open disapproval. "Good gods, what are you wearing?"

I ignored the question.

Kai took a long drink of ale.

"Is that your breakfast?" I asked him.

He shrugged. "It'll do."

I shook my head. "No. It won't."

First things first though. The two women who'd brought this food the night before now came in seeking to gather the trays. Apparently, it was not unusual to leave such things all night. My mother would never have stood for such slovenly neglect. I turned to the women.

"What are your names?"

One was short and plump, the other tall and spindly. They both looked at my dress and hair in some confusion, and I suddenly realized why Miriam had been on the verge of arguing. I hardly appeared as the lady of the house.

"I'm Betty," the plump one answered. "And this is Matilda . . . my lady."

I nodded. "I want this hall swept out, and then I want the floor scrubbed. I want all the cobwebs swept down, and I want the walls prepared for tapestries."

They both stared at me as if they'd not heard correctly, but Sebastian's face went still. "Tapestries?"

"Yes. Mother sent four tapestries from storage in the manor."

My family might be impoverished as far as ready money, but we had an endless supply of possessions. Had my father been able to sell any of it, he might have saved me the indignity of this marriage, but he'd not dared. Once a great family begins quietly selling off heirlooms, their financial need becomes public knowledge no matter how hard they try to keep the secret.

So, my parents might have taken a good deal of money from Jarrod Volodane, but to help save face regarding my dowry, they'd sent vases, dishes, goblets, paintings, casks of wine from my grandfather's day, boxes of tea, and tapestries. If anyone asked Jarrod about my dowry, he would have a ready answer.

My father's sense of family honor knew no bounds.

Still, my answer delighted Sebastian. "Tapestries!" he exclaimed, smiling.

Kai said nothing, but he wasn't really given time as Sebastian turned to Betty and Matilda. "You heard your new lady."

My orders seemed to have struck the women as bizarre. Still, upon Sebastian's urging, they sprang into action.

"I'll get the brooms," Matilda said.

With the cleaning of the hall underway, I looked again at the remnants of breakfast and sighed. "I suppose I'd better go and sort out the kitchen."

Sebastian stepped closer with his expression shifting to concern. "Shall I come with you? I fear the women in the kitchen are not as biddable as Betty and Matilda."

With every fiber of my being, I wanted to jump at his offer. The thought of Sebastian's support was beyond tempting. It had been easy enough to order the cleaning of the hall. But the knot in my stomach returned at the thought of sorting out menus with women who would most likely resent me.

Two things stopped me from accepting his help. First, he was not my husband, and even though Rolf wasn't here, I felt it might be unwise to show too much dependence on Sebastian. And second, Kai was watching me carefully again. I remembered his challenge from the night before.

I needed to show him that I could manage this house myself. I needed to show them all.

"Thank you," I told Sebastian, "but I can speak to the cooks."

"Suit yourself, but don't say you weren't warned."

He did not inspire more confidence. Turning, I left the main hall and was promptly embarrassed when I had to ask Betty directions to the kitchen. She was helpful enough and pointed down a passage leading west.

"All the way to the end, my lady. You'll see the entrance on the right and a door leading outside to the gardens straight ahead."

I thanked her and headed onward. Her words about the gardens caused me to alter my plans briefly. In all honesty, I'd not been expecting gardens, even though it was summer. This place didn't seem well run enough for anyone to have been placed in charge of a kitchen garden.

As I reached the end of the passage, I saw the open entrance to the kitchen, but instead of turning right, I stepped outside into the morning air. Though overcast, thankfully, it was not raining, and a bit of sun peeked through the clouds.

To my astonishment, I found myself looking at a large square of well-tended vegetables: potatoes, carrots, onions, cabbages, peas, and beans. Beyond it was an herb garden, and beyond that was a strawberry patch. Looking to the right, I saw a thriving chicken coop with fat hens pecking at the ground. There must be eggs.

I could hardly believe my eyes. Why hadn't any of this been served to the lords of the hall since my arrival?

A man in his early thirties, with a bent back, was on his knees in the herb garden. I approached him with quick steps.

"Good morning," I said, admiring his work. "What lovely herbs. Your parsley looks especially fine."

He blinked in surprise and confusion, as if wondering who I was.

"Forgive me," I said awkwardly. "I am the new lady here. I have married Rolf."

Blushing wildly, the man stood up, wiping his hands on his pants. "My lady, I had no idea that . . . no one told me."

His own embarrassment somehow eased mine, and I smiled. "You are the gardener here?"

Of course, this was obvious, but it gave him a chance to nod. "Yes, I am Patrick."

I smiled again. "Well, you're quite skilled, and I shall mention this to my husband. But first I want to see what is being done with these vegetables in the kitchens."

He blushed again as I turned away.

Having seen this abundance of readily available food, my curiosity over what I would find in the kitchen only grew.

I reentered the keep and walked through the open archway into the kitchen, and there I found three women among the ovens and pots and pans. One of them, the eldest, was quietly kneading bread on a table. She was slender with graying hair pulled back in a bun.

The other two women were barely past twenty, and they sat at a smaller, second table laughing and chatting with each other over mugs of steaming tea and plates of scrambled eggs with strawberries on the side.

At the sight of this, all my nervousness fled, and when I thought on what Sebastian and Kai, young lords of the keep, had eaten for their own breakfast, anger rose inside me. How would my mother have handled this?

The woman making bread saw me first and froze. Then the other two looked up. One of them was strikingly pretty with black hair, pale skin, and a charming smatter of freckles. The other one was somewhat stocky with reddish hair pulled back at the nape of her neck.

The guilt washing over that second one's face let me know these women were not ignorant of my presence as Patrick had been. They knew of my existence and my arrival.

However, the pretty one expressed no guilt whatsoever. She nearly sneered at me as she took in my dress and my hair. The mild regret I'd felt upon greeting Betty and Matilda was nothing in comparison to what I felt now. I should have listened to Miriam. I should have donned the muslin gown and earrings and let her pile up my hair.

"What do you want?" the pretty girl said in open contempt.

"Lavonia!" the older woman gasped, but the redhead took her cue from the one called Lavonia and crossed her arms sullenly.

The elder woman admonished the second girl, "And Cora. This is your new lady."

I stared only at Lavonia. Though I'd never found myself in a situation like this before, I instinctively knew I was being tested, and I couldn't show an ounce of weakness. Reaching inside myself, I channeled the cold strength and imperious nature of my mother.

"What do I want?" I repeated in my mother's haughty voice and was rewarded by seeing Cora, the redheaded girl, shrink back in uncertainty. "I came to see why two sons of this house are eating moldy cheese for breakfast." I let my eyes fall to the eggs and strawberries.

How had Jarrod let things fall into this state? Had it happened slowly over the years?

The slim older woman came around the table, her face chagrined. "My lady," she began, and I heard an apology in her voice. "Would Sebastian and Kai like something else?"

She knew the household schedule well enough to know that Jarrod and Rolf were out.

"If they want something else, they'll send for it," Lavonia interrupted.

Even taking their ages into account, I was not certain of the hierarchy here. The elder woman did not appear to be in charge.

"What is your name?" I asked her.

"Ester, my lady."

I nodded. "Ester, will that bread you're making be baked by midday?"

"Yes, my lady."

I spoke only to her. "I haven't taken stock of the larder, but I brought some things with me from Chaumont. In a short while, I'll have boxes of tea and several casks of wine brought in. At midday, I will send Matilda and Betty to you. I want trays prepared with slices of fresh bread with butter, bowls of strawberries, boiled eggs, and several pots of tea. I want this carried up to the hall for any of the men who come in to eat. Is that clear?"

"Yes, my lady."

"If they want anything, they'll send for it," Lavonia repeated angrily.

I looked her up and down as if she were an insect—as my mother would have done—and then turned back to Ester. "I assume there is ham in the larder?"

She nodded and glanced nervously at Lavonia.

"Do you know how to make cream sauce?" I asked Ester.

"Yes, my lady."

"For dinner tonight, you will make roasted potatoes and a large dish of peas in cream sauce. You will heat a ham, slice it, and lay it out on a tray. I'll have decanters sent in, and I want two decanters of red wine drawn from the casks." I paused. "I will send Betty and Matilda right at dusk this evening, and everything will be ready for them to carry out. Is that clear?"

"Yes, my lady."

I looked again to Lavonia. "I trust you will be of help with this if you wish to keep your place in this house."

"Is that a threat?" Her pretty face twisted with anger. "Lord Jarrod will hear of this!"

In my mother's voice, I answered, "I certainly hope so."

I swept from the room.

* * * *

By evening, I took a short break from my work to run upstairs and let Miriam lace me into a silk gown and pile up my hair. I wore the diamond pendant.

When I came back down, I looked the part of lady of the house.

Upon reaching the main hall, I heard masculine voices and walked in to find Jarrod, Rolf, Sebastian, and Kai all there. Jarrod and Rolf were both looking about the place in surprise, for it had indeed undergone something of a transformation.

For one, it was clean.

The newly scrubbed table had been laid with white cloths, porcelain plates, and pewter goblets. All of these had come from Chaumont Manor. Four enormous tapestries hung on the walls, and I think my mother chose them well. They bore vibrant vivid colors and all four of them depicted a story in sequence of men hunting a pack of wolves. My parents had never cared for these, as they were from before my grandfather's time, but Mother had guessed Jarrod would like them.

From the look on his face, he did.

The half dozen spaniels still wriggled about the men, seeking attention. I had no intention of displacing these dogs from the hall. This was their home. I simply intended to make certain the maids cleaned up after them.

"Dinner will be served shortly," I said from the archway.

All the men turned as I walked in.

"You approve of the changes?" I asked Jarrod.

He glanced at the table and the nearest tapestry. Then he walked over and picked up an engraved pewter goblet. "I do. I wouldn't know how to buy any of this with all the money in the land." He nodded to Rolf. "We've made a better bargain than I realized."

I supposed this was high praise coming from Jarrod.

At that moment, Betty and Matilda came in carrying trays of sliced ham, roasted potatoes, peas in cream sauce, and two decanters of wine.

"Shall we sit down?" I suggested.

With a snort of laughter, Jarrod shook his head as if amused. "A good bargain indeed." Then he looked again at Rolf. "Now I want a grandson."

* * * *

That night, Rolf came to my room again.

"My father was pleased with the hall and with dinner," he said.

I found his praise strangely gratifying. "So was Sebastian. He even helped hang the tapestries."

Rolf's face clouded. "Of course he did."

The dislike in his voice was clear. Last night, I'd noticed his affection for his youngest brother, but this warmth did not spread to Sebastian. I wondered why.

With nothing else to say, I climbed into the bed again, and Rolf joined me.

He treated me gently, and when he kissed me, I tried to respond and kiss him back. The rest of the act was over quickly. As I knew what was coming, it was not so invasive this time, but I still couldn't help feeling the entire act was merely a duty on both our parts.

Though I'd never expected to marry and had never given it much thought, in the back of my mind, I somehow thought there should be . . . more.

Chapter 3

As the weeks passed, I somehow became "the lady" of Volodane Hall.

While my mother hadn't had time to have a proper trousseau made for me, she'd sent bolts of velvet and silk from our stores, and Miriam was a skilled seamstress. With some regret, I retired my comfortable old blue wool and was not seen in it again. I had a part to play now, and if I wished to survive, I needed to look that part.

In addition, though Jarrod was somewhat tight with money, he was soon more than aware of my value as a keeper of his home, and he put me in charge of the household accounts. This gave me the freedom to order food and goods from the village when necessary. I never visited the village, but I arranged to hire a laundry woman. While the care of my own gowns was left to Miriam, I ordered washings of all four of the men's clothing, along with sheets, blankets, and curtains.

Almost before I knew it, the rhythms of daily life here had become familiar. Jarrod and Rolf were often out overseeing the land or running drills with the guards. Kai spent much of his time in training with a sword, even though the family did not appear to be at war with anyone. Sebastian spent his time playing cards with the guards . . . or talking with me.

I learned a good deal from him. My question about the guards' food source was soon answered, as they had their own cook—a man—and supplies were delivered directly to him. Apparently, the guards ate a good deal of boiled oats and mutton stew.

I learned that Jarrod, Rolf, and Sebastian all loved Kai, but Rolf and Sebastian had no brotherly love for each other, and Jarrod had no affection for Sebastian either, nor did he seem to require any work or assistance from his second son. This didn't faze Sebastian at all. He was popular among the guards, as he was both a gracious winner and loser at cards, and he seemed to have several close friends among them, especially a handsome young man called Daveed.

Inside the family, Sebastian was quite content with the company of Kai and me. He often told me how glad he was that I'd come to live here, and he offered more than once to deal with problems of difficult servants for me—especially with the kitchen staff.

"I'm embarrassed things had become so lax in the first place," he once apologized. "It wasn't always like this. Until a few years ago, we hadn't stood around the table eating whatever was served. I'm not quite sure how that happened, but you shouldn't be expected to clean up the mess entirely on your own."

Tempted as I was at times, I never once took him up on his offers. He was not my husband, and Rolf was, and Rolf respected only strength. Even with what little I could sense from him, I sensed that much. As a result, I could never show weakness. I couldn't allow myself to lean on Sebastian.

Rolf and I carried onward. We seldom spoke, but he was never unkind.

Soon enough though, the rhythms of the house were interrupted when Jarrod sought me out to tell me he'd arranged for a formal dinner, the first hosted here in many years. I found his plans to bring his family "up in the world" to be steady and methodical. First, he had spent years gaining and keeping wealth. Then he had purchased me. Now, he was putting me to use.

I had no illusions about his expectations.

"Who is coming?" I asked.

"Lord Allemond Monvílle, his wife, and his brother," he answered. "Their lands border our southern line, and I'm trying to buy a section of forest covered in oak. The timber alone is worth the purchase."

"Lord Allemond?" I repeated, surprised. He was on the Council of Nobles. He was also a friend of my father's and had visited Chaumont at least once a year since I was a child. "He's selling his land?" That seemed unlikely.

Jarrod's eyes sharpened. "You know him?"

"Yes."

"Good. Try to remember what dishes he likes and what kind of wine. He's only coming to look down his nose at me. I want him off guard by what he finds."

Considering the arrogance of Lord Allemond, I suspected Jarrod was probably right. Neighboring lands or not, I could hardly imagine the Monvílles even considering an invitation to dine with the Volodanes, and selling Jarrod land seemed beyond the realm of possibility.

The household burst into activity. Matilda began cleaning madly. Miriam worked hard to create a gown for me. With Betty's help, I started sewing clothes for the men.

Sebastian was particular about his clothes being perfectly tailored, and so he came to my room for a fitting. This event gave me a clearer understanding of how his mind worked. Within moments of walking through the door, he pulled his long-sleeved tunic over his head and tossed it onto the bed. He was bare-chested beneath it. He bore a scar on his left collarbone. Betty and I were both mildly startled by his action, but we recovered quickly, and she picked up the white shirt she'd been making for him. I couldn't take my eyes off his arms. I'd wondered why he was the only man in the family who traveled without a weapon.

Apparently, he didn't.

Sebastian had a long, sheathed dagger strapped to each of his forearms. The hilt of the dagger on the left arm was ornate, with pearl inlay. The one on his right arm was quite plain, with a tan hilt. Unlike his father and brothers, he didn't strike openly. He would keep his weapons hidden until the last moment.

He noticed me staring, and I glanced away.

Not long after his fitting, I closeted myself away with him to plan menus. I was too concerned with the upcoming evening's success not to take advantage of his help.

"We'll need at least three savory courses," I told him. "Fish, poultry, and then either beef or lamb."

He nodded. "I think beef would be best. I'll arrange for several roasts. The poultry course is easy. We can have Patrick kill some of our own chickens. Can you handle the fish?"

"Yes, Ester told me there is a fish monger in the village. I'll send an order and have four large river salmon delivered. I know Lord Allemond enjoys salmon. We'll need a sauce for the side though."

"A simple white sauce," Sebastian suggested. "Ester makes a delicious white sauce."

In bits and pieces, I'd learned that Ester had been with the family for years, since Rolf was a boy, and she had apparently once been a fine cook, but the slow breakdown of household order had left her without support from the family, and I feared she was now being bullied by the likes of Lavonia.

"What about dessert?" Sebastian asked, bringing me back to the task at hand.

Although I'd never planned a formal menu before, together, Sebastian I did quite well, and I submitted our list to Ester who was pleased by our choices and went to work with Patrick arranging for the fruits and vegetables. All seemed to be in hand until mid-morning of the day of the dinner when Jarrod and Rolf walked into the main hall where I was busy experimenting with centerpieces. Though Patrick maintained fine vegetable gardens, the Volodanes grew no flowers, and I was having to make due with what I could find growing wild.

"Is everything ready?" Jarrod asked with an edge in his voice.

I turned to face him. "Yes, I think so."

"It better be," he warned. "I want Allemond impressed by what he finds here."

I wasn't certain anything would impress Lord Allemond, but I could at least make sure nothing went wrong. The salmon had just been delivered and were now in cold storage in the cellars.

My mind was so busy on running details through my head that I was caught completely off guard when Jarrod said, "And you know I'll expect your help with this land deal. I want your best efforts."

My eyes widened. For an instant, I couldn't draw breath. My father had *told* him. Then my shock began to fade. Of course, Father told him. Jarrod had been expecting the beautiful Helena and arrived at Chaumont to find he'd have to make due with me. What better way to sweeten the deal than to tell Jarrod about my ability?

I had so much hoped to leave that part of my life behind.

With my mouth tight, I asked, "Who do you most wish me to focus upon? Allemond himself? Or is his brother handling the financial arrangements for him? I hope Father told you I can only read one person a day, and there are limits."

Rolf frowned in confusion, and Jarrod's expression went still.

"What do you mean by 'read'?" he asked slowly.

In a split second I realized how foolish I'd been. My father hadn't told him anything. Jarrod's mention of my help must have referred to me using my manners and family influence to throw Allemond off guard.

"Nothing," I responded, sounding nervous as I stepped away. "I thought you wished me to gauge his reactions and offer counsel later."

In a flash, his right hand snaked out and grabbed my wrist. I gasped as he jerked me up against his chest. I'd never had a man use his strength against me before, and the pain in my arm was startling.

Rolf's face flickered in alarm, but he didn't move. I could expect no help from him.

"Don't lie to me," Jarrod ordered, speaking close to my face. "What did you mean?"

On instinct, I used my free hand to try and loosen his fingers. I don't think he noticed.

I was terrible at lying, and he was no fool. The only option now seemed the truth.

"I would sometimes read people for my father," I rushed to say, hoping he'd let go of my wrist. "To see if they were honest. The Chaumont women can sometimes do this. My great aunt could and so can I."

He jerked my arm again, and I couldn't help crying out.

"To see if they're honest?" he pressed.

At this point, the pain in my arm was nearly blinding, and I had no choice but to keep talking.

"I can see the person's intent and sometimes pick up flashes of images! How else do you think my father borrowed so much money with no one finding out? Before we ever mentioned money, Father would have me read a potential lender to make certain he was discreet."

Jarrod's grip loosened slightly. He looked to Rolf and then back to me. "So . . . you're telling me you can read Allemond at dinner and let me know later if the deal he offers is honest or not?"

"Yes."

Without warning, his grip tightened again. "And what's to stop you from using this on one of us?"

"I would never! My father made me swear to only do readings under his direct orders."

"And you'll swear the same thing here?"

"Yes," I answered and then added, "my lord."

He smiled without warmth. "I think it's time you started calling me Father."

* * * *

As soon as he let go, I fled from the hall and hurried down the passage toward the stairs to the tower. I wanted a few moments in my room. In addition to being unsettled by the scene in the hall—and having stupidly given away my secret—my wrist was turning purple, and I needed to change into a long-sleeved dress.

Unfortunately, I made it only halfway to the entrance to the tower when Betty came trotting behind me. "My lady."

Holding back a sigh, I stopped. "Yes?"

"Lavonia is asking for you in the kitchen. She says the fish has gone bad."

All other concerns vanished. By some miracle, Lavonia had actually volunteered to prepare and bake the salmon, leaving Ester free to focus on the sauces and other courses. But the salmon was to be the first, and therefore most important, course. I'd paid well for fish caught that very morning, and I'd checked them myself upon delivery.

"Gone bad?"

"That's what she says, my lady."

Poor Betty appeared distraught, and I couldn't help a rush of pity. She was a good servant and didn't like being the bearer of bad news.

"Don't worry," I told her. "I'll go and see about it now. I'm sure she's just being overcautious."

I wasn't sure of any such thing, but I did an about-face and headed west toward the kitchen. Upon arriving, I found it a busy place, as it should be with a formal dinner planned for that night.

Ester was rolling crusts for strawberry tarts, and two girls I'd hired for temporary help were scrubbing pots in a large washbasin. Cora sat peeling potatoes.

Lavonia appeared to be supervising.

Relations between Lavonia and myself had not improved, but so long as she followed orders, I had as little to do with her as possible.

"Betty says there is a problem with the fish?" I asked, stepping through the archway.

Lavonia turned with her usual poorly hidden sneer. "They're spoilt. We can't use them."

Ester stopped rolling, and everyone was listening to us.

My nerves were already on edge, and I didn't have time for this nonsense. "I checked them myself upon delivery. Those fish were caught this morning."

"They're down in the cellar, in the coolest room," Lavonia said. "You want to come down with me to check them?"

Her eyes had narrowed and something in her voice caught my attention. My encounter with Jarrod had given away a part of myself that I would have preferred to leave behind. More, I had just promised him that I'd never read anyone without his orders, and all my instincts went against even considering such a thing.

Reading someone else's intentions tired me quickly, and I could only do one thorough reading a day before I was spent. Tonight, Jarrod would expect me to do a deep reading of Allemond, so I couldn't do a deep reading of Lavonia now.

Still, in this moment, I had little doubt that she was up to something.

Reaching out, using minimal effort, I tried to pick up only her surface thoughts, hoping I would see something useful without expending myself too much.

A nearly overwhelming flash of hatred hit me like a wall. I fought to keep my expression still. She hated me with a passion. Her life had been easy before my arrival, and she saw me as an overbearing taskmaster who had changed her life for the worse. Then I saw an image, a plan of her leading me alone to check the fish. They would be the same fresh salmon I'd already checked.

But days ago, she'd charmed the son of a fish monger into selling her four salmon—for a low price—that she'd let spoil in the sun. I saw an image in her mind of her preparing and sending out the spoiled salmon for tonight's dinner, and then in the aftermath, claiming she had warned me in front of all the kitchen staff, and that she'd shown me the spoiled fish, and I had insisted she serve it anyway.

She was going to ruin Jarrod's dinner party and blame me.

I pulled from her thoughts and stared at her for a moment. She began to fidget.

Looking to Ester, I said, "If I send you Matilda to help chop vegetables, can you manage the dinner with the girls you have here, but without Lavonia?"

A flash of something nearly unreadable, possibly hope, crossed Ester's eyes. "Yes, my lady. I can manage."

I turned back to Lavonia. "You are dismissed. I'll make sure you have a month's wages, but if you are not gone from this house within an hour, I will have a guard escort you out the gates."

Her mouth fell open, and her features twisted. "You can't do that! I'll tell Lord Jarrod!"

I briefly wondered if the girl was sharing Jarrod's bed on occasion, but it hardly mattered. "And what if I show him the spoiled fish you've hidden behind the hen house?" I countered, "And of your plan to ruin his dinner for Lord Allemond?"

Ester's face registered stark surprise but not disbelief.

Cora's shone with guilt. She knew.

Lavonia went speechless.

"You have an hour," I told her. "I'll make sure you receive your wages."

Going pale, Lavonia fled the kitchen, and my gaze drifted to Cora. "Do you wish to go with her?"

She drew in a sharp breath. "No, my lady."

I looked about the room. "Ester is in charge here, and you will all address her as Miss Ester from now on. Anyone who cannot follow her instructions without complaint will follow the path of Lavonia."

I nodded once to Ester and left the kitchen.

Even though I'd not probed Lavonia's thoughts very deeply, I felt drained, knowing I should never put myself in a position to attempt two readings in a day. My head hurt. So did my wrist.

* * * *

That night, I sat at the dressing table in my room as Miriam curled my hair with her small heated iron. Instead of piling it up tonight, she let it hang loose but drew several strands in the front over my forehead and pinned them with a small jeweled clip. Finally she put touches of kohl at the corners of my eyes and beet juice on my lips.

I stood.

She'd finished my new gown that morning, and looking at myself in the mirror, I could hardly believe the results. The gown was of burgundy silk with a v-neckline. Tight at the waist, it swept down into a voluminous skirt that moved gracefully when I walked. Thankfully, it was long sleeved and covered my now black and purple wrist. I wore a ruby pendant with matching earrings—that had once belonged to Helena.

"I don't look anything like myself anymore," I commented.

"You look beautiful," Miriam answered simply. "You should go down."

"Thank, you, Miriam," I said. "For the dress."

She smiled tiredly. I knew she'd probably been up half the night.

Leaving my room, I headed downstairs and heard voices in the hall. My mother always allowed the guests to arrive before making an entrance, so I had decided to follow her example.

Stopping at the entrance to the hall, I looked in to take of stock of what awaited me. All four Volodanes were there, wearing the new clothing Betty and I had made for them—with some input from Sebastian.

I thought Kai looked especially fine in a sleeveless black tunic. It suited his tall form, and his long hair hung down past his shoulders.

Sebastian wore a high-collared jacket over a white shirt, and he cut a dashing figure. My husband and Jarrod both wore new tunics with long sleeves, and they looked well too.

The hall was clean and properly arranged. There were white cloths on the table along with porcelain plates, silver cutlery, and pewter goblets. I'd made centerpieces from wild growing roses and lilacs. For tonight, I'd had the cheerful spaniels housed in the barracks with several of the guards who'd promised to look after them.

My gaze drifted to the guests: Lord Allemond, his wife, Rosamund, and his brother, Phillipe. Several of the Volodane guards stood discreetly near the walls, along with several of the Monvilles'. This was customary.

Lord Allemond glanced at the table several times with what I could only describe as consternation. He was a striking man, in his late forties with an impressive head of waving silver hair. Lady Rosamund had once been considered lovely, but now her generous curves were thickening and her face was heavily lined. She wore diamonds and a velvet gown of dark green.

With a deep breath, I stepped forward and entered the hall.

Allemond was the first one to see me, followed shortly by everyone else, but I couldn't help a stab of satisfaction at the flicker of uncertainty that passed over his face. "Megan?"

He recovered quickly.

I smiled and held out one hand—as my mother would have done. "My lord. It's been too long."

Jarrod stared at me as well. He'd never seen me with my hair down loose or wearing a v-neck dress.

Lady Rosamund must have been equally surprised by the sight of me, but she was a creature of my mother's ilk and showed nothing besides false pleasure. "Megan," she said, kissing my cheek. "We were saddened to hear of your sister's passing and surprised to hear of your marriage."

Her words were intended as sharp barbs, to point out that I was a secondary replacement in an unfortunate match, and even so, only here by virtue of my sister's death. I smiled and kissed her in return. "Thank you for your kind thoughts. It's so good to have guests in the hall."

Phillipe, who was younger than his brother, leaned over and kissed my hand. "My dear," he said, although in my entire life, he'd never taken notice of me before.

At the sight of this, Rolf's face darkened, which surprised me. I'd hardly thought him capable of feeling jealousy. Perhaps it was merely ownership.

"Shall we all sit and enjoy some wine before dinner?" I asked.

This was the signal for everyone to be seated. Wine was always served before dinner at these gatherings. Jarrod said nothing and took his cues from me. He sat at the head of the table, and I made suggestions for everyone else.

Smiling at Lady Rosamund, I said, "I fear we are outnumbered by the men."

At this, even her expression flickered with uncertainty. She'd sat across from me at a table many times, and she'd certainly never heard me attempt a playful comment. Until that moment, I'd not realized how much I had changed. Though it was not a change I'd wanted or asked for, I had been greatly altered by the expectations of Jarrod and even quiet Rolf. He never made requests, but I knew he wanted me to please his father.

As we all took our seats, Lord Allemond examined the porcelain dishes and pewter goblets.

"From Chaumont Manor, I assume?" he posed, sounding every inch a snob.

"Part of my dowry," I answered diplomatically, "and I think they grace my new father's table well."

Allemond shifted in his chair. It was clear that none of this was playing out as he'd expected. He'd most likely expected to find me a shadow of my painfully quiet former self, abused and cowed by the brutes of Volodane Hall. He'd expected an embarrassing show on Jarrod's part in attempting to host a dinner—a peasant with money playing at being a lord.

Betty and Matilda poured wine. It was from the best cask my parents had sent, but I made a mental note to talk to Jarrod soon about acquiring more. He would need decent wine if he planned to continue entertaining.

Phillipe and Lady Rosamund both took a sip, and I could see they were not pleased at its good quality.

Not long after, the fish course arrived. Again, Betty and Matilda quietly served.

I was so nervous that I wasn't certain how much I could eat, but I did taste the salmon. It was perfect, just barely cooked through and still slightly moist. Lord Allemond tasted it and the displeased expression on his face brought me an embarrassing amount of satisfaction. He'd not expected the food to be perfect.

Glancing down the table, I could see Jarrod enjoying his guests' smug disappointment. Seeing that, I tried to amend my attitude. It was unkind to take pleasure in the discomfort of others. But I knew my role here.

After that, as further courses were served, Sebastian took over the conversation. Neither Jarrod, Rolf, or Kai had anything to say to the Monvilles, but Sebastian was better at small talk, and he kept our guests suitably entertained. Lady Rosamund hung on his every word, and I couldn't help noticing how her eyes continued to move from his hair, over his face, and down to his arms.

Poor Kai appeared especially uncomfortable in the mix, and he brightened only once when Phillipe spoke to him directly. "I'm sorry I didn't arrange any matches for entertainment here tonight. There wasn't time, but I've always been astonished watching you in the ring at Partheney."

I had no idea what he meant by "match" or "ring," but Kai actually smiled at him. "Thank you. Next time perhaps. We have plenty of room here."

Before I could learn more about this, Rolf entered the conversation to ask about their wheat crop.

Somehow, we made it to dessert. No one had mentioned the land deal as of yet, but I knew the men would not discuss it over the table.

Then, just as we were finishing strawberry tarts with cream sauce, one of the Monvílle guards carried in a small harp. Watching this, Allemond frowned at his wife.

"Oh, my dear," she said, sound strained. "I had quite forgotten."

They must have given the guard instructions earlier.

"You brought a harp?" Sebastian asked.

That did seem odd.

"Yes . . ." Lady Rosamund began. "As a wedding gift. We have not heard Megan play in some time and hoped to impose upon her." She looked at Jarrod. "Forgive my presumption, but I did not think you would posses such an instrument here."

The Monvílles were then rewarded by the moment of discomfort on the part of the Volodanes, and I raced to think of what to say. No one had told them I played the harp. Of Helena's many, many talents, music was not among them, and I had often entertained my parents' guests. Even then, getting up in front of people had been difficult for me, but I obeyed my parents.

Once again, the Monvílles had hoped to embarrass Jarrod, probably thinking that I would be too shattered by my newfound existence to consider such a public display of myself. Even more, that the harp would look ridiculously out-of-place at Volodane Hall.

Looking directly at Jarrod, I said, "Father, would you like me to play?"

In this way, I placed him back in control of the situation, as if the decision to hear music tonight was entirely his.

He nodded.

Sebastian raised an eyebrow at me quizzically.

Standing, I went to the harp and settled myself. Then I drew upon the strings to test them. It was a good instrument. First, I played a lively, cheerful tune—or as lively as one can play on a harp—and I glanced over to see the astonishment on Jarrod's face.

I should have told him before, but it had never occurred to me.

When I finished, Phillipe called out, "Sing us a ballad. The one about the girl who drowns."

Lady Rosamund smiled tightly. "Of course. Megan has such a sweet, clear voice."

Again, her words were barbs, for my voice would certainly never fill a large room, and she meant to point this out. But I could carry a tune and hit the highest notes with a pleasing sound as opposed to the screech of many young noblewomen.

Rolf and Kai glanced at each other in open surprise, as if uncertain this scene was playing out in their own hall.

When I began to sing, everyone fell silent. Even Betty and Matilda stopped moving. The ballad was a sad one about two star-crossed lovers who tried to escape their families, each one taking a different ship to meet up on the shores of another country.

The girl's ship is caught is a storm, and she is lost.

In the last stanza, she speaks to her love:

When you look at the harsh waves
When you look at the sea
When your long life is ending
You will still see me

I allowed the final note to hang in the air. When I looked up, Rolf stared back at me, and then he began to clap. The others joined him quickly, even Kai.

"I think that might be enough music," Lady Rosamund said.

By way of answer, Jarrod stood, and I was glad he knew enough to cue the others. It was customary after dessert and entertainment for the guests to walk about a dining hall, sipping wine, looking at tapestries, and visiting with one another.

I also knew this was the time the men would conduct business, and I quietly made my way to Jarrod, Rolf, and Lord Allemond where they stood near the hearth.

Discussion of the land purchase was already underway.

"I do think you should ride the day after next and meet me at the old hunting lodge," Allemond was saying. "My gamekeeper swears some of the trees have bark beetles. I haven't seen an issue, but with such rumors, it would be wise for both of us if you and Rolf come out and check for yourselves before money changes hands."

Jarrod was a cautious man by nature, and he listened carefully. "The day after tomorrow?"

"Yes, I'm free that afternoon."

The situation appeared straightforward enough. There had been a report of bark beetles, which would damage the value of any lumber taken out, and Allemond wanted Jarrod and Rolf to check trees at random themselves.

I was nervous. In the past, I'd occasionally tried to do two readings in a day and had sometimes failed in the second attempt. Though I was still drained from my reading that morning, I had no choice but to try here. Focusing my mind, I reached out to connect with Allemond's, and as had happened with Lavonia, a wall of emotion hit me. It was so strong I nearly lost my composure. Hatred and fear seethed through him. Bracing myself, I reached deeper until snippets of his thoughts grew clear.

No such men on the Council of Nobles . . .

Cannot be allowed to happen . . .

Nearly lost inside his mind, I felt the things he felt. He feared the Volodanes rising to greater power, and the events of tonight had driven his fear into panic. He saw Jarrod and Rolf as a threat, as brutish, uneducated men who could never be allowed to push themselves into the realm of civilized men or decisions that affected the nation.

His thoughts rolled forward to the suggested meeting, and I saw a clear image of a lodge surrounded by oak trees. He envisioned himself out front of the lodge, on his horse, with two other men, one on each side of him, and a few guards behind. Inside his mind, I took note of the two men at his sides.

One was enormous, with a dark beard and black leather armor, on a bay warhorse. The other was wiry with a scar on his forehead. He rode a great roan stallion.

Jarrod and Rolf soon entered his vision of what would play out, and they rode up with perhaps ten guards.

As they approached the lodge, dozens of men suddenly charged from the trees on horseback, swinging swords and surrounding them. Allemond envisioned himself just watching, but the two men with him rode into the fray.

The large, bearded man charged straight at Rolf, coming at him from behind as he fought two attackers on his right. This man took Rolf's head off in the first swing. Several other men were rushing Jarrod . . .

I stumbled backward and pulled out of Allemond's mind. I couldn't look anymore. He dreamed of murdering Jarrod and Rolf. He was planning their deaths.

Rolf stepped toward me and reached out with one hand. "Are you all right?"

Faint from overtaxing myself, I tried to smile. "It's nothing. Perhaps the fire is too warm?"

Neither of the other two men had even noticed.

"You'll ride to meet me?" Allemond pressed. "The day after tomorrow?" Though it was deftly done, Jarrod glanced at me. I shook my head once at him.

"I'll have to check and see what needs our attention that day," Jarrod answered. Then he yawned. "Let's talk over breakfast."

As the Monville border was a half day's ride, they would need to spend the night here and ride out in the morning. This was one area where I could not do much to make Jarrod appear as a proper host. The old keep didn't boast many guest rooms, but I had managed to have several rooms prepared on the third floor of the tower. At least the bedding was clean.

However, Allemond seemed taken aback by Jarrod's response. He'd expected a quick assent to his sensible suggestion.

"I don't see why we cannot decide this now . . ." He trailed off as Jarrod walked away from him.

"It grows late," Jarrod announced. "Time to retire."

This was clearly an order, but Lady Rosamund and Phillipe took the time to say proper good nights before joining with Lord Allemond and leaving with Betty to be shown to their rooms. Allemond's face was dark. I doubted anything about this evening had gone as he'd planned.

Once our guests were out of the hall, Jarrod looked to Sebastian and Kai. "Out. Both of you."

Sebastian glanced at me. "You did well."

"So did you," I managed to answer, but I felt so drained I had trouble staying on my feet.

A few moments later, Jarrod, Rolf, and I were alone in the hall, and Jarrod turned to me.

"Well?" he demanded.

Too weary to even attempt to soften the blow, I answered. "He plans to have you and Rolf murdered the day you go to meet him at the hunting lodge."

It was difficult to shock Jarrod, but his eyes widened.

"What?" Rolf asked.

"He has men waiting in the trees," I went on, "and two men at his sides who he envisions joining the attack. You would be outnumbered."

Regaining his composure, Jarrod leaned close. "What did the two men at his sides look like?"

"One was large, with a dark beard and black leather armor. The other was smaller . . . with a scar on his forehead."

My description produced an immediate effect.

Rolf drew in a harsh breath. "Father, there's no way she could ever have met Magnus and Berrick."

Both men were silent for a few seconds, but I could see they believed me. They believed I had seen Allemond's plans in his mind.

"What do we do?" Rolf asked his father. "Kill them first?"

Jarrod shook his head. "No, murdering the Monvílles won't progress our cause. We let them go in the morning. I'll put off the meeting at the lodge, but I'll find a way to buy that land." He sounded so determined I did not doubt him.

Reaching up, I touched my temple.

"She's tired," Rolf said. "Let her go to bed."

"What?" Jarrod asked, coming from his thoughts. "Oh, yes." He waved one hand. "Off with you, girl."

Grateful to Rolf, I left the hall.

* * * *

Once upstairs, I was equally grateful to get undressed and have Miriam help me into a nightgown. Just being alone with her in my room eased the throbbing in my head.

"Did the evening go well, my lady?" she asked.

How could I possibly answer that? From Jarrod's perspective, it had been a grand success. From the Monvílles' perspective, it had been an unmitigated disaster.

So, I supposed the answer to Miriam's question would be yes.

Before I could speak, the door opened and Rolf walked in. I gave Miriam a quick nod. She hurried from the room, closing the door behind herself.

"Megan," Rolf breathed.

I looked over at him, as he'd never spoken to me in such a soft tone. He stood there watching me in a kind of wonder.

"I almost couldn't believe what was happening tonight," he said. "The greenish tinge on Allemond's arrogant face . . . the dinner . . . you at that harp." He shook his head. "I've gone along with Father these past years to humor him. There was nothing else I could do. But I never thought we had any chance to reach the heights he's imagined, not until now."

I listened, frozen, as he stepped closer.

"You are everything I have lacked, and I had no idea until tonight," he went on. "You and I could go so far together. I could gain a seat on the Council of Nobles. We could shape the nation's policies."

My breaths were shallow. No one had ever spoken to me like this before. I'd had no idea Rolf was capable of speaking so many words. Looking into his face, I didn't see love or desire, but I did see respect, admiration, and value.

Reaching out, he touched my face and then leaned down to kiss me. This time, it felt different. He was not performing a duty, and when I kissed him back, neither was I.

His words echoed in my ears.

You and I could go so far together.

I touched his chest and stood on my tiptoes to kiss him more easily. We might not have fire or passion or love, but perhaps we were developing mutual respect and need.

And for me—who'd never once been valued—the prospect of respect and need could be just as seductive as love.

For the first time since arriving here, I couldn't wait to see what tomorrow would bring.

Chapter 4

By the time the Monvílles were ready to leave the following morning, of course, Jarrod hadn't committed to any sort of meeting to inspect the trees for bark beetles.

He simply told Lord Allemond, "I'll send word to you as soon as we can arrange the spare time."

While this answer must have frustrated Allemond, it wasn't a refusal, and so he offered a strained smile. "Let me know any time that is convenient. I'll look for your message."

With that, we said our polite good-byes. Lady Rosamund hypocritically kissed my cheek. She cast one long glance at Sebastian, and then their retinue mounted up and rode from the courtyard.

Afterward, I wondered if Jarrod would wish to speak more on what I'd seen in Lord Allemond's mind.

He didn't.

I wondered if he would make mention of me having dismissed Lavonia.

He didn't.

Instead, all four of the men proceeded into their normal daily tasks. Sebastian headed off to the barracks, most likely to play cards. Kai had a sparring session. Jarrod and Rolf rode out to check the state of the apple orchards.

I headed off to the kitchens for a task I believed would be expected of me, something my mother had always done the day after a banquet.

As I entered the kitchen, Ester smiled. "Was the meal last night to Lord Jarrod's liking?"

"It was perfect. He could not have been more pleased. Thank you so much." I looked at the other girls, including Cora. "And thank you. I know you all worked hard."

Cora had been watching me nervously, but she appeared to relax at my words. This made me glad, as it convinced me she wanted to keep her position and that perhaps without Lavonia's influence, she might work out well.

I turned back to Ester. "So, how much food is left? How many of us will be needed to carry it down?"

She looked back at me in puzzlement. "Carry it down?"

"To the village."

I wondered about her confusion. It was common practice for the lady of any noble household to have all the leftovers collected the morning after a banquet and then help take them down to the nearest village to be given to the poor.

Ester didn't appear familiar with this custom.

Quickly, I explained it.

"Oh, I don't think so, my lady," she said, shaking her head. "The master wouldn't like that at all. He'd be angry." She paused. "Did you ask Lord Rolf?"

I hadn't. It had never occurred to me. In my previous world, this practice was tradition.

"No."

"You'd best ask him."

Jarrod and Rolf were both gone, but for the first time, I felt uncertain regarding the limits of my power in the realm of the kitchen. If Ester said Jarrod would be displeased, even angered, by a charitable act, I felt I ought to listen.

After nodding, I moved on to other duties.

However, that night, we were served the leftover beef and chicken for dinner, and I decided not to ask Jarrod or Rolf after all. They did things differently here, and I would need to adjust.

The days began to pass, and no one mentioned the Monvilles again. Rolf and I continued to come to know each other a little better, but the only time we spent alone was in my room at night. He never sought my company otherwise nor offered to take me riding on the land. I wasn't unhappy, but I wondered when I might once again leave the confines of the manor.

Two weeks following the banquet, Jarrod came home earlier than usual and sent for me. I found him the dining hall. The day was warm, and so no fire had been lit, but he stood by the hearth.

"You wished to see me?" I asked absently. I'd been taking stock of the larder with Ester and wanted to get back.

Turning, he studied my face for a moment. "You're a Volodane now, girl. Not a Chaumont."

Suddenly, he had my full attention.

"Of course," I answered cautiously.

"At the end of summer, the Council of Nobles convenes at the castle in Partheney."

I already knew this. The council of twelve always met in late summer, and the king attended as well.

After a pause, he added, "I want an invitation."

"Why? There is currently no open seat on the council."

"Doesn't matter. I want to be there for the gathering," Jarrod said flatly. "I want an invitation."

"I can't arrange that for you."

"Your father can."

At this, I walked over to him, tilting my head up to see his hawkish features. "He can, but I'm not certain he would. Do you wish me to ask him?"

"No, I want you to make sure. Write and tell him that unless he gains us an invitation, I'll spread word that the Chaumonts are nearly bankrupt, that he had no dowry to give you, and that I paid him for your hand."

"I can't tell him that."

His eyes narrowed. "Oh, I think you can, and I won't even need to bruise your arm this time. I think you'll do it for Rolf."

We stood watching each other without speaking. My mind flashed back to Rolf's tenderness the night of the banquet, of the things he'd said to me.

You and I could go so far together. I could gain a seat on the Council of Nobles. We could shape the nation's policies.

"I trust you have paper and quill?" Jarrod asked.

"Yes."

"Good."

That evening, I wrote to my father.

* * * *

While I awaited an answer, a message arrived for me.

I knew it probably wouldn't be from my father, as not enough time had passed, and I somewhat taken aback to see it was from Lady Violette Cornett.

My dear Megan,

Or should I call you Lady Volodane now?

How pleased I was to hear of your marriage! The baron and I have planned a brief house party, only three days, beginning the week after next. We should so like to see you and your new family. The manor will be bursting, but we have plenty of guest rooms.

Do let me know if you can attend, and be certain to tell young Kai to bring his sword as the baron is planning lively entertainments.

With affection,
Violette

I read the note twice, nonplussed. She wrote as if we were friends, and I barely knew her. I had seen her while accompanying my father in Partheney, but I didn't recall her ever speaking to me. She and her husband, Henri, were minor nobility, but they were widely known for giving lavish house parties that lasted for days. Although I'd never attended such an event, my parents had. These parties were one of the few social engagements where my father claimed he didn't need me—or my ability. Later, I learned from my sister that she and I didn't take part because the Cornett house parties had a rather wild reputation, with guests sometimes waking up in the wrong beds.

Why would Violette invite the Volodanes to one of their house parties? Did they believe Jarrod and Rolf's star was on the rise due to a mix of wealth and new social connection? Did they wish to establish a friendship in the early days? It was possible.

That night, before dinner, I took the note to Jarrod and let him read it.

His eyes scanned the paper, and he looked up. "Henri Cornett isn't on the Council of Nobles."

"No, but I'd guess there will be several men in attendance who *are* on the council. This is a sign you're being accepted into society."

Slowly, he nodded. "Write back and accept."

Over dinner that night, he made the announcement that we'd all be attending, and the reactions from his sons were varied. Rolf appeared quietly interested. He glanced at me as if I were to thank for the invitation.

Sebastian was openly pleased. "The Cornetts? Really? We'd best keep our wits about us. The rumors of some of their gatherings are scandalous."

But he said "scandalous" as if it was something to be anticipated.

Only Kai balked. "I'm not going. That sounds like three days on the fourth plane of hell to me."

"You're going," Jarrod stated flatly. "Lady Violette mentioned you by name and told you to bring your sword."

I'd wondered about that line in the letter. For one, Kai would never go anywhere without his sword. Still, no one explained it to me, but Kai stopped arguing and didn't seem so reticent anymore.

The next week was a blur of activity as Miriam and I spent hours each day sewing new clothes for everyone, and I made packing lists.

Jarrod nearly had a fit when he saw the gifts I'd had loaded into a wagon: casks of wine, fine tea, and early apples from the Volodane orchard.

"It's expected," I explained. "We'll look like peasants if we arrive empty-handed."

He frowned but thankfully deferred to my knowledge of such matters.

Finally, the day of our departure arrived.

The Cornetts' estate was to the east of ours, and Jarrod estimated that if we left early in the morning, we could reach our destination by that same evening.

He and Rolf rode at the head of our party. Kai rode with the guards, and I rode beside Sebastian with Miriam directly behind us. The day was fine, and I enjoyed the ride. It felt good to be outside again.

"You look happy," Sebastian observed.

"I am." Then I grew thoughtful. "Or at least I am right now. But I haven't the faintest idea what we're heading into or exactly why we were invited. I'm hoping the Cornetts simply believe your family is on the rise and they wish to make early inroads."

"I couldn't care less why we were invited," he answered. "I intend to have a good time."

As Jarrod had gauged, we arrived in the early evening.

Even in the fading light, I could see the Cornetts' manor was large and exquisite, with a white-painted stucco façade and a stylish black front door. At the sight of it, Jarrod expressed a flash of hesitation, but it came and went quickly.

Upon dismounting, we were met by several servants and shown inside the manor. A tall woman in a starched white apron approached us in the entryway.

"My lord and lady and the other guests are dressing for dinner. Please follow me, and I'll show you to your rooms." She paused and looked to me. "Is it acceptable for you and Lord Rolf to share?"

"Yes. Thank you."

Not all married nobles shared rooms, even as guests.

Dressing for dinner was nothing unusual to me, but it still was for the men, and they all followed my lead, remaining silent and following the tall woman, who I assumed was the housekeeper. We were shown our various rooms. We changed into evening attire and were shown back downstairs.

As we walked toward the back of the manor, I saw a large archway leading to a great dining chamber, and my stomach tightened.

I was about to represent my new family to a pack of nobles who were all probably hoping the Volodanes would provide entertainment by behaving like the brutes everyone thought them to be.

Tonight, I wore a red velvet gown and Helena's diamond pendant.

As I entered the dining hall on Rolf's arm, numerous heads turned. I judged there to be about forty people and focused my attention entirely on the smiling woman walking toward me.

"Megan, my dear," Lady Violette exclaimed, kissing both my cheeks.

She was beautiful, tiny and pale with black hair. Though she must be in her late thirties, she looked ten years younger. Both her greeting and her kisses felt different from Lady Rosamund's.

I almost believed Violette was delighted to see me, and that we'd been friends before tonight.

She greeted the men with me just as warmly, and I could see Jarrod was somewhat thrown off-balance by her beauty. That surprised me. I'd never seen him affected by a woman.

But Violette stopped on Sebastian, taking in the sight of his face, clothing, and dark hair. "Goodness, where have you been hiding?"

"Cast off in the wastelands." He smiled and his eyes sparkled.

I could see right away that those two were kindred spirits, both of them loved wit and pleasure above all else. She took his arm and led him into the room. We followed.

The next few moments were a blur of greetings or introductions. I knew most everyone by name and face. My parents were not in attendance.

Rolf did well, greeting men and asking about pending crops. In a different way from Sebastian, he was becoming a natural at conducting himself among the nobles. I could see the other men responding to him as one of their own.

Jarrod and Kai both managed to nod politely, but I could see Jarrod felt out of his element and Kai was nearly overwhelmed.

"Megan, darling," said a female voice to my left.

Turning, I was rendered speechless for a few seconds by the sight of Lady Rosamund Monvíle.

Looking over her shoulder, I saw Lord Allemond chatting with his brother, Phillipe.

"My lady," I said, recovering myself and letting her kiss me.

Violette released Sebastian's arm to join us. "Rosamund was the one who suggested I invite you," our hostess confessed. "I must say I'm so glad she did."

I blinked. Rosamund had wrangled this invitation?

"It was Lord Allemond's idea," Rosamund put in with a strained smiled. "He insisted."

"Well then, I'm glad he did," Violette answered, not appearing to note any tension. Perhaps she didn't. I was beginning to like her, but a warning bell sounded in the back of my mind.

Why would Lord Allemond insist that his wife arrange an invitation for us? He hated the Volodanes. I'd need to look for a way to speak to Jarrod quietly as soon as possible.

Rosamund's eyes raked over Sebastian, and the dinner gong sounded.

Unfortunately, I was seated between Baron Cornett and an aging gentleman, Viscount Bretagne. Jarrod was seated well down the table. I would never read Lord Allemond without Jarrod's instructions. My father had trained me well in this regard for good reason. As I could only do one deep reading tonight, there may be someone else Jarrod might wish me to read, and he'd be displeased if I couldn't accommodate his wish.

The room was filled with men with whom he may be seeking connection. I did notice him glancing at Allemond once or twice, but he didn't appear concerned. Whatever Allemond's agenda here, he was no great danger to any of us at the dinner table.

I was tired from the long day's ride and nearly winced when Lady Violette announced dancing after dinner. Somehow, I stayed on my feet and kept a smile on my face as I danced with Rolf. I got Kai out on the floor twice, and to my surprise, he seemed to enjoy himself. Perhaps he liked having something to do.

Nothing about the evening struck me as remotely scandalous. I did notice a few men and women in low conversations with people to whom they weren't married, but that was all. Even Sebastian, who'd expressed a plan to enjoy himself, spent much of the night speaking with Viscount Bretagne's handsome son, Richard.

Finally, people began to drift away, and I felt it late enough to say our good nights.

Soon, with great relief, I found myself in bed beneath a down comforter with Rolf beside me.

"I found out Lord Allemond initially suggested our invitation," I told him.

"Truly?" He frowned. "Perhaps he thought to provide us with another chance to embarrass ourselves."

"Perhaps. I hope it's nothing more. Remember he's not above violence."

"I doubt he'd try anything here, but I'll speak to my father first thing tomorrow."

Feeling better that this was out of my hands, I leaned back into my pillow.

Propping himself up on one elbow, Rolf touched my face. "Allemond or not, we wouldn't be here without you, and I very much want to be here."

Again, I couldn't help drinking in his value of me.

"You did well tonight," I answered. "Everyone saw you as one of their own."

"I never thought I'd have the chance to try."

"Surely you've been invited to some dinners or events."

"No. Never. We've sometimes gone to Partheney when Kai's entered a tournament, but none of the other noble families had much to do with us."

"Tournaments?" I asked. "As in competition via combat?"

He kissed my forehead. "You'll see tomorrow."

Then he kissed my mouth, and we spoke no more.

Chapter 5

Everyone slept until midday and then spent time dressing. In the mid-afternoon we gathered in the dining hall for a casual buffet-styled meal.

As the afternoon waned, Henri Cornett walked to the archway and announced, "I think it's time. Shall we go below?"

Kai's eyes glittered, and I looked up to Rolf.

"What's happening?"

"A small tournament, just for betting and entertainment. I heard some of the men discussing it last night."

Of course, I knew what the word "tournament" meant, but I still didn't quite understand how such a practice would fit into this house party. We all followed Henri out the dining room, down a passage, and through a door near the end.

I found myself in a stairwell leading downward. At the bottom of the stairs, I stepped out into a large underground chamber with no windows. Torches in brackets on the walls provided flickering light.

Rows of benches had been built in a circle all around the room, and standing on the top bench, I looked down into a pit on the floor below, about forty paces in circumference.

"An arena," Rolf supplied.

The Cornetts had an arena built in their cellar? Had my parents ever stood here?

Kai left us, and I didn't see where he went, but Sebastian and Jarrod stepped downward over the benches to find a place nearer the front.

They sat.

Rolf and I followed to join them. I ended up sitting between Sebastian and my husband. All around us, people began finding seats, chattering to each other, and I began feeling some trepidation over what was about to transpire.

"Who's up first?" Sebastian asked.

"I'm not sure," Rolf answered, "but I heard there would only be five matches, so I doubt they'd put Kai up too early. They'd want to save him for the end."

There was a door at the back of the pit area below. That door opened and two men emerged. One of them was young Richard Bretagne and the other was a stranger, a stocky man in a leather hauberk.

Both carried swords.

I understood we were about to see a fight, but some of this still eluded me.

"Who's the other man?" I whispered to Sebastian.

"Probably a mercenary," he answered. "This isn't a formal competition, just a bit of sport, so Henri must have hired a few men for the day."

Standing, Lord Henri called, "Second blood!"

I glanced to Sebastian again.

Seeing my discomfort, he leaned closer. "It's all right. They'll only spar with each other, and no one aims for the face. The first man to strike a second cut on his opponent wins."

"Oh, and Kai will take part in this?"

"Wait until you see him. He started competing at sixteen, and he's never lost a match."

I felt myself relaxing somewhat. Even if the men would cut each other once or twice, this didn't sound like too violent a blood sport, and there were rules.

Sebastian looked over my head at Rolf. "Two silver pieces on Richard."

Rolf studied the mercenary for a moment. "Done."

Others around us began calling bets.

Henri stood waiting until all bets were placed. I could see him enjoying his role as host for this portion of the entertainment.

Once the small crowd fell silent, he nodded to Richard.

Within seconds, the bout began. Richard was slender but quick. His opponent was larger, stronger, and a little slower. The two men circled each other and then the mercenary took a swing. Richard dodged it easily and cut the man on the shoulder.

Sebastian and a few others cheered.

But as Richard drew his sword back to block, the mercenary took a back swing that was faster than I would have expected, and he nicked Richard's collarbone. A line of blood flowed out.

This time, more of the small crowd cheered. It seemed most people had bet on Richard's opponent.

The two men circled again, each one taking a few feints but not striking. Then, without warning, Richard darted forward and slashed. He barely missed, but the other man took advantage of the moment and stuck Richard across the arm, cutting through his wool shirt.

"Second blood!" Henri called.

The crowd cheered again.

"Bad luck," Rolf said to Sebastian. "That's two silvers."

"The afternoon's not over yet," his brother answered.

Down in the pit, Richard smiled openly at his opponent, and the two men shook hands. I relaxed even further. Although I'd never seen anything like this, it did appear to be more of a game than anything else.

More matches followed, all between one of the nobles and a paid fighter or soldier Henri had hired. Each fight was similar to Richard's with a display of footwork and circling and swinging. One of the nobles won and then two of the mercenaries, but each match ended with smiles and the shaking of hands. By the close of the fourth match though, Sebastian owed Rolf five silvers. Jarrod never placed a bet.

Finally, I heard a few loud cheers and looked down to see Kai coming out the door and taking his place in the pit for the final match.

People in the crowd were smiling. They might not invite the Volodanes to house parties, but apparently, quite a few of them had already seen Kai fight.

"No one will bet against him," Rolf said in my ear. "This one is just for show."

I watched in anticipation, my expectations high . . . but then I looked at Kai's opponent. He was tall with long arms. His head was shaved and beads of sweat ran down his temples. It wasn't warm down here.

There was a sheen across his face, and his eyes were glazed. He gripped the hilt of his sword tightly.

"Something's wrong," I whispered to Rolf. "You need to stop this."

He glanced down at me. "Don't say that aloud. You'll embarrass Kai."

The fear inside me grew as the two men began circling each other. This mercenary was different from the others. His expression was desperate.

"Ask your father if I can read that man," I begged Rolf in a low whisper.

I dared not act without permission as Jarrod might want me to read one of the nobles later, and I dared not use up my strength now without his agreement.

"Megan, quiet," Rolf answered in what almost sounded like annoyance. "Kai knows what he's doing."

As if to entertain the crowd, Kai flipped his sword once and caught it. People applauded and cheered.

Then, in a flash, he moved fluidly inside his opponent's guard and nicked the man's shoulder.

As he continued moving past the man and was turning back, the mercenary abandoned all rules of the match and swung for Kai's face, slicing his cheek open. Unprepared for this, Kai stumbled, and the man swung downward, cutting through the back of his right knee.

"No!" Sebastian cried, jumping to his feet.

People in the crowd gasped.

But it was too late. Kai fell backwards onto the floor of the pit. The man gripped the hilt of his sword with both hands and rammed it through Kai's chest.

Sebastian was screaming. He and Rolf both jumped down into the pit, but guards were pouring out the lower door, and one of them reached the scene on the ground first. That guard thrust a dagger through the side of the mercenary's throat.

"No!" Sebastian cried again, still running, and he shoved the guard away.

I knew why. He wanted someone to question.

Rolf was on his knees beside Kai, his face a mask of disbelief.

Kai's eyes were open, but he wasn't breathing. He was dead. Had he been expecting a death match, he could have defended himself, but he'd gone out only to spar. Jarrod stood beside me with his eyes on his dead son, as if unable to absorb what had just happened.

The guard who'd killed the mercenary wore a light green tabard bearing the crest of the Monvílles.

I looked instantly to the Monvílles. Both Rosamund and Phillipe were on their feet with expressions of equal shock. Only Allemond remained calm and seated.

I knew I should wait for permission from Jarrod, but this wasn't my old world, and the rules here were different. Focusing all my strength, I reached out for Allemond's thoughts, and a wall of satisfaction hit me.

His thoughts and emotions rushed through me as he looked down. He'd been frustrated by Jarrod's continued postponements to ride out to meet him, so he'd decided to try another tactic.

He found an ex-soldier who'd married, had children, and tried his hand at farming. A bad crop had forced the soldier to borrow money at high interest. Another poor year had left him in dire straits. He and his family were about to be turned from their home to starve.

Allemond had offered to pay the entire debt and interest if the man would kill Kai in the ring. This man had killed before, many times, and he agreed.

He'd probably known he was signing his own death warrant as well, but at least he'd saved his family.

Allemond sat looking down at Kai's dead body with great satisfaction. Kai was the one the others had loved. Allemond had spotted that much at the dinner party at the Volodanes. Now, not only had their numbers been decreased by one, but the three other men would be thrown into mourning. They would be careless and easier to manipulate.

I pulled from Allemond's mind and looked down into the pit. Rolf was still on his knees, his face white. Sebastian wept openly as if he didn't care who saw him.

* * * *

Not long after, Jarrod, Sebastian, Rolf, and myself were alone in a cellar room beneath the manor. Kai's body had been laid out, and Lord Henri had ordered we be given a moment of privacy.

Kai's eyes had been closed, and his long, brown hair spread out around his head on the table. There was a bloody hole in his chest where his heart should have been.

The pain and rage in the room were palpable.

Jarrod could barely speak. Sebastian couldn't seem to stop moving, and Rolf simply stood by his dead younger brother.

Quietly, I told them what I'd seen in Allemond's mind, and Rolf's eyes lifted to my face.

"I'll kill him," Rolf whispered.

"What do you mean, you *saw* these things in Allemond's mind?" Sebastian asked.

Jarrod raised a hand. "Not now." His breathing was ragged. "That's why his guard reached them first. He ordered the mercenary to be killed so the man couldn't be questioned."

Rolf started for the door. "I'll kill him," he repeated.

"No!" Jarrod barked. "You cannot start a blood feud here!"

Rolf whirled, glaring.

"There's no proof," Jarrod added. "If you run a sword through Allemond, we'll lose all the ground we've gained."

"I don't care! Kai is dead, and you don't seem to . . ." Rolf trailed off and choked once. "Kai is dead, and I'm killing his killer."

"Let me do it," Sebastian said quietly. His eyes locked on Jarrod. "Give me a free hand, and there won't be a blood feud."

Rolf shook his head. "Father, no. You can't turn him loose. There's no telling what he'll do."

"I know exactly what *you'll* do," Jarrod returned. "You'll walk out there and attack Allemond with no proof. What will you say? That your wife read his mind?" He turned to Sebastian. "No, blood feud?"

Sebastian shook his head. "Give me one more night here. No one will even blame me."

Slowly, Jarrod nodded. "All right."

Rolf exhaled through his teeth.

After that, Sebastian walked back to the table and leaned over Kai's body. For a moment I thought he would begin weeping again. I didn't know what to say or do. I wanted to offer comfort but didn't know how. I wanted to weep for Kai myself, but I felt an outsider in this scene, someone who had no part in this mourning.

Light footsteps sounded outside the room, and Lady Violette walked in. The regret on her lovely face was genuine.

"Forgive the intrusion. My lord Jarrod, I cannot tell you how sorry we are for your loss, and we cannot fathom how this happened. I assure you that my husband is questioning the other men he hired for today's match, to see if they know anything. He will get to the bottom of this, but there is no way we can amends."

"It's not your fault," Jarrod answered, but his voice was strained. He loved Kai as much as Rolf and Sebastian did. "None of us blame you."

"Perhaps the man was mad?" Sebastian said to her. "He hated nobles?"

"Perhaps so." She seemed quite relieved by both their responses. "But please don't take Kai's body and ride out tonight. Stay here at least until morning. Dinner will be served, but we've cancelled any dancing. Stay and let us try to offer comfort."

Jarrod glanced to Sebastian and then back to Violette. "Thank you, my lady. We'll stay tonight."

* * * *

That night, at dinner, I couldn't help feeling anxious. We were all supposed to pretend we knew nothing and were as lost regarding Kai's death as everyone else.

I could feel that Rolf was on the edge of his own self-control, but he obeyed his father and simply avoided speaking to any of the Monvilles. In my mind, I kept seeing Kai laid out on that table, his life cut off in such a brutal and senseless way.

I wish I understood what Sebastian was going to do.

I knew better than to ask him.

Everyone was kind to us, and when Lord Allemond offered me his condolences, I managed to accept gracefully. Thankfully, he didn't approach Rolf.

To my surprise, Sebastian not only accepted such sympathies, he treated Allemond like an old friend, and he sat with Lady Rosamund at dinner. I was convinced that neither Rosamund nor Phillipe knew anything of Allemond's carefully orchestrated murder of Kai.

Still, I wondered what Sebastian was thinking by sitting with Lady Rosamund all evening, and letting her comfort him as if he were a child. She patted his hand and stroked his back and spoke softly in his ear. I noticed Lord Allemond glancing at them once or twice and frowning.

Rolf didn't speak much to anyone, but no one seemed to expect him to.

Somehow, we made it through dessert and the after-dinner conversation and were able to excuse ourselves.

Alone in a guest room with Rolf, I sank down on the bed. "I'm so sorry," I said. "I know how you loved him."

He came over to sit beside me. "I wanted to avenge him. Father was right to stop me, but he shouldn't have given Sebastian a free hand."

"What will Sebastian do?"

"I've no idea. That's the problem. There's something broken inside him. He doesn't think or feel like other people."

I found that an unfair assessment of Sebastian. Yes, he could be sly, but he was also capable of kindness, loyalty, and protection.

Rolf put his face in his hands. "I can't believe Kai's gone."

Scooting backward, I piled some pillows against the headboard. "Let me hold you. Please."

I needed this as much as he did. To my relief, he moved to me and laid his face against my stomach. I held him with both arms, rocking him gently.

He let me.

After a while, we both fell asleep like that, and the next thing I knew, I was awakened by the sound of a woman screaming.

Rolf sat up.

Loud voices and running feet came from beyond our door. Rolf bolted for the door, and I followed. He was faster than me, but I could see a small gathering down at the end of the passage. Lady Violette, Lord Henri, and several other guests must have had heard the screams. Jarrod was there. Coming to a stop near Rolf, I looked through an open doorway, into a room, and I went cold.

Lady Rosamund was on the bed of her guest room, on her knees, pressed up against the headboard, clutching the front of her gown.

Sebastian stood in the middle of the room over Allemond's dead body. He had his pearl-handled dagger in his right hand, and Allemond's hand gripped a dagger as well. But I had seen it before. It was Sebastian's other blade, the plain one with the tan handle.

Blood flowed from a wound in Allemond's throat and spread around him on the floor.

"What happened?" Lord Henri demanded.

This was the second death on the same day in his home.

Sebastian appeared distraught, but I could see the calm in his eyes.

He put his free hand to his head. "I didn't . . . I would never have . . ." Looking down, he leaned over and picked up a small beaded purse on the floor. "Lady Rosamund must have dropped this earlier in the hall. I found it and brought it back to her. Lord Allemond came upon us in here, and he . . . he misunderstood and attacked me. I had no choice but to defend myself." He turned to Rosamund. "My lady, forgive me."

Henri was still staring at the scene. "Rosamund?" he asked. "Is this true?"

Her eyes were wide, moving from her dead husband, to Sebastian, to Henri. "Yes," she answered. "It's as he says. He brought me back my purse and my husband came to my room and found us and misunderstood. He flew into a rage. Sebastian had no choice."

And then I thought on her earlier attentions to Sebastian, and I realized what he'd done. It appeared Rosamund and Allemond had separate guest rooms. Sebastian had accepted an assignation with her and then somehow arranged for Lord Allemond to come see his wife.

Sebastian probably had a message sent.

Upon Allemond's arrival, Sebastian had killed him and placed a dagger in his hand and Rosamund had begun screaming.

But now, she was faced with a number of her peers asking questions. A little secret bed hopping could be overlooked so long as it wasn't noticed. But a great lady like her being caught openly cavorting with a handsome young Volodane was something else entirely. She couldn't let the truth be exposed. She'd lose her reputation and doors would be slammed in her face.

If she didn't support Sebastian's story, she would be ruined.

"It's as he says," she repeated.

I don't know if everyone believed this, but it didn't matter. They both told the same story: Sebastian had been forced to defend himself.

Lord Allemond was dead, and for Rolf and Jarrod, honor had been served.

But when I looked back to Sebastian, I could see that his pain had not been eased. I wasn't sure it ever would be.

Chapter 6

We made the journey home and buried Kai in the family graveyard beside his mother. I had not seen this place before, as it was situated well beyond the kitchen gardens.

"I'll have wild flowers placed on their graves as often as possible," I promised Sebastian.

He nodded but didn't answer.

There was nothing else for me to do but go inside the keep and oversee the unpacking.

Betty found me almost right away and handed me a letter. "From your father, my lady."

"Thank you."

I took it to my room to read in private. I'd never seen my father threatened before, and I wasn't sure how he'd react.

Bracing myself, I unsealed the letter and opened it. The message was brief.

Dear Megan,

I understand your new father's interest in receiving an invitation to attend the gathering. I can most certainly arrange for this.

But your mother and I have found ourselves in some difficulties, and two hundred pieces of silver would solve our current issues. If Jarrod can assist in this matter, I can be of assistance to him.

With affection,
Your Father

I stared at the note. He harbored no affection for me. Really, the man had nerves of iron. He'd completely ignored Jarrod's threat and instead made an offer of his own: money in exchange for the invitation.

Taking the letter, I went downstairs and found Betty.

"Where is Lord Jarrod?"

I didn't think he'd leave the keep grounds today.

"He's out in the barracks," she answered.

Heading down the main passage, I left the keep, walked to the barracks, and entered. The place smelled musty, but I stood in a large main room with tables. The men must eat in here.

Jarrod stood a few paces away conferring with a few guards.

He appeared surprised at the sight of me. I never came out here. Waving off the guards, he closed the distance between us.

I held out the letter. "From my father."

Taking the paper, he scanned it once and looked up at me.

"I'm sorry," I said instantly. "I did make your threat clear."

"Don't be sorry. This is what I expected."

"It is?"

"Of course. I'll have the money put together before dinner. You prepare an answer."

It seemed Jarrod knew my father better than I did.

* * * *

The summer passed swiftly.

Kai's absence was like a hole in the family. But while Jarrod and Rolf appeared to slowly recover, Sebastian did not.

I understood why. Kai had been the only one who loved him, and now he felt alone. I tried to make up for this as much as I could, and I spent time with him, but I had to be cautious. He wasn't my husband, and a woman in my position had to be careful offering even sisterly attention to her husband's brother.

As the harvest came to a close, we sat down for dinner one night and Jarrod made an announcement.

"I've received our invitation to the gathering at Partheney," he said. "We leave next week."

Rolf started slightly, but I could see the excitement dawning on his face.

Sebastian looked stunned but not pleased. "What? No. That's not possible."

Jarrod snorted. "And how would you know what's possible? We're invited. We're staying in rooms at the castle, and we'll be inputting Rolf's name for the open seat on the council."

Rolf inhaled and gripped the table as he absorbed this news.

"Open seat?" Sebastian repeated.

"For Allemond's replacement," Jarrod answered, taking a long drink of wine from a goblet. "Thanks to you."

Sebastian stood. "I didn't kill him to leave an open seat on the council."

"All the same, it's there."

Stepping back, Sebastian shook his head. "I'm not going. I always go to the house in Rennes for the first month of autumn, and you know it. I won't give it up."

I didn't know what he meant.

A muscle in Jarrod's jaw twitched. "You'll go where I tell you."

Sebastian pointed at Rolf. "I'll not lift a finger to help you put him on the council!" He looked to me. "And neither should you! I assume we all have you to thank for this kind invitation?"

Without waiting for an answer, he turned and strode from the hall.

"Let me go after him," I asked Rolf. "He's distraught."

"Leave him be," Rolf answered.

He and Jarrod turned to discussing the pending journey to Partheney. I sat looking down at my plate.

* * * *

I'd taken to rising early to make sure Rolf and Jarrod had a decent breakfast before they set off on any duties for the day.

Sebastian never came down until later.

But the following morning, shortly after Rolf and Jarrod had left, and I was having the breakfast trays cleared away, Sebastian walked in to the hall wearing a black wool shirt, canvas pants, and boots.

"Get your cloak," he told me. "I need to show you something."

His face was unreadable.

"Wait here," I said. "I'll be right back."

After fetching my cloak, I found him waiting outside the archway of the hall. Without another word, he grasped my hand and led me outside the keep. Two saddled horses awaited us in the courtyard.

At the sight of them, I tried to pull back, but he didn't let go.

"Mount up," he ordered.

"Where are we going?"

"To the village. Get on the horse or I'll put you up myself."

He'd never once bullied me before. He'd certainly never threatened to use his strength against me.

I stared at him.

He sighed. "Please, Megan. We won't be gone long."

As he sounded more like himself now, I moved for the nearest horse and let him hand me up. He mounted the other horse and led the way. When we approached the front gates, I saw they were already opened and none of the guards there questioned Sebastian.

We rode out into the trees and down the path toward the village. After trotting a short distance, I pulled my horse to a walk and so did he.

"What did you mean last night by the 'house in Rennes'?" I asked.

"We own a second house in the city of Rennes. It belonged to my mother. Every autumn, I spend a month there doing exactly as I please. You may not have noticed, but Father needs me at social events enough to offer a reward. He occasionally needs me for other services too. So long as I play the part of dutiful son for eleven months out of the year, he lets me have one to myself."

I thought on that. Of course, I'd noticed that Jarrod relied on Sebastian at dinner parties. I wondered what other things he might ask of Sebastian, and I tried not to think on Allemond's death.

"I've gone along with Father's dreams of power to humor him," he continued, "and I'll admit I did want to go to the Cornetts when we were first invited. But it never once occurred to me that Rolf might actually gain a seat on the council. Not once."

"Why don't you want him to have a seat?" I asked.

"You're about to see."

We approached the village, often referred to Volodane Village. I'd only seen it the evening I arrived here, and we'd ridden through quickly. But I remembered the people vanishing at the sight of us.

Sebastian rode right in.

The village spread out around us. There were about fifty circular wattle and daub huts with thatched roofs, a few shops, a smithy, and a sturdy log dwelling that probably served as a common house. But in the daylight, I could see holes in many roofs and decay in the shops and dwellings.

It was a shabby, sad little place.

At the sight of us, the nearest people began slipping away.

"Stop," Sebastian ordered in a clear voice.

Down on the ground, to my right, a young mother in a threadbare dress froze in fear as she held the hand of a small boy.

"Take a good look at them," Sebastian said to me.

The woman was perhaps eighteen, but she was so thin. Her face was pinched and her dry hair was pulled back at the nape of her neck. The boy was no better, wearing pants with holes and no shoes. His arms were like twigs.

Sebastian nodded to the woman and she fled.

An uncomfortable wave passed through me. In addition to focusing on a single person and reading thoughts, I also had an unfortunate tendency to absorb strong emotions or sensations if enough people around me experienced the same feelings. Right now, all I could feel was fear, hunger, and despair.

Sebastian wasn't finished.

He grasped the rein of my horse and led me farther inside, forcing me to see the conditions in which these people lived. The old and the young were all thin, and some were ill. The despair grew until it became nearly overwhelming.

"Please. I need to leave."

Something in my voice must have reached him because he immediately started for the edge of the village, leading me all the way out.

We hadn't been inside long, but I was struggling to breathe. I'd never seen people in such a condition. I'd never felt such misery.

"Something must be done," I choked out. "Does your father know how bad things are?"

He looked at me as if I were simple. "Does he know? He's the one who's ensured they live like this. He's even instated the old laws by which most of the people can't fish in the streams or set snares for rabbits. Only a few people have license to fish or hunt and they have to either sell what they catch to us or sell it to anyone who can afford it and then pay my father over half of what they earn."

"Over half?"

"Megan, where do think all our wealth comes from? This place is just one village. Father bleeds them dry in taxes and then keeps the money or crops for himself, and do you know who he sends out to face these people to collect that money?"

I didn't want to hear the answer and closed my eyes.

"Rolf," he bit off. "Do you know what reward Rolf receives for his hard work?"

I kept silent.

"He receives a portion of the profits to pay our guards or hire more, and he has a number of them riding the perimeter of our property."

I opened my eyes. "Why would he do that?"

"Because he's paranoid, and he believes military force is the answer to everything. He feels the same way about the nation. Has he never spoken to you of his concerns that the king needs to increase the size of our military?"

I shook my head, but Rolf never spoke to me about much.

Sweeping one hand toward the village, Sebastian said, "Imagine what the country might look like if Rolf was making decisions on a larger scale? He'd tax without thought or mercy and build up our armies . . . just in case we need to go to war or defend ourselves. That's how he thinks. Is this what you want for the nation? People sucked dry to fund the military?"

Sitting on my horse, I was reeling. I'd lived in Volodane Hall for months, and if Sebastian was right, I knew nothing of the truth of my husband's ambitions.

"Whether you realize it or not," Sebastian went on, "you have a good deal of power inside this family. We've come further in three months than the last five years, and that's all due to you." He shook his head at me. "Don't help Rolf gain a seat on the council. Don't do it, Megan."

As I gazed back toward the village, I let his words sink in.

Perhaps I did have power. Perhaps it was time I used it.

Chapter 7

The next day, Sebastian packed up and left for Rennes. Jarrod didn't try to stop him. Perhaps he realized such efforts would only result in an ugly battle that could produce more harm than good . . . and he still might need Sebastian's help in the future.

For now, he had me to smooth over any socializing.

"I'll be home in a month," Sebastian said.

I never told Rolf about our visit to the village.

The following week, Rolf, Jared, and I were on our way to Partheney. It was a four-day journey, and we brought a large retinue of guards.

I often rode beside Miriam, so Rolf and I didn't speak much during the day, but we stayed at inns along way, and he was attentive at night, kissing me more deeply than ever before. Jarrod would never openly admit to my being essential in this venture, but Rolf acknowledged my importance without reservation.

He valued me for what I could do, and a part of me basked in his appreciation. I'd never been appreciated before, and it was seductive. Another part of couldn't forget how Sebastian had opened my eyes, and yet, I had no intention of disappointing Rolf.

Another plan was forming.

Near the end of the fourth day we arrived at the glorious city of Partheney, located on the west coast of the nation. The city stretched for miles, but it spread out around a hill and at the top of the hill was an enormous eight-towered castle. Our king had several castles, but he resided here in the autumn.

Much of the city itself had no walls as it had grown outward over the centuries, but the poorer citizens lived on the outskirts and the more affluent lived closer to the castle. Jarrod knew the roads well, and he led the way through the crowded streets.

Upon reaching the outer wall of the castle, he presented a letter, which I took to be the invitation he'd mentioned, and the castle guards ushered us through the gatehouse. Once inside the wall, we crossed a bridge and then passed through a second gatehouse and entered the vast courtyard of the castle.

It was alive with activity as guards bearing the colors of different noble houses all seemed to be giving orders regarding the distribution of luggage or stabling horses or housing men.

Our own men began to dismount and engage in the same sorts of activities.

Before I realized it, Rolf was on the ground beside me, and he reached up to lift me down.

"Where to now?" he asked. "We've never stayed at the castle."

I made sure Miriam was with us, and then I looked around until I saw a middle-aged soldier in a light blue and yellow tabard, the king's colors.

"Captain Trevar?" I called.

At the sight of me, he stopped what he was doing and came over, his eyes taking in Jarrod and Rolf in some surprise.

"My lady?" he asked.

"Can you please have us escorted inside? We should already have rooms prepared."

"Yes, my lady."

I'd known Captain Trevar since I was a girl, but he'd never seen me in the company of anyone besides my father. Still, we were clearly royal guests, and he called out to another man.

"Sergeant, see Lady Megan and her group inside. Find someone to show them to their rooms."

"Yes, sir."

Jarrod glanced down at me. "Deftly done," he said quietly.

"Not for a daughter of the Chaumonts," I answered.

He frowned. "You're a Volodane now."

"Of course."

* * * *

That night, we attended a large, informal dinner in the great hall of the castle. There were tables everywhere laden with food and drink. Everyone milled around, sitting when and where they chose and walking when they chose.

The king sat at a table up on a pedestal, but he didn't stand on ceremony tonight, and occasionally spoke to people standing in front of the table—while he ate—before turning to someone sitting on his left or right.

Jarrod and Rolf both seemed more comfortable with this arrangement than with a formal dinner where all eyes seemed to be upon them and they were expected to contribute to a single discussion.

I was just about to sit down when I looked across the hall and saw my parents enter. My mother was tall and imperious as always, my father alert. Both were dressed impeccably.

Upon seeing me, they came straight for us. Mother didn't bother kissing my cheek.

"Megan," she said, with a nod.

An unwanted flash of anger rose inside me. She had absolutely no idea what kind of life she'd sent me to. Nor did she care. She'd not written me a single letter to ask how I fared or if I was happy.

For all she knew, Rolf could have beaten me with a riding crop every night.

"Mother," I responded.

My father looked to Jarrod. "So, you wish to throw Rolf's name in for the open seat on the council? Rather poor taste as one of your other sons ran a dagger through Monville's throat, don't you think?"

So, he knew the whole story. Normally, though, he wasn't so openly cutting—more subtle. His manner suggested he was a good deal more bothered by Jarrod's threat to expose him than he'd sounded in that letter he sent.

"My dear," Mother said with a hint of warning. "Lord Jarrod, please accept our condolences on the death of Kai. I enjoyed his company during your visit."

Jarrod's tight expression flickered. "Thank you." His eyes locked on my father. "I'd like to speak to you alone tomorrow. Perhaps before lunch?"

I could see the resentment under the skin of my father's face, but Jarrod had him over more than one barrel, and he couldn't afford to offer offense.

"A walk in the courtyard?" Father suggested.

"Fine."

At that, my father took my mother's arm. "Forgive us. We have so many people to greet."

They walked away.

"Puffed-up snob," Jarrod said quietly. "You wouldn't know he'd borrowed the money for those clothes on his back."

I couldn't argue.

* * * *

Rolf stayed late in the hall after dinner to speak with some of the men, but I made my excuses and went to our room. Miriam had just slipped a white nightgown over my head when a single knock sounded and Jarrod walked in. He didn't seem remotely abashed by my state of undress. I grabbed a silk robe off the bed and donned it.

He glanced at Miriam. "Out."

This brought a flash of alarm. Jarrod had never sought me out in a private bedroom before. But what could I do?

"It's all right, Miriam. Please excuse us."

After a moment's hesitation, she slipped out. He followed her with his eyes.

"Pretty girl, that. I never noticed before."

"How can I help you?"

His attention swung back to me. "You can drop the haughty act for one. We're here on business, and tomorrow, you'll get to work."

"Doing what?"

"Dredging up dirt. Rolf needs at least six votes, and so far, we've only got three for certain."

"You've already managed to secure three?"

I was surprised. There were normally twelve noblemen on the council, and all of them were much like my father, of the oldest blood. With Allemond Monvíle gone, that left eleven men, so Rolf would have to garner at least six votes to carry the open seat. No one of Rolf's low status had ever come close to attaining a seat.

He nodded. "I've got your father in my pocket, and I'll drive that home tomorrow. We can count on him. I've also got Lords Paquet and Sauvage cornered."

"How?"

"Never you mind. You're not the only one who knows how to learn secrets. But we've got their votes. That leaves three more, and the council convenes in five days. That's not much time."

"What is it you wish me to do?"

I had a sinking feeling I already knew.

He laughed without humor, and his eyes moved up and down my silk robe. I wished Rolf would come in.

"Do? You're not a fool, girl. You know exactly what to do. Start reading men on the council and find something we can use."

What he was asking was not as easy as he made it sound.

"I can only do one deep reading a day," I reminded him.

"I know that, so you'd better choose right. Start with Lord Moreau. I'd wager next year's taxes he's as corrupt as they come."

"And if I do find some dirty little secret he won't want exposed?"

"Bring it to me. I'll do the rest."

Well, that was a relief. For a moment, I thought he might ask me to handle the blackmail. Now that I had my instructions, I only wanted him to leave.

Channeling my mother, I drew myself up. "Of course. Now if you'll excuse me, it has been a long day." I hoped to sound withering.

It didn't work.

Instead, he closed the distance between us and grabbed my wrist again, jerking me up against him. His grip was painful.

"Don't try that on me, girl, or I'll leave a few bruises where they won't show. And if you can't get me something I can use in the next five days, you'll find out what else I can do. You understand me?"

I was afraid of him. I didn't want to be, but I was.

"Yes."

He let go and started for the door. "Get started tomorrow."

* * * *

The next four days were some of the worst in my life. In addition to fearing Jarrod, I genuinely wanted to help Rolf. I was ever mindful of what Sebastian had shown and told me, but I believed I could both support my husband and temper some of his baser drives.

As instructed, on the first day, I began by seeking out Lord Moreau before dinner. There was a crowd in the great hall, and I drew him off for a goblet of wine. This was easy. He seemed interested in speaking with me, as he was as stunned as everyone else by Rolf putting his name up for Allemond's seat.

"How many men have requested to be considered?" I asked.

"Four others," he answered but didn't offer their names.

"Only four? Hopefully none of them will have any secrets that might prevent their election."

Although this was an odd thing to say, it produced the desired effect. I focused fully on his thoughts as his mind instantly went to his own secrets.

Though his financial situation was not as bad as my father's, he was having difficulties. Three nights ago, he'd been here at the castle playing cards. The king's first cousin, the Duke of Ariennes, had joined the game, and Lord Moreau ended up playing credit—hoping to win a large hand.

Instead, he'd lost four hundred pieces of silver to the duke. With a smile, Moreau had promised to pay the debt before leaving for home.

He couldn't. He didn't have the money, and he couldn't borrow it from anyone here lest his situation become known. His plan was to wait until after the council's vote and then fake receiving a note that his wife was ill at home. She'd not accompanied him this year. He hoped the duke would believe he'd simply forgotten the debt due to panic over his wife's health. Once home and away from the other nobles, he might be able to raise the money. Or . . . the duke was incredibly wealthy, and he might even overlook the debt out of sympathy for Moreau dealing with an ill wife.

After reading these thoughts, I pulled from Lord Moreau's mind and excused myself. All Jarrod would have to do was threaten to put a word into the duke's ear that Moreau planned to leave without paying. Then the issue would become a matter of honor and payment would be demanded. When it was discovered that Moreau couldn't pay, his standing would be ruined.

I took this information directly to Jarrod.

He smiled and nodded. "Good."

We had four votes.

The next day I went after Baron Augustine. He was an old friend of my family's and falling into conversation with him was easy. However, once I'd gotten him to focus on secrets, I was uneasy by what I found in his mind. He was worried and unsettled. He'd been embroiled in somewhat hurried negotiations with Viscount Bretagne—to marry his daughter to the viscount's son, Richard.

The wedding was to take place here at the castle in a week.

Unfortunately, Augustine's daughter was two months pregnant, by one of the house guards, and he was desperate that the wedding should take place before Richard learned of this. Afterward, the Bretagnes would keep the secret for the sake of their own family's honor.

After reading his thoughts, I wavered. This information would give Jarrod a good deal of power that stretched far into the future. Should the child prove to be male, it would mean the heir to the Bretagne was illegitimate, and Jarrod wouldn't hesitate to use this against them.

Still, I had little choice.

Jarrod would be waiting tonight and expect me to have something of use.

He was thrilled when I told him and actually patted me on the back. "Good girl."

I wondered if he knew how condescending he sounded.

We had five votes.

The next day proved a disaster. I decided to go after the oldest man on the council. At the age of sixty-two, Lord Cloutier had held his seat the longest. I tried him because I thought anyone who'd been in power for so long must have some secret he wished to be kept.

To my alarm, as I read him, I found nothing. He was a man of ethics with nothing to hide.

Jarrod snarled when I told him. He raised one hand but stopped himself and didn't strike me.

"You've got two days," he said.

On the fourth day, at a gathering for lunch, I tried Lord du Guay. He was a quiet man, and I wondered if his mild demeanor might be a cover for something darker. I was not wrong, but once I got him to turn his mind to any harbored secrets, what I saw was beyond unsettling. I almost recoiled from his thoughts.

He was man with penchant for what I'd heard referred to as "rough wooing." As a girl, I'd never known what it meant. Living with the Volodanes, I could imagine a bit more, but in truth I had no real idea.

Lord du Guay liked violence with sex, and he liked to be the one meting out the violence. His wife knew of this penchant, but he valued her and cared deeply what she thought, so he'd convinced her that he'd managed to box up all his blacker needs and desires and put them away.

He had not.

Last month, he'd given in and raped his wife's new lady's maid, and in the process he'd also choked her. He'd not meant to kill her, but he had. Tragically, none of his peers would care much about the life of a maid, but his wife had been fond of the girl.

In panic, he'd disposed of the body himself, burying it in the forest behind his manor.

Feeling ill, I drew myself from his thoughts and excused myself.

All Jarrod need do was threaten to send a fast rider with a message for du Guay's wife.

But this time, I didn't go to Jarrod first.

When it was time to dress for dinner, I met Rolf in our room, and I sent Miriam away.

He glanced at me. "Don't you need her to lace you up and do your hair?"

I didn't answer. "Do you know what your father has had me doing these past days?"

He frowned. "Yes."

His frown was colored by discomfort. Did he prefer to think he might win the seat on his own merit as opposed to blackmail?

"We now have the votes of five men in our pockets, and I have information that will ensure the sixth."

Discomfort vanished. "You do? Have you told my father?"

I shook my head. "Not yet. I want something first."

In all the time we'd been together, I'd never asked him for anything and I wasn't sure how he'd react.

"You want something?" he asked. He looked at me as if I were a stranger. "What? Money?"

"When have I ever been interested in money? Once you have the seat, you'll turn your hand to increasing the nation's military. I don't want you draining the common people dry in your efforts."

His expression turned incredulous first and then angry. He stepped closer, towering over me. "Are you telling me you wish a voice in national affairs?"

I didn't flinch. "Yes. You need me to secure the seat at all. After that, in the years to come, you'll need me to know who is on your side and who has turned against you. You'll need me the length of your career in politics, and I am saying that if you wish for my help, you'll give consideration to the lives and needs of the people."

He stared at me, speechless.

"I'm not saying I don't believe in a strong military," I went on. "I'm simply saying that while on the council, you should suggest other methods for raising funds than increasing taxes until the towns and villages are starving. If the people are strong, the nation is strong. Surely you understand that."

His expression wavered, but he still looked at me as if I were a stranger to him. "And from where else should we raise these funds?"

"You can start with the coffers of the nobles themselves. Go to those who can most afford to be patriotic. In the case of war, you'll need the common men to fight. Strong, loyal men volunteer and fight well. Weak, starving men have to be conscripted. Strong women left at home can work the farms. This is only wise policy."

He stepped back. "Megan," he whispered.

"I want a voice in some matters," I said. "Do we have a bargain?"

He was quiet for a long moment and then slowly nodded.

Turning away, I headed for the door. "I'll go to your father now."

* * * *

When the council met to vote, they cloistered themselves away around a long table inside a room with two solid oak doors.

At least sixty people stood in the large passage outside those doors, awaiting the result.

Jarrod, Rolf, and I stood together. My mother was not there.

People spoke in hushed tones, speculating on which of the men might be voted into a seat of such power. None of them had any idea that the outcome was already a forgone conclusion.

The meeting didn't last long,

When the doors opened and the men emerged, Lord Cloutier led the way. His face was ashen, and when he spoke, his voice held disbelief.

"The seat has been won by Lord Rolf Volodane."

Gasps resounded.

However, once the shock passed, people quickly began to congratulate Rolf. Jarrod stood glowing beside his son.

My own father appeared as stunned as everyone else, and he moved over beside me. "Five other men voted for him," he whispered in what sounded like horror. "You know that I had to, but I cannot fathom what just happened in there."

"Can you not?" I challenged him.

His eyes flashed to my face as the truth dawned. "You . . .?"

I couldn't help a wave of satisfaction. He'd thrown me away like yesterday's refuse so that he might pay a few debts. Now, he was reaping what he'd sown.

Rolf Volodane held a seat on the Council of Nobles.

Chapter 8

We stayed in Partheney for another month so that the council and the king could debate matters of state. In that time, Rolf began gaining respect, and he found a kindred spirit in Lord Sauvage, who had long wanted to increase the nation's border patrols.

As opposed to growing proud or arrogant, Rolf became more self-assured—which was different. In private, he told me everything that was discussed in council meetings, and I offered my thoughts.

I don't believe he ever did this with Jarrod.

In mid-autumn, we traveled back home and arrived at Volodane Hall in the early afternoon. I had been pondering a number of plans to try and improve the lives of the people in the village and outlying areas, but as of yet, I hadn't approached Rolf.

All such thoughts vanished when we entered the dining hall to find Sebastian sitting at a table playing cards with a few guards.

"Sebastian," I called, hurrying to him. "You're back!"

He stood and I gave him a quick embrace, not caring what anyone else thought. I'd missed him. Rolf and I were partners, but Sebastian was a friend.

He smiled and hugged me back. Then he looked over at his father and brother. "And how fares the ambitious ones?" he asked. "Not too disappointed, I hope."

"Not at all," Rolf answered coolly. "I won the seat."

Sebastian's face went momentarily blank. Then he looked down at me as if I'd betrayed him. "He won the seat?"

I glanced away. I couldn't meet his eyes, but I would find him later and explain everything. I'd not let Rolf abuse his power.

Sebastian stepped away from me and put one hand on the table.

"Will you not congratulate me, brother?" Rolf said.

Sebastian's eyes were hard. "Congratulations."

* * * *

We met again in the hall before dinner that night. Though I hadn't found an opportunity to speak to Sebastian alone, he had calmed considerably and was even apologetic to Rolf.

"Forgive my loutish behavior," he said. "You caught me off guard. I never thought you'd do it, not because you aren't capable, just because I didn't think those snobs would ever vote for one of us."

Rolf watched him carefully and then shrugged. "It's all right. I know the outcome seemed unlikely."

There were two pots of tea on the table, one large and one small.

"We'll have wine with dinner and drink a toast to you," Sebastian said, "but I brought some of that orange-spiced tea you like so much back from Rennes." He pointed to the smaller pot. None of the rest of us were fond of orange-spiced tea, but it was a favorite of Rolf's. Then Sebastian gestured to the larger pot. "I had some black tea made up for everyone else."

"Tea?" Jarrod asked. "Before dinner? I think not. Have the wine brought in."

The idea of tea before dinner was unusual, but in truth, Rolf wasn't all that fond of wine, and he loved spiced tea. Sebastian knew that. Was he making a peace offering?

Rolf blinked as if uncertain how to respond to his brother. "Thank you," he said finally.

A flicker, something unreadable, passed through Sebastian's eyes. Something was very wrong here.

I had to act.

I knew I shouldn't.

What I was about to do broke every rule my father had taught me: *Never read one of your own.* Sebastian was a young lord of my own house now. It was wrong to invade his thoughts, but this didn't stop me.

Focusing completely on Sebastian, I was hit by a wall of desperation. He'd depended on me, on what he'd both shown and told me, to keep Rolf off the council. He feared for the future of the nation with Rolf in power.

There was hemlock in the orange-spiced tea.

He was about to poison his own brother.

I pulled from his mind. Keeping my expression serene, I smiled at Rolf and walked toward the table. "Stay there. I'll pour a cup for you."

Reaching out, I lifted the pot and then pretended it was too heavy, and I dropped it. The lid came off, and the contents splashed all the over the floor. Beside me, Sebastian drew a sharp breath, but I looked back to Rolf.

"Oh, I am sorry. It was heavier than I anticipated. Should I have Ester make more?"

He waved me off. "No, let's just sit down to dinner. I'm more hungry than anything else."

I called Betty to clean up the mess and then serve dinner.

We all sat down, but I could feel Sebastian's eyes on me.

* * * *

Long after Rolf had fallen asleep that night, I slipped from my bed, donned my silk dressing gown, and left my room.

This late, the keep was silent, but I walked as quietly as possible to the end of the passage right where it curved inside the tower. Although I had never before visited my planned destination, I knew where it was located, and I stopped outside of Sebastian's room.

After taking a few seconds to gather myself, I knocked.

Nothing happened, but I didn't leave, and I didn't knock again.

Finally, the door opened, and he stood there dressed in nothing but a pair of loose black pants. He wasn't surprised to see me.

Holding the door wider, he asked dryly, "Would you like to come in?"

"No."

Being found inside his room would be disastrous. It would be bad enough if anyone saw us standing at his open door. But this couldn't wait until tomorrow.

He raised one brow. "Then to what do I owe the pleasure?"

"You tried to poison Rolf tonight. Don't do it again."

"What an imagination you have. Then again . . . one never knows what might come out of that kitchen."

"I know you're worried," I rushed on. "But you needn't be. I've spoken to Rolf and he listens to me. He's trying other methods to fund his plans. He won't have national taxes increased."

At that, Sebastian dropped all pretense. "For now!" he whispered harshly. "What do you think he'll be like in a year? Two years? You'll have lost any hold on him."

I shook my head, focusing on the scar on his collarbone. "I won't."

He leaned down closer until I could feel his breath. "You can't be sure of that."

"I can. And if you try to hurt him, I'll know. I won't say anything about tonight. I'll keep the secret, but if you ever try anything like that again, I'll know and I'll speak out. Both your father and Rolf will believe me."

"I'd be executed or at best disinherited. You would do that?"

"Yes."

In that instant, our friendship died. A sharp pain struck me at the thought, but it passed.

Turning, I walked away. I had needed my friendship with Sebastian here, but Rolf was my husband.

My loyalty was to him.

* * * *

In the year that followed, my life changed a good deal.

I turned eighteen.

Rolf and I were now important people. We held small house parties at Volodane Hall, and I was allowed not only to make improvements to the guest quarters but also to take some areas reserved for storage and turn them into guest rooms.

We were invited to stay at great houses across the nation. Sometimes Jarrod came with us, but Sebastian never did.

I'd begun having all leftovers and other food supplies sent down the village, and Jarrod never questioned me. I think perhaps Rolf spoke to him on this matter. I'd also begun whispering to Rolf about easing taxes on his own people.

We had plenty of wealth ourselves, and our lands would be improved if the people were stronger. He listened.

Soon, I found that I could live without Sebastian's friendship. We existed in a state of polite civility, and he began spending more time in Rennes now that he was no longer so necessary for Rolf to rise in position. I was lonely at first, but I adjusted, and Miriam was ever my friend.

I found myself content.

Only one thing caused true disharmony in our household.

It started off as a small concern, but it grew worse each month. Jarrod would study my stomach for signs that I carried a child. I began to dread the start of my courses. Each month, I fervently hoped they would not come, and that I would feel sick with breakfast and could tell Rolf that a child was coming. This didn't happen. A year into our marriage, with him sleeping in my bed almost every night, and no baby had quickened in my womb.

If a marriage didn't produce a child, it was common knowledge that the woman was at fault. If she should give birth only to girls and no sons, it was her fault as well.

Another year passed, and I began to feel like a failure. Miriam consulted midwives, and I was told to eat everything from asparagus to wild game birds. Nothing worked.

Jarrod made cutting remarks about me being barren, but Rolf never said a word of reproach, and I sometimes even caught him looking at me in what appeared to be pity. That was worse.

Then one night, as I made my way down the passage toward the dining hall, I heard raised voices, and I stopped.

I couldn't see Rolf or Jarrod through the archway, but I could hear them.

"Then put her aside!" Jarrod shouted. "She's done what we needed for you. Now you need a son! I didn't go through all this to have our line end! Find a wife who can give you a son."

I trembled. What would become of me then? Would my father take me back? I shuddered at the thought.

"I'll never put Megan aside," Rolf returned. "Not for anything. You must know this isn't her fault. In your heart, you must."

I'd never heard him speak like that.

There was no answer at first, and then Jarrod asked tightly, "What do you mean?"

"You remember Bess. Of course you do. And Jane? And Eliza? I never made a secret of any mistress I took from the housemaids or the village. Father, Bess slept in my bed for the better part of a year, and there was no issue between us." His own voice grew strained. "I've never made a child with any woman."

I couldn't imagine what it cost a man like Rolf to admit this.

"That means nothing," Jarrod shot back.

"It does. You could pack the hall with new wives for me, and you wouldn't have your grandson. At least not from me, and I wouldn't pin much hope on Sebastian."

"Then it was all for nothing," Jarrod said more quietly.

"Not to me. I've been more fortunate than I ever could have hoped, and I won't waste it wishing for something that will never happen. I plan to live the life I have."

Who knew my husband had such thoughts and feelings?

I almost wept with relief. He didn't blame me for his lack of a son, and more, he did not seem to care.

Resuming my path, I let my heels click more loudly so they would hear me coming.

"Good evening," I said upon entering. "Ester's prepared a turkey for dinner."

* * * *

The years passed, and Rolf was voted as the head of the Council of Nobles. He often conferred with the king. With my guidance, he proved a good leader, and he never stopped conferring with me on important matters.

We did not have a passionate love.

We did not have a child.

But we had mutual respect and value of each other . . . and we had a good deal of power.

* * * *

The world around me vanished, and I found myself standing once again in the storage room of my parents' manor, staring into the right panel of the three-tiered mirror.

I stumbled backward, fighting to take in air, thinking on all that I had just seen.

But the dark-haired woman was now looking out from the center panel.

"That would be my life with Rolf?" I gasped.

"That would be the outcome of the first choice," she answered. "But now those memories will vanish, and you'll go back to the beginning, to the wedding day once again, to live out the second choice."

"Wait!" I cried. "I won't remember anything of what I just saw?"

"To the beginning once more," she answered. "To live out the second choice."

My mind went blank, and the storage room vanished.

I found myself back in my family's dining hall. It was my wedding day.

Chairs had been set up in rows, and guests were seated in them. I wore a gown of pale ivory and held my father's arm as he walked me past the guests toward the far end of the hall.

Flowers in tall vases graced that same end, and a local magistrate stood there with a book in his hands.

Beside the magistrate stood Sebastian. I had chosen him.

He smiled.

The Second Choice
Sebastian

Chapter 9

The first time I laid eyes upon Volodane Hall, I was wet, damp, and struggling not to give way to misery.

Not long after my wedding at Chaumont, I'd been swept up in a journey north with my new husband, his father, both his brothers, and their retinue of guards. Sebastian told me the ride would take two days. He was the only one of the men who spoke to me. Kai pretended I didn't exist, and Rolf seemed to seethe in quiet anger that I'd not chosen him.

My one comfort was that I'd been allowed to bring Miriam with me.

Another blessing to this arrangement was that as Jarrod paid for rooms at inns along the way, Miriam and I were given a room to ourselves, so as of yet, I'd not been expected to share a bed with Sebastian.

Though it was early summer, the farther north we traveled, the thicker grew the trees and the darker grew the sky. Near the end of the second day, a cold drizzle began to fall, soaking through my cloak.

We passed through a village and headed toward a rise.

"We're almost there," Sebastian said, riding beside me. Even in my misery, I noted he sounded worried as he added, "But you'll need to brace yourself."

As we came over the rise, I gained my first view in the fading light. My hands tensed on the reins as I fought to keep from expressing dismay. A squat keep loomed up from out of the surrounding forest. Even at a distance, its dark profile looked worn and ill kept.

Sebastian glanced at me. I was lost for words and could only imagine the inside.

Jarrod urged his mount forward, rode up to the gates, and called out. A moment later, a loud grinding sounded, like timber creaking across timber, and the gates opened. We rode inside to a small, muddy courtyard, and as the men began dismounting, the flurry of activity that followed kept me from taking in much more.

"Put your hands on my shoulders," someone said from below.

Shivering and looking down, I saw Sebastian standing below. Without even thinking, I put my hands on his shoulders and let him lift me off the horse. He held me steady for a few moments.

Kai lifted Miriam down. Poor Miriam. What had I dragged her into?

Jarrod called back toward us, "Kai! Get the women inside."

"As if we need him to tell us that," Sebastian whispered in my ear. "Come on."

Miriam and I were ushered across the courtyard to the main doors of the keep. Inside we passed through an entryway and into a wide passage. Neither of the men slowed down.

At the end of the passage, we emerged into a great hall with a fireplace large enough that I could have stood inside. In addition, half a dozen small spaniels came running toward us, wriggling and whining for attention.

One of them came running and jumped into Kai's arms. He caught the dog and smiled as she licked his face.

"Lacey, stop."

The fire in the hearth had been lit, but I couldn't stop shivering.

Sebastian looked down at me in concern. Turning, he called to a guard down the passage, "You! Have your lady's travel trunk carried up to her room." Then he called, "Betty!"

A plump serving woman with a pleasant face came bustling forward. "Yes, my lord?"

"Show your lady up to her room." He looked down to me again. "Go on and get out of those wet things. Put on your nightclothes if you wish. I'll have food brought up."

The thought of retiring to a private room and not having to come out again tonight filled me with relief.

Wordlessly, I nodded and took Miriam's arm as we followed Betty from the hall.

I'd not seen much of my new home, but in the moment I didn't care.

* * * *

Thankfully, the room I was given on the second floor of the single tower was not entirely awful.

It was a woman's room.

The furniture was old, faded, and in need of a polish, but the four-poster bed was large, with a thick, eyelet comforter. The dressing table was well crafted from rich-toned mahogany. A matching wardrobe stood beside it. A moth-eaten tapestry covered one wall.

Miriam stood in the center of the room taking in the furnishings. Her face was pale and stricken.

One of my chests had been carried and set at the end of the bed. "See if I have a clean nightgown in there," I said.

We hadn't eaten since midday, and I longed for a cup of steaming tea, but I was more concerned with being warm and dry. Miriam began unlacing my travel gown.

"As soon we've finished with me," I said, "we'll see about your room and clothing. You need to get out of those wet things too."

I couldn't help wondering how often it rained here in the summer.

Together, we peeled off my clothing, and she slipped a dry nightgown over my head. I sighed in pleasure.

"Let me brush out your hair," she said. "Tonight is . . ." she trailed off and then finished, "your first night in your husband's home."

My pleasure vanished. Would Sebastian expect to sleep in here? Of course, I'd known that side of things was coming, but until Miriam had spoken, I hadn't wondered if it would be tonight.

"Come and sit," she said from the dressing table.

I sat and let her brush out my hair until it fell in slightly damp waves down my back.

I couldn't stop thinking about what might happen if Sebastian came up. My mother hadn't told me much about what to expect.

"Miriam?" I asked, wondering if she knew.

She never heard the rest of the question as the door cracked open. I could see its reflection in the mirror. Sebastian pushed it all the way open with one shoulder. He carried a tray himself.

"Dinner as promised," he said cheerfully. "Such as it is."

Miriam and I both froze at the sight of him standing there. When he saw our faces, his cheerful countenance faded. There was nothing threatening about him, but he was still a man standing in a bedroom chamber with two women who barely knew him.

Using his head, he motioned toward the door and spoke to Miriam. "Go on out. Betty will show you to your room."

She hesitated but had no choice. With a nod, she left us, and Sebastian used his shoulder to close the door.

We were alone.

"No need to look as if you're going to the executioner's block," he said. "I promise I don't bite."

I didn't find his humor comforting.

With a sigh, he walked to the side table and set down the tray. Then he grasped the bottom of his tunic. "Don't be shocked. I know this isn't manly to admit, but I'm freezing."

He pulled off his tunic first and then the damp wool shirt beneath it. I knew from experience that wearing wet wool was unpleasant at best. There was a dagger strapped to each of his forearms, and he removed the sheaths. After this, he dropped onto the bed and took off his boots.

"That's better," he said. Thankfully, he left his pants on, but they looked dryer than his tunic and shirt.

Half turning, he arranged all the pillows up against the headboard and patted a spot on the bed beside him. "Come sit here."

I stared at him, not moving. He had a scar on his left collarbone.

His tone hardened. "Megan, come here."

This was an order, and it was one of the first things I came to learn about Sebastian. He always asked politely the first time. Then he gave an order.

Slowly, I climbed up onto the bed beside him.

"Lean back against the pillows," he said.

He reached for the tray and set it on the bed between us. For the first time, I examined its contents. There was a jug of wine, two goblets, a chunk of cheese, bread, and butter.

"I know it's not much, but it was the best I could manage," he said, pouring the wine. "I fear you'll find it an uphill climb trying to put the staff of this household together. We've let things go a bit lax."

"I'll do my best." This was the first thing I'd said since he'd entered, and my voice sounded small.

He stopped pouring and leaned closer. "You don't need to be afraid of me. I'd never hurt you, and I'll never let anyone else hurt you." He handed me a goblet. "You did something I've never managed, and I'll be grateful for the rest of my life. Here, have some of this cheese."

He broke off a small chunk and handed it to me.

Taking the cheese, I couldn't help asking, "What did I do?"

"You wiped that self-satisfied, arrogant expression off Rolf's face, that's what you did. I'll never forget the moment when you picked me. I thought he'd have an apoplexy." Sebastian smiled. "It was glorious. The daughter of the Chaumonts chose me over the paragon son, right there in front of everyone. You have my undying loyalty."

Did he hate Rolf so much?

He buttered a piece of bread for me as if I were a child. "Eat this."

I began to enjoy myself. It was like having a picnic in bed.

"Was this room your mother's?" I asked.

He nodded, taking a long drink of wine.

"When did she die?"

"When Kai was born. Poor Kai. He blames himself, but none of the rest of us do."

The house had been without a lady for twenty years. That explained much.

"You can trust Kai," Sebastian went on. "He may glower and spit a little, but he has a good heart underneath, the best. Stay as far away from Rolf as you can though. He won't forgive you for choosing me. And don't ever trust a thing my father says. His only goal is to raise our family's status, and if there's a line he won't cross, I haven't seen it yet."

While eating my bread and butter, I appeared to be receiving a rapid lesson on family dynamics.

"I was never intended for marriage," I offered. "My sister, Helena, was supposed to be here now. She died the same day you all arrived at the manor."

We'd finished eating, and he put the tray back on the side table. "So this has all come as a bit of a rude awakening to you then, hasn't it?"

Unbidden tears sprang to my eyes. He understood. I nodded.

He lay down with his head on the pillows, reached out, and pulled me against his chest. Oddly, I wasn't afraid of him. I settled my head against his shoulder.

"You won't regret anything," he said. "I'll take care of you."

No one had ever offered to take care of me before.

He kissed the top of my head. "You're tired. Close your eyes. Tonight we'll just sleep."

Right then, I fell in love with him. He was more concerned about me than he was about himself. I'd made the right choice.

* * * *

The next morning when I awoke, he was gone.

Miriam brought me water for washing, and then she took out the yellow muslin gown for me to wear. With a frown, I thought longingly of my simple blue-gray wool gown. I'd managed to stash it in the chest when my mother wasn't looking. It was old and had probably been washed too many times, but it was warm and comfortable and made me feel like myself.

Still . . . Sebastian was my husband now, and he seemed to care about appearances.

Without protest, I let Miriam lace me into the yellow muslin. She put up hair and found a small choker of white pearls my mother had sent.

I looked the part of lady of the house.

"Your other chests should be up soon," Miriam said. "I'll stay and unpack your things."

"All right. I'd best go down."

And so, with that, I headed out of the room, down the passage, and down the curving stairs of the tower. I had an aging keep to try and put in order. I'd only glimpsed the great hall the night before, but I'd seen enough to know it was filthy.

The first things I saw upon entering the hall were Sebastian and Kai, standing by the table. The pack of spaniels wriggled at their feet.

Kai's eyes were locked on me as I approached. As always, anger seemed to rise from his skin. I couldn't help wondering about Sebastian's assessment of his younger brother.

But Sebastian took in my dress and hair and smiled. "You're lovely."

Then I looked down at what they were eating. It appeared to be the remnants of moldy cheese. Their mugs held ale.

Kai took a long drink of his ale.

"Is that your breakfast?" I asked him.

He shrugged. "It'll do."

I shook my head. "No. It won't."

Two women entered to gather up the breakfast tray. I remembered Betty from last night. The other woman was tall and spindly.

"Do you have any instructions for Betty and Matilda?" Sebastian asked me pointedly.

Was this a cue for me to take charge?

I spoke to the women. "I want this hall swept out, and then I want the floor scrubbed. I want all the cobwebs swept down, and I want the walls prepared for tapestries."

They both stared at me as if they'd not heard correctly, but Sebastian's face lit up. "Tapestries?"

Kai said nothing, but he wasn't really given time as Sebastian turned to Betty and Matilda. "You heard your new lady. Get started."

Did I need him to back up my instructions? I wasn't sure.

"I'll get the brooms," Matilda said.

With the cleaning of the hall underway, I looked again at the remnants of breakfast. "I suppose I'd better go and sort out the kitchen."

Sebastian nodded. "I'll come with you. The women in the kitchen aren't as biddable as Betty and Matilda."

To my shame, his words brought relief. He'd promised to protect me, and although I knew I should start setting a more authoritative precedent, I welcomed the thought of him standing beside me as I faced down the women in the kitchen—who would most likely resent being ordered about by a seventeen-year-old girl, suddenly foisted upon them as their new lady.

Sebastian and I left the hall and walked down a long side passage. "The entrance to the kitchen is up ahead on the right, and beyond that is a door that leads out to the gardens."

"Gardens?"

"Yes, at least we boast a decent kitchen garden, although lately, few vegetables have made it to the table. Honestly, I haven't been down this way myself in some time."

We walked through the open archway into the kitchen, and there we found three women among the ovens and pots and pans. One of them, the eldest, was quietly kneading bread on a table. She was slender with graying hair pulled back in a bun.

The other two women were barely past twenty, and they sat at a smaller, second table laughing and chatting with each other over mugs of steaming tea and plates of scrambled eggs with strawberries on the side.

At the sight of this, Sebastian went still.

The woman making bread saw us first.

"My lord," she said in alarm. "Can I help you?"

Then the other two looked up. One of them was strikingly pretty with black hair, pale skin, and a fetching smatter of freckles. The other one was somewhat stocky with reddish hair pulled back at the nape of her neck.

"I thought to introduce my lady to the kitchen staff," Sebastian said coldly.

"Of course," the older woman answered, wiping her hands. Speaking to me, she said, "I'm Ester, my lady, and this is Lavonia and Cora." She pointed first to the dark-haired girl and then to the redhead.

"It seems you could have done slightly better with our breakfast this morning," Sebastian said, his gaze on the scrambled eggs, strawberries, and steaming tea.

To my astonishment, Lavonia leaned back and crossed her arms. "If you wanted something else, you should have sent for it."

"Lavonia!" Ester gasped.

Sebastian held up one hand. "You have a new mistress, and from now on she will be giving the instructions, and if any of you wish to keep your place here, you'll obey her as if the orders came from me or my father." He turned to me. "Do you have instructions?"

My tongue felt tied. He'd taken full charge here—for which I was grateful—and then, without warning, had turned to me. I didn't wish to disappoint him or make him sorry for his protection.

What would my mother have ordered? I tried to sound like the lady of the keep.

"Ester," I said. "Will that bread you're making be baked by midday?"

"Yes, my lady."

"I haven't taken stock of the larder, but I brought some things with me from Chaumont. In a short while, I'll have boxes of tea and several casks of wine brought in. At midday, I'll send Matilda and Betty to you. I'd like trays prepared with slices of fresh bread with butter, bowls of berries, boiled eggs, and several pots of tea for any of the men who come in to eat. Can you manage that?"

"Yes, my lady."

From the table, Lavonia glared at me.

"Is there is ham in the larder?" I asked Ester.

She nodded and glanced nervously at Lavonia.

"For dinner tonight," I continued, "you'll make roasted potatoes and a large dish of peas in cream sauce, if those vegetables are available. Please heat a ham, slice it, and lay it out on a tray. I'll have decanters sent in, and I want two decanters of red wine drawn from the casks." I paused. "I'll send Betty and Matilda right at dusk this evening."

"Yes, my lady."

Sebastian smiled, but again it was cold. "There, all planned out for today, but you should ready yourselves for changes around here, and clearly...it's about time."

He turned and took my arm.

As he walked down the passage, I could see the anger in his eyes. "Ester's a good sort," he said, "but if those girls give you any trouble, you tell me, and I'll handle it. We've let things get far too lax around here."

I nodded. This was all unfamiliar ground for me, and I was beyond grateful for his help. If there was trouble, I could go to him.

Right now, I wanted to get back and see to the work being done in the great hall.

* * * *

By evening, I left my duties and ran upstairs and let Miriam lace me into a silk gown and re-style my hair. I wore the diamond pendant.

When I came back down, I looked ready for a proper dinner.

Upon reaching the main hall, I heard masculine voices and walked in to find Jarrod, Rolf, Sebastian, and Kai all there. Jarrod and Rolf were both looking about the place in surprise, for it had indeed undergone something of a transformation.

The newly scrubbed table had been laid with white cloths, porcelain plates, and pewter goblets. All of these had come from Chaumont Manor. Four enormous tapestries hung on the walls, and I think my mother chose them well.

The half dozen spaniels still wriggled about the men, seeking attention.

"Dinner will be served shortly," I said from the archway.

All four men turned as I walked in. Sebastian smiled. Rolf glowered. It was clear to me that he and I would never be friends. He frightened me a little. Kai eyed my silk gown and glanced away.

"You approve of the changes?" I asked Jarrod.

He walked over and picked up an engraved pewter goblet. "I do. I wouldn't know how to buy any of this." He nodded to Sebastian. "We've made a better bargain than I realized."

Sebastian's eyes glittered, and Rolf's face was like thunder.

Right then, Betty and Matilda came in carrying trays of sliced ham, roasted potatoes, peas in cream sauce, and two decanters of wine.

"Shall we sit down?" I suggested.

"A good bargain indeed," Jarrod said. He looked again to Sebastian. "Now I want a grandson."

* * * *

That night Sebastian came to my room with two goblets and a decanter of wine. I'd already had wine with dinner and didn't want any more. I was in my nightgown. He set the wine on a stand beside the bed and dismissed Miriam. Then he jumped onto the bed, pulled off his boots, and leaned back against the headboard.

"That was the perfect meal," he said. "Rolf barely managed to choke it down."

Hesitantly, I asked, "You dislike him so much?"

"Dislike him? By the gods, that's an understatement. He's a bully beyond description, and he's viewed me as nearly useless since the day I was born. So does Father for that matter, all because I don't see the world as they do."

"How do you see it?"

"There's more to life than gaining wealth and power and smiting one's enemies. A good deal more. But that's the scope of their world. That's why Rolf can't figure out why you chose me."

I didn't understand what he meant. My own father cared for little besides wealth, power, and social standing. Isn't that what most men cared for? What did Sebastian care for?

Seeing my confusion, he patted the bed. "Let's not talk of such serious things."

Without hesitation, I went to him. He poured himself a goblet of wine, drank it in several swallows, and then stripped down to a pair of white underdrawers. I'd never seen a man in such a state of undress.

He did all this while still sitting on the bed with me, and something about his actions felt intimate.

I touched the scar on his collarbone. "How did you get that?"

"Rolf caught me with a blade when I was about twelve. I can't remember what we were fighting over. A horse, I think."

I tried to imagine him fighting with Rolf as a boy, but I couldn't see him as anything but a man. It was difficult not to be affected by his appearance, his dark hair and handsome face. His body was lean with tight muscles. I wondered what it would feel like if he touched his mouth to mine.

Putting the goblet aside, he pulled me up against his chest. I trembled once. Would we consummate the marriage tonight?

He kissed the top of my head again. "You've had a long day. Get some sleep."

I knew I should be relieved. Of course I should. But a part of me couldn't help being confused . . . even disappointed.

Chapter 10

As the weeks passed, I continued trying to become the lady of Volodane Hall.

Almost before I knew it, the rhythms of daily life here had become familiar. Jarrod and Rolf were often out overseeing the land or running drills with the guards. Kai spent much of his time in training with a sword, although I wasn't entirely sure why he put so much time into this. Sebastian spent most of his time playing cards with the guards or talking with me.

He had a close friend among the guards, a young blond-haired, blue-eyed man named Daveed who took an instant dislike to me. He wasn't openly impolite, but he tensed whenever I drew near. When I asked Sebastian about this, he brushed it off.

I ended up having as little to do with the kitchen staff as possible. Their workload had been doubled—or more—now that they were expected to serve proper meals, and the younger women blamed me.

I began sending for Ester when I wanted to go over menus, and she'd come out to the dining hall to sit with me at the table. One day, I noticed she looked weary.

"Ester, are you receiving enough help from Lavonia and Cora?"

"Yes, my lady."

I didn't believe her and knew I should do something about it, but Sebastian had made it clear that if any problems arose, he was to handle them. As I hadn't encountered any problems myself, I didn't wish to cause trouble.

And I had other worries.

He continued to sleep in my bed night after night, but he never touched me other than to pull me up against himself or to kiss the top of my head. Did he not find me attractive? Should I do something to instigate? What would that be?

Although I didn't know everything about the actual mechanics, I did know that unless a man and woman "came together" (as I'd heard it said) in bed, no baby would be created. Soon enough, Jarrod would start to wonder why I wasn't with child.

I loved Sebastian. No one had ever protected nor treated me with more kindness than him. We had an intimacy I'd never known. We whispered to each other and drank tea or wine in bed. But why didn't he take action to make us truly husband and wife?

The nights continued to pass.

Then one day, the rhythms of the house were interrupted when Jarrod sought me out to tell me he'd arranged for a formal dinner, the first hosted here in many years.

"Who's coming?" I asked.

"Lord Allemond Monville, his wife, and his brother. Their lands border our southern line, and I'm trying to buy a section of forest covered in oak. The timber alone is worth the purchase."

"Lord Allemond?"

Jarrod's eyes sharpened. "You know him?"

"Yes."

"Good. I expect your best efforts here. He's only coming to look down his nose at me. I want him off guard by what he finds."

That night as I readied myself for bed, Sebastian came to the room in a state of excitement.

"Father actually asked me to help make this evening impressive. He's ordered me before, but he's never asked. I want everything to go well."

"We'll make it perfect," I assured.

Miriam began working on a new gown for me. With Betty's help, I started sewing clothes for the men. Matilda began cleaning madly. Sebastian and I planned the menu with meticulous attention to detail. He wanted to start the dinner with baked salmon in a simple white sauce.

Two days before the dinner, I couldn't find him and I wanted to ask him about centerpieces. I thought he might be in the barracks playing cards.

As I stepped out into the courtyard, I nearly ran into Rolf, who was on his way in. Normally, he wasn't home at this time of day, and the near collision unnerved me. My head barely reached his chest.

He looked down with his usual angry glower, but to my surprise, he spoke.

"And how are you enjoying life with your new husband?" he asked. "I assume by now you've realized you made the wrong choice."

He sounded so sure of himself. Did he *know* there was something not quite right with the marriage?

But I understood Rolf better than he might think. Rolf respected only strength, and showing him any sort of weakness was a mistake. Drawing myself up, I channeled my mother's voice.

"If my other two options were you or Kai, I'd say I made the only choice."

With that, I swept past him, feeling better than I had since my arrival. It felt good to stand up to Rolf and not find myself in need of Sebastian's protection.

* * * *

Mid-morning, the day of the dinner party, I was in the great hall experimenting with centerpieces. The Volodanes grew no flowers, and Sebastian had asked me to see what I could do with wild flowers. He badly wanted to impress his father, to show that he too could contribute skills that would help raise the status of the family, and I was determined to do everything possible to help him.

I had a bouquet of wild roses in my hand when Jarrod and Sebastian walked in.

"Is everything ready?" Jarrod asked.

I turned to face him. "Yes, I think so."

"It better be," he warned. "I want Allemond impressed by what he finds here."

I wasn't sure anything would impress Lord Allemond, but I could at least make sure nothing went wrong. The salmon had just been delivered and were now in cold storage in the cellars.

My mind was so busy running details through my head that I was caught unawares when Jarrod said, "And you know I'll expect your help with this land deal. I want your best efforts."

For an instant, I couldn't draw breath. My father had *told* him. Of course Father told him. I had so much hoped to leave that part of my life behind me.

Feeling defeated, I asked, "Who do you most wish me to focus upon? Allemond himself or his brother? I hope Father told you I can read only one person in a day."

Jarrod stared at me. "What do you mean by 'read'?" he asked slowly.

Then I realized my mistake. He didn't know anything. His mention of my help must have referred to me using my manners and family influence to throw Allemond off guard.

"Nothing," I answered. "I thought you wished me to gauge his reactions and offer counsel later."

In a flash, his right hand snaked out and grabbed my wrist. I gasped as he jerked me up against his chest. The pain in my arm was startling, but it only lasted a few seconds.

Before I knew what was happening, Sebastian snarled and bolted forward and shoved his father away from me.

"Don't touch her!"

I stumbled forward as I was released, and both men faced each other. Jarrod appeared more stunned than anything else, but his fist was drawn back ready to strike. He hesitated. Sebastian wasn't as tall as his father, but he was younger and his tightly muscled body looked like a coiled spring.

The tension was thick until Sebastian took a step back. "The dinner will be perfect if you give me a free hand," he said, "and Megan will provide all the help you need with the guests. Just don't touch her. She's mine. You do as you like with the rest of us, but not her."

Jarrod was so thrown by Sebastian's behavior that he seemed to have forgotten all about me. Sebastian motioned toward the archway with his head.

"Go," he told me.

I hurried for the passage, wondering what they might say to each other after I was gone. Sebastian couldn't know it, but he'd just done me a great service. Jarrod didn't know about my ability, and I would never make such a mistake again. If he knew what I could do, he'd use me at every chance he had, ordering me to read his enemies or people he doubted. I longed to leave that part of my life behind and never invade anyone's mind again.

Due to Sebastian's protection, I'd kept my secret.

The near-conflict left me weary, and I decided to go up to my room and take just a few moments for myself.

I'd made it only halfway to the entrance to the tower when Betty came trotting behind me. "My lady."

I stopped. "Yes?"

"Lavonia is asking for you in the kitchen. She says the fish has gone bad."

"Gone bad?"

"That's what she says, my lady."

"I'm coming."

I'd not dealt with Lavonia since that first meeting, so I didn't know her well. She had volunteered to do the fish course and was probably being overly cautious. Doing an about-face, I headed west toward the kitchen. Upon arriving, I found it a busy place.

Ester was rolling crusts for strawberry tarts, and two girls Sebastian had hired for temporary help were scrubbing pots in a large washbasin. Cora sat peeling potatoes.

Lavonia appeared to be supervising.

"Betty says there's a problem with the fish?" I asked, stepping through the archway.

Lavonia turned. "They're spoilt. We can't use them."

When she spoke, she gave the impression that I was last person in the world she wished to see.

Ester stopped rolling, and everyone was listening to us.

"Those fish were caught this morning," I answered. "I checked them myself. Where have they been stored?"

"They're down in the cellar, in the coolest room," Lavonia said. "You want to come down with me to check them?"

This seemed wise to me, and now I was concerned. If the salmon had somehow gone bad, we had little time to replace them, and Sebastian had been so particular about that dish as the first course.

I followed Lavonia down to the cellar where four large salmon had been placed in cold storage. Leaning over, I touched several of them. They were firm and fresh.

"Oh, Lavonia, these are fine."

"You're sure. I thought I smelled something bad."

I sniffed several of the fish and smelled nothing wrong. "No, you can prepare them later today."

She nodded tersely, and we headed back up.

After I left the kitchen and was on my way down the passage, I saw Sebastian coming toward me.

"Is your wrist all right?" he asked and then frowned. "Why are you here? Is anything wrong?"

"Lavonia said she was worried about the salmon, but I just checked them and they're fine."

His gaze moved down the passage toward the kitchen. "Lavonia told you that?"

"Yes, she's preparing the dish. Why?"

He smiled at me. "No reason. Why don't you go rest for a bit? You've not stopped all morning."

He passed by me, continuing on.

* * * *

That evening, I headed for the dining hall at precisely the right moment. My mother had always preferred to make an entrance at dinner parties, and I'd decided to follow her example.

Tonight, my hair hung loose with several strands in the front over my forehead and pinned up with a small jeweled clip. I wore kohl at the corners of my eyes and beet juice on my lips. My gown was burgundy silk with a v-neckline.

I stopped at the entrance of the hall to see what waited me.

All four Volodanes were there, wearing the new clothing Betty and I had made for them. Sebastian wore a high-collared jacket over a white shirt, and he cut a dashing figure.

He was the first one to spot me standing there, and he smiled with warmth in his eyes.

The hall was clean and properly arranged. There were white cloths on the table along with porcelain plates, silver cutlery, and pewter goblets. I'd done the centerpieces with wild growing roses and lilacs.

My gaze drifted to the guests: Lord Allemond, his wife Rosamund, and his brother, Phillipe. Several of the Volodane guards stood discreetly near the walls, along with several of the Monvílles'.

Taking a deep breath, I stepped forward and entered the hall.

Lord Allemond spotted me next, and I couldn't help a stab of satisfaction at the flicker of uncertainty that passed over his face. "Megan?"

The sight of me must have equally surprised Lady Rosamund, but she showed nothing besides false pleasure, kissing my cheeks and making politely cutting remarks that I pretended not to understand. I did notice her stealing occasional appreciative glances at Sebastian, but who could blame her? Most women would find him striking.

"Shall we all sit and enjoy some wine before dinner?" I asked.

As we took our seats, Lord Allemond examined the porcelain dishes and pewter goblets.

"From Chaumont Manor, I assume?" he posed.

"Part of my dowry," I answered diplomatically, "and I think they grace my new father's table well."

I could see the silent glee in Sebastian's eyes, and it gave me joy. After all our hard work, everything was perfect. Allemond shifted in his chair. It was clear that none of this was playing out as he'd expected.

Betty and Matilda poured wine from the best cask my parents had sent. Phillipe and Lady Rosamund both took a sip, frowning at its fine quality.

Not long after, the fish course arrived. Again, Betty and Matilda quietly served.

"How are your parents, my dear?" Lady Rosamund asked me, but even as she spoke, she stole another glance at Sebastian.

"Very well, I think," I answered. "I haven't had much time to write them."

In truth, I'd written two letters to my mother, and she hadn't answered.

"No, I can see you've been busy," Rosamund answered, another cutting barb for the Volodanes on how I had transformed the hall.

Once everyone had been served a portion of the salmon, she, Phillipe, and Jarrod raised their forks at the same time. I lifted mine, anxious that this first course should meet their standards. The fish was covered in white sauce, and as I took a small forkful, I heard the sounds of gagging.

My eyes flew up.

Lady Rosamund was gagging, and Phillipe was spitting.

Jarrod spat out a mouthful of salmon and jumped to his feet. "What in the name of the gods . . .?"

"What?" Sebastian asked in alarm. "What is it?"

Quickly scraping off the white sauce, I took a sniff at my salmon and nearly choked from the smell. "No one eat the fish!" I cried. "Put down your forks."

Rolf, Kai, and Allemond all dropped their forks. Kai and Rolf appeared distressed, but Allemond's eyes glowed with delight. This was exactly what he'd been hoping for. Rosamund and Phillipe both continued to gag or choke. Rosamund was turning greenish, and I feared she'd swallowed an entire bite.

"Betty!" I called. "Help me."

I hurried to Rosamund, grasping her shoulders. "Try to retch, my lady," I said. "You must bring it back up."

Though this hardly was what anyone would wish at a formal dinner table, I feared for her safety if she could not purge herself. She could fall ill from food poisoning.

A moment later, the fish came back up.

My eyes rose to Sebastian.

His face was desperate, almost manic, and my heart nearly broke at the sight. He'd wanted nothing to be less than perfect, and this was a disaster. I couldn't understand it.

Rosamund still looked very ill, and Phillipe was now slightly green. They would both need to lie down.

"Betty, Matilda, please help our guests to their rooms." I leaned down to Rosamund. "I'll be in to see you shortly, just as soon as I've seen to some things in here."

She barely nodded and allowed herself to be led away by Betty. Matilda helped Phillipe.

Lord Allemond hadn't touched his fish, so he remained in the hall.

"My lord," I said to him. "I am so sorry. If you'll allow me to have this cleared away, I can have the beef course brought in."

Though his expression was dour, I knew he was pleased beyond description. He raised one hand. "Thank you, my dear, but I think I have had enough . . . dinner."

Sebastian blanched, and I ached for him.

"What in all the hells happened?" Jarrod demanded.

Sebastian whirled and strode for the archway. "Wait here and I'll find out."

Everyone else was on his feet by now.

I walked to Allemond. "Are you sure I can't have something else brought in?"

"No, I should check on my lady soon," he answered, picking up his goblet of wine and looking to Jarrod. "But I would like to discuss a few aspects of this land deal. Can we speak now?"

Though Jarrod was still shaken over the catastrophe that was supposed to be his family's first formal dinner in society, he managed to nod and grab his own goblet. He, Allemond, and Rolf moved over the hearth to speak in low voices. I wasn't listening closely, but I did hear the phrase, "Bark beetles."

Kai moved up beside me, gazing down at the table. "What do you think happened?" he whispered.

"I don't know. We were so careful."

The trio of men by the hearth continued speaking until I heard Jarrod say, "All right then. The day after tomorrow."

Allemond said his good nights and left the hall.

Jarrod turned to glare at me, and I feared what he was about to say, but he never had time. Sebastian came striding back in, and the sight him startled everyone. There was blood all over the back of his right hand.

Beads of sweat ran down his angry face. "It was deliberate!"

I'd never seen him like this and ran to him. "You're bleeding."

"It's not mine," he answered, but he was looking at Jarrod and not me. "One of the kitchen maids, Lavonia, did it on purpose. She hid spoiled fish behind the hen house and used those instead of the fresh ones."

Jarrod closed the distance between them. "Why? Was she bribed?"

"Worse than that. She did it to discredit Megan. To make it look like Megan ordered spoiled fish to be served."

Jarrod's eyes narrowed. "And how do you know the fish Megan ordered were still fresh?"

"Because I checked them myself before lunch."

"Lavonia has admitted to this?" I asked, feeling numb.

He nodded. "And Cora knew as well. I asked a few questions and made a few threats, and the story came out. I've locked Lavonia down in a cellar room. I'll handle this myself." He ran his hands through his hair and some of the blood smeared across the side of his head. "Father, I'm so sorry."

Jarrod turned away. "Sorry doesn't change anything."

Sebastian closed his eyes with his hands still up on his head. Kai appeared distressed, but now Rolf looked smug.

* * * *

Later, alone with Sebastian in my room, I hoped to comfort him, but he was beyond comfort, pacing back and forth at the end of the bed.

"That bitch," he said. "I thought she might be up to something. That's why I went down to the cellar after talking to you in the passage."

"You couldn't have known."

"Oh, yes, I could. I wouldn't put anything past her. She sleeps in Father's bed now and then, and she probably thought he'd protect her if anything went wrong. That's a joke. But what astonishes me is she genuinely seemed to believe you'd be blamed for all this. She never thought anyone would even glance her way, which makes her stupid as well as cruel."

"Sebastian . . . whose blood is that?"

"Hers. Who did you think?"

"You struck Lavonia?"

"I'll do more than that before this is finished. Or I may just leave her in that cellar room."

I went cold. Yes, the girl had done wrong, but he sounded dangerous.

"You can't leave in there all night," I said. "Does she have any water? Surely, you should just dismiss her and send her off. Losing her position here is punishment enough."

He didn't answer and kept pacing. He was like a stranger to me.

"No, she'll pay," he said finally. "I haven't decided quite how yet, but she'll pay."

"How long will you leave her in there?"

Angrily, he turned to me. "Stay out of this, Megan. I know none of this is your fault, but don't interfere now."

It was an odd sensation, being afraid of Sebastian. Though I wasn't afraid of him hurting me, what would he do to Lavonia?

"Come to bed," I said quietly. "Let me clean up your hand."

Slowly, he exhaled and sat on the bed. I fetched a rag and the basin of water on my table.

"Father won't forget," he whispered. "If he lives to be a hundred, he'll never forget that I ruined his first attempt to hold a formal dinner."

At the pain in his voice, I drew his head against my shoulder.

* * * *

Late in the night, as he finally slept beside me, I listened to him breathe. Nothing would make up for what happened tonight, and he was most likely correct in his assessment of his father: Jarrod would never forget and never forgive.

Of course, Lavonia was to blame, but Sebastian's talk of punishing her seemed far beyond the crime. The kitchen girls had been allowed to wax lazy for years, and then one day, they'd been expected to work much harder.

Some of them blamed me for this turn of events.

Lavonia probably saw herself as justified in attempting to discredit me.

She wasn't suited to work in the kitchen, and she'd betrayed the family she served, but the proper punishment for that was a dismissal.

As Sebastian slept, I slipped from the bed and donned my silk dressing gown. Going quietly to my dressing table, I took up a small pouch of money I'd brought with me from Chaumont. Then I tiptoed to the door and opened it, desperately hoping he wouldn't awake. He didn't, and I left the room.

I went down to the main floor, to the west passage, and I paused in front of Ester's door. After gathering myself, I knocked softly.

A moment later, she opened it and peered out. "My lady?"

"Where did he lock Lavonia? Do you know?"

Her expression was strained, and she didn't appear to have been awakened. Perhaps she couldn't sleep either. "Foolish girl. I was so busy with the tarts I didn't even watch what she was doing. If I'd known, I've have stopped her."

"I know you would have, but do you know where she is?"

She nodded. "He made me lock her in myself."

"You have the key?"

Again, she nodded.

"My husband is angry beyond cause," I said, "and I fear for Lavonia's safety. If you give me the keys and tell me where to go, I'll let her out, but she'll have to leave the grounds tonight."

After a brief hesitation, Ester opened the door all the way. She put a robe over her nightgown and lifted a set of keys from the wall. She took up a candle lantern that had been glowing on her nightstand. "I'll come. He left her in quite a state."

Though I had no wish to involve Ester, I wasn't about to refuse her help. Together, we went downstairs into the cellars and down a passage with a dirt floor. Ester stopped before a stout wooden door and unlocked it.

When she held the candle lantern high, we both looked inside. Lavonia was huddled back against the far wall, but I could see her face. Her mouth was split on one side and her eye was swollen shut. There was no food, water, or even a bucket in which she might relieve herself.

"Ester?" she said in what sounded like hope, and she started to rise. Then she saw me and balked.

"Come on," Ester said. "We need to get you out."

I held up the pouch of money. "You have to escape the grounds tonight, and you must hurry."

"Escape? No. This is my home."

She still didn't grasp the gravity of the situation.

Ester shook her head. "There's nothing for it now. I think Lord Sebastian means to leave you in here, or worse."

"Take this money," I said. "Can you sweet talk one of the guards into letting you out?"

"She should be able to," Ester answered. "Shanyel is on watch tonight, and he's always been partial to her."

"Lord Sebastian would leave me in here?" Lavonia asked. "With nothing?"

"You crossed him," I answered, and then I couldn't help asking, "Did you really think I would be blamed?"

Her battered face turned sullen. "Everyone in the kitchen heard me tell you the fish was bad, and you ordered me to cook it. Of course, they'd blame you." Her voice broke. "I just wanted things to go back to the way they were."

With a sad shake of her head, Ester took the pouch from me and pressed it into Lavonia's hand. "Run. Go to Shanyel and have him let you out the gate. Walk south to Cerantes, that's the nearest town, and try to find work. That's the best we can do for you now. Whatever you do, don't let Lord Sebastian find you."

This last piece of advice had an effect, and Lavonia finally seemed to realize she was in danger. With one last hard look at me, she hurried for the stairs up to the main floor.

Ester sighed and relocked the door.

Both of us stood in silence.

I had no idea how this would play out now or what the repercussions might be, and I was anxious. If there was one thing I'd learned tonight, it was this: Don't ever cross Sebastian.

Chapter 11

The next morning, I woke up alone. I hadn't even felt Sebastian rise and leave the room. I agonized over my actions in the middle of the previous night but didn't regret them. I simply wondered what would happen when Sebastian learned of my interference. Ester was the only one with a key, and I wouldn't let her take the blame.

Pushing such worries aside, I dressed without Miriam's help and went downstairs to check on our guests. With Betty's assistance, I got Rosamund and Phillipe to both eat some boiled oats and drink a little tea, and then the Monvílles announced they wished to go home.

I understood this and walked out with them to the courtyard.

By the time Jarrod, Rolf, and Kai joined us, Sebastian still hadn't made an appearance, and I wondered where he was. Was he too embarrassed to face everyone?

The Monvílles had brought a wagon for their luggage, but it was full. I even noticed the bottom of a half-covered harp near the end of the wagon's bed. Why would they have brought a harp? I didn't ask.

Concerned about Rosamund riding a horse though, I suggested that Jarrod loan them another wagon—which he gladly did. I piled blankets in the back and made a bed so she could rest for the half day journey.

This morning, Lord Allemond had thawed a good deal and was surprisingly friendly to Jarrod and Rolf.

"Tomorrow then?" Allemond asked.

"Yes, we'll meet you at the old hunting lodge in the north quarter," Jarrod answered.

"Good. I'm sure you'll find everything in order, but I think it's best you check for yourself."

With that, our guests rode out.

Jarrod wasn't happy, but he didn't seem angry anymore. At least the land deal was progressing. I turned and went back into the keep before he could say anything to me, and I found myself walking down the passage toward the kitchen. Though I still fretted over the situation with Lavonia, I had a duty to perform today.

As I entered the kitchen, Cora was the first person I saw, and I stopped upon seeing the dark bruise on the left side of her face. I could only imagine the scene that had taken place in here last night.

"Are you all right?" I asked instantly.

"Yes, my lady." She sounded on the edge of tears.

Ester was making bread, and we locked eyes for a few seconds. Two women in a conspiracy.

"I assume there is a good deal of food left since so little of it was served," I said. "How many of us will be needed to carry it down?"

Ester frowned slightly in puzzlement. "Carry it down?"

"To the village."

It was common practice for the lady of any noble household to have all the leftovers collected the morning after a banquet and then help take them down to the nearest village to be given to the poor. Ester didn't appear familiar with this custom, and so I explained it.

"Oh, no," she said, shaking her head. "The master wouldn't like that, and I wouldn't ask him about it today." She paused. "Did you ask Lord Sebastian?"

I hadn't, and considering his probable state of mind, I decided not to try.

Leaving the kitchen, I felt the need for fresh air and walked out the back door into the garden. This place always cheered me with the vegetables, berries, and herbs.

Slowly, I made my way toward the hen house, and then I heard a familiar voice: Sebastian.

"This is where she hid them, out here so they could further spoil. You should have seen my father's face. I don't think I'll ever be able to recover from this."

"Well, at least one thing has come of it," a male voice answered. "You're finally spending some time with me."

"Daveed, don't push me," Sebastian warned. "Not today."

I paused in mid-step. Sebastian was out behind the hen house with Daveed, his handsome friend from the guards, the one who didn't like me.

"When should I push you?" Daveed asked, sounding petulant. "I never see you anymore, and you spend every night with that slip of a girl."

"She's my wife. What would you have me do?"

"You said she'd never choose you."

"Because I didn't think she would! What young noble woman wouldn't choose Rolf? He's the eldest son. But for some reason, she did pick me."

"Then don't pretend you're not enjoying it."

"Daveed! Not today. I mean it."

They both fell silent

A feeling of discomfort grew in my stomach. I didn't understand this conversation. What did Daveed mean by accusing Sebastian of spending his nights with me, as if this were something wrong?

Footsteps sounded, and Sebastian came around the side of the hen house. At the sight of me, he didn't even break stride.

"Megan, where are the Monvílles?"

"They've gone."

"Are you looking for me?"

"No, I was just walking, but I'm glad to see you."

Reaching out, he grasped the back of my head. "You're the only one who never asks anything of me. Why is that?"

"I love you," I answered simply.

"You do, don't you?"

Letting go of my head, he offered me his arm, and I took it. But as we walked back toward the keep, two things troubled me. First, he hadn't even mentioned checking on Lavonia or letting her out. This was both a blessing and a concern to me. Second, I couldn't stop thinking on his strange conversation with Daveed.

* * * *

The following morning, Jarrod and Rolf prepared to ride out. Apparently, the night of the disastrous dinner, they'd made a plan to meet Lord Allemond to inspect some trees in regards to the upcoming land deal.

Sebastian, Kai, and I walked out to the courtyard with them. Ten of our guards were already mounted and waiting. Daveed was among them.

Wearing their chain armor and swords, Jarrod and Rolf looked every inch the hardened men I thought them to be. I hoped they might find some middle ground to form at least an outward-appearing friendship with a man like Lord Allemond, but it didn't seem likely.

Jarrod swung up onto his horse, and I stood below him.

"Should we wait dinner for you or should I just have Ester keep something warm?" I asked.

"We're meeting in the north sector of his lands," he answered. "It's almost a half day's ride out and then back again. If we're not home by dinner, go ahead and eat."

I nodded and stepped back, but as I turned, I saw Sebastian standing beside Daveed's horse. He had one hand on the horse's shoulder, and Daveed was leaning down so they could speak without being overheard.

There was nothing unusual about this. It was common for a lord of any keep to speak with one of the house guards. Still, the discomfort in my stomach rose up again. They both looked so intense.

Finally, Sebastian patted Daveed's leg and stepped away. "All right," he said. "I'm sorry again, and I'll see you tonight."

Rolf was watching them. Then he looked at me. I held his gaze without flinching.

Jarrod wheeled his horse and the entire contingent cantered toward the gate.

Kai, Sebastian, and I remained in the courtyard until they were out of sight.

"Well, we have the place to ourselves," Sebastian said. "Rather a pleasant thought. What shall we do with our day? How about a game of cards?"

I smiled. "You two play. I thought I'd see about hanging some wildflowers to dry. That way, next winter we can have a little color on the table when we need it. Also, I need to make sure Betty and Matilda have seen to cleaning the guest rooms."

"Industrious thing," he teased.

He and Kai headed off together, and I went to my duties.

The day passed slowly for me as I alternately dreaded and expected Sebastian to give an order regarding the fate of Lavonia. He never said a word. Even though I'd already ensured her safety, it troubled me that to his knowledge, she'd been locked in a room without water since the night before last. Had she still been in there, she'd be suffering terribly. How long could a person live without water?

Not long past dusk, I met Sebastian and Kai in the great hall.

"Your father said we should go ahead and eat if they hadn't returned yet, so I've ordered dinner be brought in."

Kai nodded. "I am getting hungry."

I was gratified that relations between him and myself had improved somewhat, though we still seldom spoke. When we were in a room together, he often followed me with his eyes, but he was no longer hostile. I believed in time, he and I could be friends.

The three of us sat down at the table.

Betty and Matilda carried in trays of beef, potatoes, and carrots. As the beef was left over from the dinner party, I thought it might jog Sebastian into mentioning Lavonia. It didn't.

"Betty, is there bread?" Kai called.

"Yes, my lord. I'll fetch you some."

She had just turned away when a loud crashing sounded from somewhere at the front of the keep. It took me an instant to realize it was the front doors being opened hard and fast enough to slam against the walls.

"Sebastian!" a male voice nearly screamed. "Sebastian!"

Everyone in the hall froze for a second or two, and then Kai was running. Sebastian was on his heels and I ran after, down the passage for the front doors.

We reached the open doors to find Daveed on his knees panting for breath. He was bleeding from a wound on the side of his head, but he saw us coming.

"Kai . . ." he managed say. "Your father . . . get your father."

Kai ran past him as Sebastian skidded to a stop and dropped to his knees. "Daveed, you're bleeding."

I hurried after Kai, thinking to find the contingent in the courtyard and learn what had happened. But there was only one foaming horse waiting, with Jarrod draped over its back. Other guards from the barracks were running out by now.

Kai got to Jarrod first. "Father!"

Reaching up, he struggled to lift Jarrod's prone form off the horse. Once he'd done this, he dropped down while holding his father in his arms. Jarrod was unconscious and his skin was nearly white. There was an ugly slash across his stomach. His chain armor hadn't protected him.

As the other guards reached us, several knelt to see if they could help Kai with Jarrod. I knew a few of them by name.

Captain Marcel swung his head left and right. "Where's Lord Rolf? Where are the rest of our men?"

"We need to get Lord Jarrod inside and into a bed," I said.

Kai's face had turned nearly as white as his father's. "Captain, take him. Do as your lady says and get him inside." He jumped up and ran back to the open doorway. "Daveed, where is Rolf?"

I came up behind Kai to see Daveed's anguished expression.

"I'm sorry," Daveed choked. "He's gone. They're all gone. We were ambushed."

"Gone?" Sebastian repeated.

Several guards came up behind us carrying Jarrod, and I moved forward, going with them to the tower and then up to Jarrod's room.

"Lay him on the bed," I said.

Events were happening too rapidly for me to take in, and I'd not fully absorbed the announcement about Rolf, so I focused on the matter at hand: Jarrod's wound. It was still bleeding. Had it penetrated his stomach though, he would already be dead.

"Send for water," I ordered Captain Marcel.

I was no physician, but I needed to clean around the wound to better see with what we were dealing. Kai, Sebastian, and Daveed entered the room.

"Sebastian, help me with this armor," I asked.

As my husband moved to assist me, Kai looked down at us. His entire body was rigid.

"Daveed," he said. "Where is Rolf?"

The room fell silent, and Daveed wasn't looking at anyone. "Dead, back where he fell. Right as we rode up to the lodge to meet Lord Allemond, men came out of the trees . . . maybe thirty of them. We were outnumbered. They struck Rolf down first. Six of our men were dead before I got my sword from its sheath, but then I saw Lord Jarrod fighting, and he took a wound across his stomach and fell backward across his horse . . . but he didn't fall to the ground. I dropped my sword, jumped off my horse, and ran to him. I got up onto his horse with him in front of me. I grabbed the reins and tried to get him out. Somehow, we broke through and I just kept pushing the horse." He dropped his head. "I left everyone else behind."

The room fell silent again, but now Kai was shaking.

"You did the right thing," I said to Daveed. "What else could you do? Had you not tried to save Lord Jarrod, you'd both be dead."

Sebastian looked to me in gratitude, but I'd only spoken the truth.

"It was Allemond?" Kai demanded. "He planned this? He'd been planning it before arriving here as a dinner guest?"

Daveed nodded. "He must have."

"Then he's dead!" Kai spat. "Captain, prepare the men! All of them. We'll attack tonight and burn Monvílle Hall to the ground."

"No," Sebastian said, stepping forward. "Captain, stand down. Kai, we can't attack the Monvílle estate. That place is a fortress, and we'll never get past the gates. The Monvílles' outer wall is high enough for archers. We'll only lose more of our men."

"We can't just do nothing!" Kai shouted. "They killed Rolf!" His eyes were wild, and he whispered, "They killed Rolf."

Sebastian grabbed his shoulders. "I didn't say we'd do nothing."

Kai jerked away. "Then order our men to ride!"

He seemed almost out of control in growing grief, and I suspected Sebastian was right. An open attack would only further injure the Volodanes.

I stood. "It is a great offense for the lord of one house to ambush the lord of another in such an underhanded way. My father is on the Council of Nobles, and so is Allemond. Let me write to my father and tell him what happened. We can bring shame to Allemond and force the council to punish him."

Sebastian nodded. "Good. Kai, listen to her. We have to do this correctly. Let the council punish him. I swear we'll take revenge, but I won't allow any of our men to be killed in a futile attempt."

As he said this, I realized that with Rolf gone and Jarrod incapacitated, Sebastian was in charge of the keep.

Captain Marcel seemed to realize it too, as I saw his body relax. Even though he was loyal to Jarrod, he must have agreed with Sebastian here.

I looked back to Jarrod. "Everything else can wait. We need to help him. Is there a physician within riding distance?"

Sebastian shook his head. "Not that I know of."

"There's Abigail," Kai said, his voice still tense with anger. "I can ride and get her."

"No," Sebastian answered instantly. "He wouldn't want that."

"Who is Abigail?" I asked.

"A wise woman from the village just beyond our own," Kai answered. "She's a skilled healer. I've seen her at work."

"She's a witch," Sebastian said, "and Father wouldn't want her touching him."

This time, I agreed with Kai. I feared that Jarrod needed to be sewn up, and I had no training in such matters. If this Abigail was a skilled healer, I thought Kai should already be running for his horse.

But Sebastian was so adamant that I couldn't gainsay him in front of the others, so I held my tongue.

Kai's anger faded. He looked defeated and helpless.

Sebastian sent everyone out except for Kai, himself, and me. Miriam brought water and bandages and then she stayed as well.

The rest of the night was long.

We managed to clean and bandage Jarrod's wound, but nothing we did could stop the slow bleeding. He never woke up.

In the early hours of the morning, he died.

Kai knelt beside the bed with his face pressed down on his father's shoulder.

Sebastian reached down to touch Kai's back. "I'm sorry."

Jumping up, Kai moved away. "Are you?"

Turning, he strode from the room.

* * * *

The next few hours felt like a matter of going through motions.

Alone, I prepared Jarrod's body for burial, and as I finished, Sebastian walked in to see the results.

I'd cleaned away any remaining blood and dressed Jarrod in a dark blue tunic. I'd combed his hair.

"Thank you for this," Sebastian said.

I didn't know what to say.

"Kai's right, you know," he went on. "I don't feel sorry. I would change this outcome if I could. I'd have protected them had I known, but I'm not in mourning. Does that make me wicked?"

From what I'd seen, neither Jarrod nor Rolf had ever offered Sebastian a single kind word in his life.

"No," I answered. "I don't really know how I'd feel if my own father died, but I don't think I could mourn him."

Sebastian leaned down and kissed my head. "Bless you."

I could see how much he needed my absolution. Perhaps it was wrong, but I used this moment of solidarity. I used his moment of weakness.

"Would you allow me to let Lavonia out and dismiss her?" I asked. "Whatever she did, the damage hardly matters anymore."

"Mmmm?" he responded, still looking down at his father.

"Lavonia, the kitchen maid. Would you allow me to send her off?"

His expression darkened, and I could see he'd not forgiven her. But as I'd said, his reasons for holding her accountable hardly mattered anymore.

I stood tense.

Finally, he waved his hand. "Do as you see fit."

"I'll see to it now."

Before he could change his mind, I left the room and walked down to the main floor to the west passage. Upon reaching the kitchen, I found Betty, Matilda, Cora, and Ester.

Breakfast trays had been prepared.

"Oh, my lady," Betty asked. "Is it true? Is Lord Jarrod gone?"

I nodded. "I've prepared him for burial. Lord Sebastian will decide the rest of the arrangements."

The women made appropriate sad sounds, and I turned to Ester. "Lord Sebastian has given me permission to release Lavonia and dismiss her. Will you assist me?"

She started and then relief crossed her features. "Yes, my lady."

I wanted everyone out of this part of the keep so that she and I could pretend we'd brought Lavonia up and taken her out the back door.

"Cora," I said. "Please help Betty and Matilda with the trays this morning." She blinked but didn't argue. Kitchen girls rarely carried trays to the hall. All three of them left, and Ester met my eyes.

And so, because Sebastian was preoccupied with the deaths of his father and brother, he never learned that I'd already released Lavonia.

* * * *

After leaving the kitchen, I went to my room and wrote to my father. I held nothing back regarding what Allemond had done to lure out Jarrod and Rolf and then have them murdered. I asked him to bring the matter to the council and to seek justice.

I didn't know if anything would come of this. Allemond and my father were men of the same ilk, and they didn't view the Volodanes as equals. But I wrote with passion and laid the case out clearly.

Once it was finished, I wanted to show the letter to Kai, so that he would know what I'd written. I owed him that much. He'd been overruled and pushed aside. Though he'd been wrong in wanting to launch an open attack against the Monvílles, I still felt he'd been right in wanting to ride for the wise woman. Whether Jarrod would have approved or not, we should have tried every option available.

I went first to Kai's room, but he wasn't there. Then I made my way downstairs to the great hall. It was empty, so I walked into the courtyard and headed toward the barracks. Sometimes Kai could be found there.

As I reached it, Daveed came out the main door. His head was bandaged. "Are you well?" I asked.

His animosity toward me was gone. Perhaps he was grateful I'd justified his actions last night.

"I will be."

"Have you seen Kai?"

"I saw him go toward the barn earlier. He's in a bad way."

Turning, I went to the barn and slipped inside the large front doors. The smells of hay and leather reached me. Light filtered down from high windows, showing dust floating in the air. Looking across the open area in the front section, I saw Kai sitting on a crate with his face in his hands. His body wracked once.

I went to him.

All thoughts of showing him the letter vanished. He was in too much pain. Sebastian might not be in mourning, but Kai was. He had cared for his father and Rolf. Worse, I feared a rift between him and Sebastian.

"Kai?" I whispered.

He didn't look up.

"No matter what has happened," I said softly, "Sebastian only did what he thought was right. You have to forgive him."

"Why?" he asked so quietly I almost didn't hear it.

"Because you love him and because he's all you have left." I paused. "Except for me."

His body wracked again, and I reached out for him. He was so tall that even while sitting on the crate, his head was nearly level to mine, and I pulled him against me. Thankfully, instead of drawing away, he buried his face in my neck, grasped hold of me with both arms, and wept.

I held him as best I could.

Chapter 12

We buried Jarrod the next day, and Sebastian became the Lord of Volodane Hall.

As Kai, Sebastian, and I sat down for dinner that night, Kai asked, "Now what do we do?"

I thought it a good question.

"Nothing," Sebastian answered, sounding surer of himself than anyone I'd ever heard. "I've no interest in raising the status of our family or landing a seat on the Council of Nobles. Do you?"

"No."

"That was Father's dream, and Rolf's, not ours," Sebastian went on. "I only wish to live in peace and not have to deal with anyone or anything I find disagreeable."

Kai frowned. "You mean live in peace except for taking revenge upon the Monvilles?" His head swiveled toward me. "You wrote to your father?"

"Yes. I had a messenger take the letter yesterday."

Again, I didn't know what would come of that, but I hoped Allemond would at least lose his seat and face sanctions. This wouldn't be enough for Kai, but it would be something.

The days began to pass, and I awaited a response from my father. About three weeks after I'd written, a letter for me arrived. I was alone in the great hall, going over the menus when Betty brought it into me.

"Message for you, my lady."

"Thank you, Betty."

It wasn't from my father, but from Lady Violette Cornett.

My dear Megan,

*While I'd only recently heard of your marriage, I just now
learned of the deaths of your new father and brother. I send
my deepest condolences. Allemond Monville is devastated by
the tragedy, and he is still uncertain how the dispute broke out
between his men and the Volodanes'.*

Please take this invitation in the spirit with which it is meant.

*Lord Henri and I are having a house gathering the week
after next. I know you are in mourning, but Volodane Hall might
seem an isolated place right now for you and Sebastian and
Kai. Please do come and join us if you feel you can be comforted by companionship.*

With warm regards,

Violette Cornett

I held the letter in my hand, allowing the contents to sink in. Allemond
Monville was passing the incident off as a sudden dispute between his guards
and the Volodanes'. He was probably asserting that Jarrod and Rolf had
somehow been caught in the middle. I didn't know Violette Cornett well,
but she knew my family and had hosted my parents on numerous occasions.

Her words struck me as sincere, and I did believe she wished to offer us
comfort. I had little doubt that Sebastian would accept such invitation. But it
also sounded as if Violette was in the intimate circle of the Monvilles. What
if we were to attend this gathering and the Monvilles should be present?

Kai would go mad.

If he killed Allemond, the repercussions would probably
mean his own death.

I wrote Violette a kind refusal, saying we were not up to socializing yet.

Then I burned the invitation without ever showing it to Sebastian.

* * * *

In spite of his announcement—about doing nothing—after the burial
of Jarrod, Sebastian soon began making changes. He announced to me
one morning that we'd be having a guest for lunch, and so I asked Ester
to make a fish pie.

Just before the midday meal, a stocky man in a leather jerkin and
heavy boots arrived.

Sebastian introduced him to Kai and me. "This is Ethan Porter. He's to
be our land manager and tax collector. Megan, he'll be living here at the

keep. Normally, he'll eat in the kitchen, but you'll need to have a room made up for him."

Kai appeared startled. From what I understood, the Volodanes had always overseen their own lands.

For the remainder of lunch, Kai and I were ignored as Sebastian explained to Ethan about the various villages, tenant famers, and crops. The man seemed quite competent, but I still struggled with the idea of turning over such an important element of running the estate to what basically amounted to an employee.

"I'll be back in few days to settle in, my lady," Ethan said to me after lunch. "Thank you for the fine meal."

After he left, Kai asked Sebastian, "What are you doing?"

Sebastian waved one hand. "There's no sense in either one of us trying to fill Rolf's boots when it comes to the land. Father never taught us a thing. I was his great disappointment and you were his golden boy in a fighting ring. Trust me, this Ethan Porter knows what he's about. He's handled several estates. I looked into his references."

"You did this without even talking to me?"

"I assumed you'd agree," Sebastian answered, but there was an edge in his voice. He didn't like being questioned. "Oh, and I'm cutting taxes in half, possibly more. We've enough money to live three lifetimes. The silver mines alone have made us wealthy. I want to give the people here a better life. I'm also going to lift the ban on fishing and hunting."

"Of course, you're right there," Kai agreed, "but I don't like the idea of hiring a land manager. That's our place."

The edge in Sebastian's voice grew sharper. "We'll give it a try."

Several days later, Ethan Porter moved into a guest room. I saw very little of him, but he rode out every day to oversee the people, crops, and lands of the Volodanes. Sebastian conferred with him almost every night after dinner.

My father didn't respond to my letter about Allemond Monvílle, but Kai continued to ask if he had.

A week after Ethan's arrival, Sebastian announced we were having a house party. To me, this seemed much too soon following the deaths of Rolf and Jarrod, but what could I say?

"Who is coming?" I asked. "Do you have a guest list so I can send the invitations?"

"I've already done that. These are friends of mine from Rennes."

Apparently, the family owned a house in the city of Rennes, and Sebastian enjoyed spending time there when possible. But I was taken aback that he'd sent out the invitations. Only the lady of the house sent out invitations for a formal house party.

I soon realized this would not be like any house party I'd ever seen.

As opposed to planning menus, Sebastian wanted great quantities of food prepared that could be laid out on tables. We ordered hams and cheeses. He told Ester to be prepared to make numerous fruit trays. He wanted a variety of breads, cakes, and tarts baked, so many that I joined in to help in the kitchen. Cora and Ester were somewhat discomfited at the sight of me in an apron with my sleeves rolled up, but then they welcomed my help. I was no cook, but I could peel and cut up apples and roll pastry.

When Miriam saw this, she joined in too, and we both rather enjoyed ourselves. I always preferred to be occupied with something useful.

Sebastian ordered casks and casks of wine and ale.

When the guests began arriving, my confusion grew. I didn't know anyone, and none of them were from among the noble families. Most were in their early to late twenties. They laughed and spoke loudly and embraced Sebastian like old friends. They didn't seem quite sure what to say to me. I felt the same.

"Who are they?" I asked.

"I told you, friends of mine from Rennes," he answered. "Normally, I'd go to see them, but now they can come here. It's wonderful, isn't it?"

He was so happy that I tried to smile and agree.

A few hours later, a group of musicians arrived, and he told me I'd need to find rooms for them. I ended up housing them in the barracks.

That night, Betty and Matilda piled the table in the great hall with food. Casks of wine lined one wall. People in brightly colored clothing flocked in to eat and drink, but few of them sat down.

The musicians began to play.

Card and dice games spontaneously appeared, with a good deal of money exchanging hands. People danced and ate and drank and laughed. Sebastian laughed and danced along with them, and he was clearly the lord of the hall.

Kai and I were at odds among this company. He liked a card game at home, but he wasn't a gambler. He wasn't much for dancing with strangers, and he rarely drank more than a single goblet of wine or cup of ale.

As the hour grew late, the sounds grew more raucous, with people chasing each other, squealing with laughter. The spaniels who lived in here were either overexcited or frightened, and I decided we'd need to relocate them tomorrow.

Betty and Matilda worked hard to clean up dirty dishes and spilled wine, but I finally decided to find Sebastian and ask him if they could go to bed and see to the mess in the morning. Looking around, I didn't see him and tried to press pass some of the people dancing. As I neared the far end of the hall, I spotted him talking with a blond man in a burgundy tunic. I recognized the tunic because I'd made it for Sebastian.

As the man turned, I stopped.

It was Daveed, wearing Sebastian's clothing. The burgundy made his blue eyes glow.

He spotted me in the same moment and had the good taste to look abashed. What was one our house guards doing in Sebastian's clothes? My husband had a goblet of wine in his hand, and I knew he'd already had too much to drink.

Walking up, I ignored Daveed. "I'm going to send Betty and Matilda to bed. It's nearly midnight, and they'll need to be up early to help Ester and Cora start breakfast." There was so much noise around us that I had to speak up.

"By all means," Sebastian slurred. He was drunk . . . but he also looked happier than I'd ever seen him.

"If you don't mind," I added, "I think I'll go up too."

It was the height of poor manners for the hostess to leave her own gathering, but I didn't think anyone here would notice.

"Of course," he said. "Don't wait up for me. I may be late." He appeared almost relieved.

With a nod, I headed straight for Kai. He stood by himself near a card table, pretending to sip at a goblet.

"I'm going to excuse Betty and Matilda," I said, hoping he could hear me over the din, "and then go up to bed myself."

His eyes filled with hope. "Is that allowed? Can I leave too?"

"Yes."

We gathered Betty and Matilda, and the four of us fled the hall, said good night to each other and hurried to our respective rooms. I'd long since sent Miriam to bed, but I managed to unlace myself and step out of my gown.

Exhausted and troubled, I crawled under the covers. It took a while until I slept. Since my arrival here, I'd never gone to sleep without Sebastian.

* * * *

The following morning, I woke up alone.

Miriam arrived soon after, and she dressed me for the day. Neither of us said much, but I caught her eye in the mirror and asked, "Have you been downstairs?"

She shook her head.

Together, we left the room and made our way down.

The great hall was in a shamble and several of our guests had passed out on the floor near the hearth. I called in a few guards to help take them to their rooms. The poor spaniels were sleeping in a pile in the far corner. Betty and Matilda arrived soon after, and we began the clean up.

Kai walked in and looked around. "Can I do anything?"

"I think we ought to take the dogs out. I saw a man feeding Lacey ale last night. Could you take them to the barracks and ask a few of the guards to look after them?"

"Yes."

I had no idea when Sebastian might want breakfast to be served. I didn't know where he was but assumed he'd slept in his own room.

He didn't appear until after midday, looking less worse for wear than I'd expected. The hall was nearly cleaned up by then, and he kissed my face.

None of the guests had arisen yet.

"I had a wonderful night," he said. "Are you enjoying yourself?"

I was not. "Yes."

Nearly everyone else slept until the late afternoon, and then when they came in, Sebastian ordered food to be piled on the table, and to my astonishment, a repeat performance of the previous night began.

This went on for four more days.

When the guests finally left, I exhaled in relief, hoping fervently that Sebastian had needed to purge himself of the shadow of his father and brother, and that he'd been able to get *something* out of his system, and that Volodane Hall would never see such a display again.

Once everyone had gone, Kai, Sebastian, and I had a quiet dinner, and then Sebastian closeted himself away with Ethan Porter to discuss the harvest. I thought Kai should be involved in these meetings, but he wasn't.

That night, I expected Sebastian to come to me as he'd done before the house party, carrying mugs of tea or an apple to slice in bed.

He didn't.

Something had altered in our world, and I had no idea why.

He was soon busy with details of the harvest as it was time to bring in the wheat. Kai continued with his sparring sessions in the morning, but he seemed rather at a loss in the afternoons. I could see him growing more restless and unhappy.

A month later, right after the harvest, Sebastian announced another house party.

When the kitchen women heard the news, I feared Cora might give her notice. I think she would have if she'd had anywhere else to go.

* * * *

A pattern in our lives took shape.

Sebastian was never lazy or negligent in the any matter involving the estate. He was meticulous with house accounts, and he worked closely with Ethan, but every other month, he'd fill the keep with pleasure-seeking people, and the length of the house parties began to extend.

He never slept in my bed.

I longed for his company in the night.

Although I'd come to accept that there was something missing in our marriage, that we were not like other married couples, I'd never felt as close to anyone as I had to Sebastian in those early nights together.

Now I didn't even have him sleeping beside me.

I dreaded the house parties.

Three nights into the fourth gathering, I looked about the hall and didn't see Kai. Without telling Sebastian, I left the hall and went up to the third floor of the tower and knocked on the door to Kai's room. I'd never done that before.

Almost instantly, he opened it and looked out. He was still fully dressed.

"Are you all right?" I asked.

He didn't answer. It was a foolish question.

Inside, there was a table near the bed with a chessboard. "You play?" I asked.

"Yes, Rolf and I used to play all the time. He was good."

Poor Kai. He loved Sebastian, but he'd looked up to Rolf.

"If we leave the door open," I suggested, "you and I could have a few games. My father taught me."

He brightened and stepped back. I knew it was inappropriate for me to be inside his bedroom, but none of the old rules seemed to apply here anymore. We sat and began to play, and I felt myself relaxing.

He won the first game.

Not long into the second, I began to understand his strategy a little better and took his queen. He blinked. "Wait, where did that rook come from?"

I laughed and showed him. He laughed too. Kai was a gracious winner and loser.

A shadow passed over the board, and I turned my head.

Sebastian hung in the doorway. "I noticed you both gone and came to check. Are you hiding away up here?" He'd been drinking but wasn't drunk. I knew he wouldn't think twice about me being Kai's room. Sebastian wasn't that type of husband.

"Do you mind?" I asked. "It's so loud down there."

A flash of sadness passed through his eyes. "You both hate these gatherings, don't you?"

"Of course not," I lied. "We just wanted some quiet."

He nodded. "All right. I'll go back down."

After he left, Kai's enjoyment of the game was gone.

* * * *

Things came to a crisis the following night.

For Sebastian's benefit, I made an attempt to pretend I was enjoying myself. I stayed in the hall much later than usual. Kai remained as well.

I sipped at wine and tried to make conversation with Sebastian's friends.

By midnight, few of them were capable of making conversation, and I decided to make my escape. Walking past the dance floor, I started for the arch when someone stepped in front of me.

I tried to remember his name. I think it was Renaldo, the son of a prosperous wool merchant.

"Come and dance with me, beautiful lady," he slurred.

"Not now, sir," I said, trying to smile. "I was just on my way out."

As I moved to walk around him, he grasped my arm. "I insist. You must have at least once dance."

When I tried to pull my arm back, he kept ahold of me. I don't think he meant me any harm. He'd had too much to drink. But before I could say another word, a loud crack sounded and Renaldo went flying backward. He hit the floor.

Kai was beside me in a rage. "Keep away from her!"

I then realized he'd stuck Renaldo.

Sebastian came hurrying over. "Kai, what did you do?"

Renaldo wasn't moving, and his eyes were closed.

"He had his hands on Megan!" Kai shouted. "If you won't do anything, I will."

The music stopped and the hall grew quieter. Several people knelt to revive Renaldo, but Kai was now facing off with Sebastian.

"I hated the way Father treated you," Kai said. "But if he were here now, he'd be ashamed, and for once, you'd deserve it."

Whirling, he strode from the hall. Sebastian stared after him.

* * * *

The next day, the house party broke up.

By now, I'd realized that Sebastian wasn't simply sowing wild oats after being repressed by his father and older brother for so long. He believed in responsibility—and he took responsibility for the estate—but he needed other people around him who enjoyed pleasure in the same way that he did.

His alternation between work and these house parties wouldn't stop, neither would he ever give Kai any kind of authority. After a lifetime of feeling powerless, Sebastian needed to *be* in charge.

Kai would only grow bitter and miserable in this environment. He needed an occupation. He needed a purpose.

And I had to help him.

Going upstairs to my room, I sat down at the vanity and wrote a letter to Chaumont.

> *Dear Father,*
> *I require your help and am willing to help you in return.*
> *I ask that you speak to Lord Sauvage and request that he offer Kai Volodane a commissioned office in the king's army, perhaps as a lieutenant. Have him send the offer here.*
> *If you do this, I will pay off one of your creditors. You only need name the debt.*
> *Please respond at your earliest convenience.*
> *Your daughter,*
> *Megan*

Taking the letter out to the barracks, I found Captain Marcel.

"My lady," he said with the short bow. "Can I be of service?"

"I need a letter carried to my family in Chaumont as quickly as possible. Can you spare a swift rider?"

"Of course."

I knew my father wouldn't ignore my message as it contained an offer of money, but he exceeded even my expectations with his rapid response. Chaumont Manor was a two-day ride at a leisurely pace. It could be done in a day and half on a fast horse.

Three days after I sent the letter a response arrived. Father must have penned it and put someone on horse within an hour of reading my offer.

> *My dear Megan,*
> *I have already sent word to Lord Sauvage, and I'm certain*
> *he will offer to sell young Volodane a commission. From what*
> *I understand, Kai is well trained with a sword, and Sauvage*
> *would be glad to have him.*
> *The offer should arrive shortly with all the particulars.*
> *I have enclosed a note for a loan I took out last year, and I*
> *appreciate your offer of assistance.*

He didn't bother with a signature. I looked at the note for the loan. It was for five hundred silver pieces.

I took the letter down the west passage. Recently, Sebastian had had a storage room cleaned out, and he'd turned it into a study. I found him there behind his desk going over a ledger of accounts.

"May I disturb you?" I asked.

He smiled. "Please do."

I held out the letter and quickly explained what I'd done. Almost as soon as I began speaking, his smile faded.

"You'd need to pay my father's debt and buy Kai the commission," I finished. "But will you?"

"You want me to send my only brother off to serve in the king's army?"

"No." I shook my head. "I don't want you want to send him off. I want you to let him go. Will you?"

To his credit, he didn't pretend not to understand me.

"If this offer arrives and he wants it, I'll pay the commission," he said tightly.

"And my father's debt?"

"Yes."

I started for the door and then stopped. "Kai can never know about these backdoor dealings. He'll need to believe Sauvage sought him out."

Slowly, he nodded.

* * * *

The offer arrived in the evening about a week later.

I hid it and saved it until morning. I wanted to speak with Kai alone, and Sebastian rarely came down for breakfast anymore.

Walking into the great hall, I found Kai at the table, drinking tea and eating bacon.

Without even a greeting, I said, "I've received a letter from Lord Sauvage. I think you know he's a friend of my family? He enclosed an offer for you."

"For me?"

I held out the piece of paper. "He's offering you a commission as a lieutenant. If you accept, you're to report in Partheney and then take your place in the coastal border patrol."

Jumping up, he took the letter. Honestly, I'd not known how he would react, but his face came alive.

"A commission? As a lieutenant?" He was overjoyed, reading the contents of the offer several times. "But don't commissions cost a good deal of money?"

"Sebastian will pay it."

"Oh, Megan." His eyes flew up. "On the coastal patrol? I can hardly believe it." Then his face fell, and he ran his free hand through his hair. "Wait. I can't go. I can't just leave you here, not with everything that's..." He trailed off.

I fought to keep my expression still. He feared abandoning me.

"Yes, you can," I answered. "Sebastian will look out for me, and our king needs men like you on the border. We'll all be safer with you watching our shores."

This was probably a pretty lie, but it worked.

His eyes lit up with hope again.

I touched his arm. "Go, Kai. Go."

* * * *

Sebastian couldn't bring himself to see Kai off, but Miriam and I did. It was a bittersweet morning for me.

As he mounted up, I said, "Write when you can."

"I'll try, but I've never been one for writing." He paused, looking down from his horse. "If you ever need me, I'll come."

"I know."

He cantered toward the gate, and I felt the loss of him. Miriam's hand grasped mine.

"You'll always have me," she said.

I gripped down on her fingers. "We'll always have each other."

* * * *

Winter turned into spring, and spring turned into summer again.

I turned eighteen.

After Kai's departure, Sebastian expressed more concern for my happiness. Between that midwinter and summer, he held only two house parties, and in between those he spent a good deal of time with me, even taking me on a picnic once.

Occasionally, he would sleep in my bed, and we'd whisper under the covers and he'd pull me up against him to sleep. I would have liked this to happen much more often, but I'd learned never to ask more than he was capable of giving. Sebastian didn't like to be questioned and he didn't like to be pressed.

"You understand me," he whispered one night. "Sometimes I think you're the only one."

I'd long since given up on us becoming a more traditional man and wife, but it pained me that we'd never have children.

In the middle of that summer, a letter arrived from Kai.

True to his word, he hadn't written me often, so one of his infrequent letters always delighted me. This one was longer than usual, and I read parts of it aloud to Sebastian at dinner.

"He thinks next year he'll be given command of a small contingent of scouts," I said.

Sebastian shook his head. "He sounds happy, doesn't he? As if he loves riding up and down the coast looking for pirates who've landed without permission."

"He probably does."

I didn't know if Kai was a born soldier or not. I only knew that he needed a purpose.

However, there was a part of the letter I didn't read to Sebastian, and that night in my room, I read it again by the light of a candle.

> *I've never had any doubt that you somehow took a hand in helping me escape the keep, and I will always be grateful. It may surprise you to hear that I still miss home so much, not the home I left, but the one I remember. In my mind, I go over and over that day when Father and Rolf were killed, imagining ways I might have stopped it.*
>
> *For a brief span, between the time you came to live with us and the time they died, we had a true home. Then suddenly, Father and Rolf were gone and Sebastian became a stranger.*

I like my comrades here, and I've made good friends, but
they are not my own people and I sometimes feel alone. We all
need our own people. With the exception of you, mine are gone.

During the day when I'd read that section, it had made me pity Kai. Here, in the night, in the solitude of my room, it made me pity myself. To my shame, tears sprang to my eyes.

I felt alone too.

I longed for Sebastian to come through the door with an apple or a bowl of strawberries.

The hours ticked by, and he didn't. I began to feel desperate. Something about Kai's letter brought the entire last year crashing down on me, and I could no longer sit in here by myself.

Should I go to Miriam? She was dear to me.

I didn't want Miriam's company tonight. I wanted Sebastian's.

Rising from the bed, I put on my dressing robe and left the room. I went down the passage to the curve, to Sebastian's room. I'd never slept in there but didn't think he'd mind me coming to him this once. He understood loneliness better than he liked to let on.

Upon reaching his door, I almost knocked and then decided not to. He never knocked on mine, and at this hour, he may already be asleep. I could just slip in beside him. He'd understand, and he'd wake up enough to hold me.

Quietly, I cracked the door and opened it halfway.

A candle lantern glowed on the top of a table. Perhaps he wasn't asleep. My gazed shifted to the bed as I saw movement there, and I went still. Two entwined forms moved slowly together on the bed. Tightly muscled shoulders and arms glistened with sweat.

Sebastian lay above Daveed, gripping Daveed's head with both hands. His open mouth pressed against Daveed's in a way that was urgent and hungry and sensual all at the same time.

I couldn't move.

Daveed must have seen or sensed something because his head turned toward me.

An instant later, Sebastian looked over and saw me there in the doorway. "Megan!"

He jumped off Daveed, grabbed a blanket, and wrapped it around his waist. Then he came toward me so fast I back-stepped into the wall across the passage. His face was close to mine as his body held me there against the wall.

"What are you doing here?" he demanded.

Was this the wrong that had been committed tonight? I'd gone up the passage to a room where I should not?

I couldn't answer, and he seemed to realize the absurdity of the question.

"May I go to my own room?" I asked, shaking from the revelation of what I'd seen.

He stepped back. "Go. We'll talk tomorrow."

"Yes, tomorrow."

* * * *

By morning, I was a different person. I grew up that night. For over a year, I'd believed that Sebastian and I were married and he loved me and that he practiced a different type of marriage.

None of this was true.

Yes, I had chosen him, but he hadn't chosen me. All this time, he'd been in love with someone else, someone who was not me, and I'd been too blind to see it.

The next morning, he was up early and called me into his study.

There, he leaned down and studied my face.

"It's gone," he said.

"What's gone?"

"That look. The look you always give me as if the sun rises and sets around my head."

I suppose it was gone. He was in love with someone else, and he'd hidden it. I couldn't forgive him.

"I'm sorry," he said.

I didn't respond. His apology meant little.

In agitation, he put one fist to his mouth and took it away again. "I can't have this. I can't have you looking at me like that."

"What are you saying?"

"I'm saying we can't live together with you looking at me like that."

So this was my fault? Would he send me away? Where? Back to my parents? I couldn't stand the thought.

Walking away to the desk, he said, "We have to solve this." He turned to face me again. "What if I give you the house in Rennes? It was my mother's and I own it outright. I could set you up with a monthly stipend for expenses and servants?"

It took a moment for me to grasp what he was offering: my independence. We would remain married, but I'd have my own house and my household, well away from here. Once this sank in, I understood what Kai must have felt upon receiving the offer for his commission.

Then I saw the desperation in Sebastian's eyes. He wished me gone. He only wanted me here so long as I adored him. This hurt, but I kept my head and took advantage of his need.

"I want the house signed over to me, in my name," I said, "and I want no monthly stipend that can be cut off. Dip into the money from the silver mines and provide me with enough to support me for life."

My voice sounded hard, and he stared at me. "Megan . . ."

"Is it a bargain?"

He nodded.

I knew my heart should be breaking, but it wasn't. Perhaps I was my father's daughter after all.

Chapter 13

Captain Marcel led the contingent that accompanied my small party to Rennes. Upon depositing us, our guards would return to Volodane Hall directly.

In Rennes, we'd have no need of guards.

Of course, I brought Miriam. I also brought Betty and Cora. I'd not wanted to deprive Sebastian of Ester, but when I made offers to Betty and Cora, they'd both jumped at the chance to come with me.

It was nearly a day's ride to Rennes, and upon arriving, we found ourselves entering a small city. I'd never been here.

We passed through the gates into a large open-air market, and I immediately had a good feeling about our new home. The streets were clean and as we headed deeper into the city, we passed a mix of shops with brightly colored awnings and well-maintained dwellings.

Seven blocks in, Captain Marcel turned north. Two blocks later he stopped in front of a large house constructed of light-toned stone. The house boasted latticed windows with whitewashed shutters. A mix of ivy vines and white roses climbed up and around the entire front. It reminded me of a smaller version of Chaumont Manor.

"Here we are, my lady," the captain said.

I wasn't certain I'd heard him correctly. "This is the house?"

"Yes."

I dismounted and stood looking up at the windows. I don't know what I'd expected, but this was . . . more.

Miriam, Cora, and Betty climbed from the back of a wagon that carried our trunks and gazed up as well.

"This is your house, my lady?" Miriam asked.

"No," I answered firmly. "This is our house, and no one can take it from us."

* * * *

We settled in quickly, a household of women.

Miriam no longer functioned as my maid, and she lived as my friend. Cora did the cooking, and Betty did the laundry. Miriam and I helped with the cleaning. The house had a lovely front parlor, and the four of us gathered there in the evenings to sew or read aloud to each other.

Even though Sebastian had been generous with the sum he gave me, we lived simply for the most part. I'd never known the joy of living completely under my own power before. I had lived on the whims of my parents, and then I'd lived to try and please Sebastian.

Now I lived for myself.

Miriam and I learned of a group of women who organized food for the poor, and we joined them so that we might be of help. This made us feel useful, but it also offered us a chance to make new friends.

My father was appalled when he heard of my new living arrangements, and he wrote me an angry letter telling me to go home and beg Sebastian to forgive me—as of course I must be the one at fault. I assumed he feared that under the present circumstances, he'd never see another copper penny from Sebastian.

He was probably right.

A few months after I'd settled into my life in Rennes, Sebastian wrote a chatty letter with news from the hall. Although at first I'd been hesitant to open it, I found I enjoyed reading his rather caustic writing style. Time and distance had helped quell my anger toward him. I wrote back to tell him all our news.

Following this, we wrote without fail once a month.

After a year, I was even able to ask after Daveed.

Happiness has a healing effect, and I was happy. I controlled every aspect of my own life, and this suited me well.

Another year passed. I was not yet twenty-one.

Kai had written to me occasionally over the past two years. He'd been promoted to captain, and he led a small team of scouts who rooted out smugglers. At the start of the third year in my own home, a short note arrived from him to let me know he was on leave and would be passing through Rennes and wanted to stop over for several days.

We flew into a flurry of cooking and baking.

The day he arrived, Miriam and I both ran out front to greet him with an unabashed welcome.

For some reason, I'd expected to find the same Kai who'd ridden from the Volodane courtyard two and a half years ago, but he had changed. For one, his hair was cut very short, and he now wore the light blue and yellow tabard of the king's army.

He hadn't shaved for several days, so his face bore a stubble.

But he smiled at the sight of us. "Megan. Miriam."

We each took an arm.

"Prepare to be petted and spoiled," Miriam said. "You are entering a house of women."

"After the past few months, you'll get no complaint from me. I could use a little petting and spoiling."

He even sounded different, more self-assured.

"How long can you stay?" I asked.

"Three days."

We made the most of those three days, feeding him stews, fish pie, cakes, and tarts. We took him shopping at the market. One night, a group of players came through the city, and we went to see them perform. The other evenings, he told us stories of his adventures with his scouts, and how he had even once infiltrated a group of smugglers in order to catch them outright.

Cora and Betty listened on the edge of their seats, lost in the novelty of a masculine presence.

On his last night, when everyone had gone up to bed but him and myself, the two of us sat by the fire sipping small glasses of brandy.

Out of the blue, he asked, "Do you remember that letter I wrote? The long one, when you still lived at the hall?"

He'd not asked me why I left, and I hadn't offered to tell him, but I'd never forget that letter.

"Yes, I remember."

"There was more I wanted to say, a good deal more." He hesitated. "I wanted to tell you how sorry I was for the way I treated you when you first came. I thought you looked down on us, and it made me angry."

"You don't have to apologize."

"I do. Before my family ever visited Chaumont Manor, we'd been told all about Helena. I expected to see someone tall and proud with red hair, but we rode into your courtyard, and I saw you standing there in that yellow dress, so small and terrified. Then I saw your house, and I knew we'd never be good enough. That night at dinner, I was desperate for you to pick me and yet so afraid you'd pick me, the lesser of three evils, someone you didn't want."

I breathed quietly, listening to him, knowing that he needed to talk of these things but wishing he would stop.

"You picked Sebastian," he finished.

"Yes, I picked Sebastian."

"I wasn't angry in the way that Rolf was," he said. "I just thought you didn't want us, any of us, and I'm sorry."

"It doesn't matter."

"It does to me."

In the old days at the hall, I might have grasped his hand to comfort him, but now I didn't touch him.

The next day, we saw him off and made him promise to come back as soon as possible.

Cora sighed as he rode away. "It was nice having him here."

"It was," I agreed.

But I was glad to go back to the normal rhythms of our life.

* * * *

The years passed.

Miriam and I became more influential in our charity work, sometimes hosting meetings at the house.

She took up painting, and I bought a harp.

Each day was full, and we lived as we pleased.

I answered to no one.

* * * *

The world around me vanished, and I found myself standing once again in the storage room of my parents' manor, in front of the three-tiered mirror.

As before, I fought to breathe, thinking on all that I had just seen.

But the dark-haired woman was now looking out from the left-side panel.

"That would be the outcome of the second choice," she said. "Now you'll go back to the beginning, to the wedding day once again, to live out the third choice."

"Wait!" I begged. "Give me a moment."

I needed to think.

"To the beginning once more," she said. "To live out the third choice."

My mind went blank, and the storage room vanished.

I found myself back in my family's dining hall. It was my wedding day.

Chairs had been set up in rows, and guests were seated in them. I wore a gown of pale ivory and held my father's arm as he walked me past the guests toward the far end of the hall.

Flowers in tall vases graced that same end, and a local magistrate stood there with a book in his hands.

Beside the magistrate stood Kai. I had chosen him.

As he stared back at me, I could feel his anger.

The Third Choice
Kai

Chapter 14

The first time I laid eyes upon Volodane Hall, I was wet, damp, and struggling not to give way to misery.

Right after the wedding I found myself of the back of a horse for a two-day journey. Thankfully, Miriam had agreed to accompany me, and by the time we reached our destination, I'd still not been expected to share a bed with Kai. He'd not spoken to me for the entire journey.

What had I been thinking, choosing him? Whatever had possessed me?

He wasn't pleased that I'd chosen him. In this regard alone, either of his brothers would have proven a saner option.

The farther north we traveled, the sky grew darker. Though it was early summer, a cold drizzle began to fall, soaking through my cloak. None of the men seemed to notice, but Miriam and I both shivered. A part of me still couldn't believe my parents had sent me off with these strangers without a word of comfort or concern.

Finally we arrived at Volodane Hall, and yet the sight of it brought me no relief—rather just the opposite. Because of the word "hall," I'd been picturing something like an oversized hunting lodge.

But a bleak, decaying one-towered keep stood at the top of a rise.

"Home, sweet home," Sebastian said. "Such as it is."

Sitting on his horse in front of me, Kai turned around to see my reaction. I'd not expected him to do this and had no chance to hide my dismay.

Jarrod urged his mount into a canter, rode up to the gates, and called out. A moment later, I heard a grinding sound, like timber creaking across timber, and then the gates opened.

We rode inside to a small, muddy courtyard. We had several wagons of goods sent by my parents, along with my luggage. Captain Marcel began calling out orders for proper unpacking and storage. Large, growling wolfhounds stalked between the horses.

This was not a welcoming place.

Jarrod jumped to the wet ground and called back toward us, "Kai! Get the women inside."

Kai was already off his horse, but instead of reaching for me, he walked to Miriam and lifted her down. By the time her feet were settled, Sebastian was on the ground beside me.

"Put your hands on my shoulders," he ordered.

I wondered at the wisdom of accepting his help, as Kai was my husband. Though Kai clearly wasn't happier than me about us having been pressed into this marriage, I didn't want to alienate him further by seeming to depend on his brother.

Still, I was exhausted and sore from riding and had no wish to offend Sebastian either. Placing my hands on his shoulders, I let him lift me down.

After this, Miriam and I were ushered inside the front doors of the keep . . . and I was home. The foyer and main passage were both dim, but Sebastian slipped past to lead the way.

"Bring them along, Kai," he called over one shoulder, hurrying ahead. "I'll make sure the fire is stoked in the hall."

There was that word again: hall.

At the end of the passage, we emerged indeed to a large chamber with a fireplace tall enough that I could have stood inside. The sight of the already burning logs and the emanation of warmth filled me with relief. Half a dozen friendly spaniels came running toward us, wriggling and whining for attention. One of them leaped up into Kai's chest. He caught the dog with both arms and smiled.

"Lacey, stop that. You know better."

It was the first time I'd seen him smile.

Miriam grasped my hand and pointed to the hearth. "My lady?"

Nodding, I let her lead me to the warmth of the blaze. The walls were bare of any ornament or tapestry, and the floor was filthy.

Hearing heavy footsteps, I turned to see Jarrod and Rolf walk in.

Kai put down the dog.

Two serving women hurried in carrying trays, and Jarrod waved me toward the table. "Over here."

Miriam and I both moved to join him. Though my dress was damp, and I couldn't stop shivering, I was hungry and longing for a mug of tea.

I waited for Jarrod to take his seat so the rest of us could follow suit. He didn't. He stood beside the table and poured himself a mug of what looked to be ale. Then he poured another and held it out to me. I didn't care for ale.

Of course, though, I took it, and he gestured down to a tray on the table. "Help yourself."

The only items on the tray were two loaves of hardened bread and a half wheel of cheese with mold on the rind.

Kai watched my face carefully, and his resentment was unmistakable. He thought me a snob who viewed them all as far beneath myself, who viewed this place as far beneath myself. Perhaps he wasn't wrong.

Jarrod studied me as well. "The kitchen women have grown lazy. It's your place to set them into minding their tasks." He paused. "I want to have guests here soon and not be ashamed."

I shuddered at the thought of being expected to turn this keep into a place suitable for entertaining. No one had ever taught me how to run a house. But I pushed the thought aside and tried to eat a chunk of the cheese.

After a few bites, I felt too exhausted to eat.

Jarrod waved to one of the serving women. "Betty, show your new lady to her room. You know which one." He looked back to me. "Kai will be up later."

That prospect was far more daunting than the thought of running a household.

Miriam and I followed Betty.

* * * *

The room I was given on the second floor of the single tower was a woman's room, or it once had been.

Two candles burned on a bed stand, providing sufficient light.

Walking to the dressing table, I gazed into the mirror and cringed, as I was more bedraggled than I'd realized. Miriam stood in the center of the room, taking in the furnishings. Her face was pale and stricken.

What had I dragged her into?

One of my chests had been carried and set at the end of the bed. "See if I have a nightgown in there."

Springing into action, she peeled off my dress and my shift and then helped me into a long white nightgown. I grew anxious over what would happen tonight. My mother hadn't told me much of what took place between men and women in the dark.

Miriam must have sensed my thoughts. "Try not to worry, my lady."

Just as she'd begun attempting to dry my hair, the door opened, and Kai walked in.

He still wore his sword and chain armor. His entire body was rigid, and I could hear him breathing as he glared at me. Glancing at Miriam, he motioned toward the door with his head. "Go."

Taking in his expression, she hesitated. "My lady?"

This only seemed to make him angrier, and so I told her, "It's all right. Have someone show you to your room."

She slipped out, and I stood facing Kai alone. Most women probably would have found him handsome, with his young, clean-shaven face and long hair. I only saw a tall, strong man who didn't like me. Worse, I belonged to him. He could do anything he wanted and I couldn't stop him and no one would care.

For the first time since our wedding, I realized the full extent of my situation, and I was afraid. If only he had talked to me a little before now. But he hadn't. We'd barely exchanged a few words.

He didn't take his eyes from my face.

"You don't want me," he said. "Like all your kind, you look down on us. On me."

"That's not true."

"You do want me? Then say it. Say the words."

I couldn't say it. He was an angry stranger, and I was afraid of him.

At my silence, he whirled and left the room.

A flood of relief passed through me, but this was followed by a different kind of fear. What would happen now? I had no protector here, and my husband cared nothing for my welfare. In fact, he seemed to want me gone. Whatever I did, I couldn't allow myself to make any kind of mistake nor do anything for which I might be blamed. There would be no one to take my side.

Shivering, I crawled beneath the covers of the bed.

I was in a room surrounded by someone else's things. This wasn't my home, and the Volodanes weren't my family. I never thought to miss my parents, but at least I knew what they expected of me. I even missed Helena.

What would she have done in my place?

No doubt she'd have won Kai over by now, and he'd be on his knees, willing to kill or die for her.

I wasn't Helena, not even close. He didn't like me.

I was alone.

Tears leaked from my eyes and disappeared into the pillow.

* * * *

The next morning Miriam brought me water for washing, but I could see she was concerned when she entered the room, glancing at me furtively.

"Are you well, my lady?" she asked.

Was she worried Kai had brutalized me last night?

"Yes," I answered. "Perfectly well."

I didn't bother to elaborate. I didn't wish to share that my new husband had walked out the door only moments after he'd entered.

She pulled the yellow muslin gown from a chest.

"No," I said. "I'll wear my old blue wool. It's warmer."

It was a simple gown of blue-gray that had been washed too many times, but it was soft and fit me well. Kai couldn't care less how I was dressed or what I looked like, so why shouldn't I give myself this one comfort?

Once dressed, I had Miriam weave my hair into its usual thick braid and I pushed the new shorter strands behind my ears. I felt more like myself.

"I'm going down," I told Miriam. "Would you sort through the chests and put my gowns in the wardrobe?"

"Of course, my lady."

I left the room, headed down the passage, and then down the curving stairs of the tower. If Kai wouldn't treat me as his wife, my only task here was to try and put the aging keep in order. If I was to maintain any kind of value to the Volodanes, I couldn't make a mistake. I had to be successful, and yet I wasn't sure of my own power here. It seemed wise to attempt to neither understep nor overstep my bounds, and this would be a thin line to walk.

I decided to begin in the filthy main hall.

The first things I saw upon entering were Sebastian and Kai, standing by the table, eating the rest of the cheese from the previous night. The pack of spaniels wriggled at their feet.

Sebastian took in the sight of me and frowned in open disapproval. "Good gods, what are you wearing?"

I ignored the question.

Kai watched me walk in, but I had no idea what he was thinking. As always, he simply struck me as angry. He took a long drink of ale.

"Is that your breakfast?" I asked him.

He shrugged. "It'll do."

The last thing I wanted to do was disagree with him. At least he'd spoken to me. That was something.

The two women who'd brought this food the night before now came in seeking to gather the trays. Betty was short and plump. The other woman was tall and spindly. They both looked at my dress and hair in some confusion. I suddenly realized that I hardly appeared as the lady of the house.

"This is Matilda . . . my lady," Betty explained, motioning to her companion.

I nodded. "I would like this hall swept out, and I want the floor scrubbed. Then I'd like all the cobwebs swept down and the walls prepared for tapestries."

"My lady?" Betty asked, as if she hadn't heard me correctly.

I wavered. Was I allowed to give such orders? No one had explained the extent of my role here, and Kai's treatment had left me walking on eggshells.

Sebastian's face brightened. "Tapestries?"

"Yes. Mother sent four tapestries from storage in the manor."

Kai said nothing, but Sebastian turned to Betty and Matilda. "You heard your new lady."

At his urging, they sprang into action.

With the cleaning of the hall underway, I looked again at the remnants of breakfast and sighed. "I suppose I had better go and sort out the kitchen."

Sebastian stepped closer. "Shall I come with you? I fear the women in the kitchen are not as biddable as Betty and Matilda."

With all my heart, I wanted to jump at his offer. The thought of Sebastian's support was beyond tempting. But Kai was still watching me carefully. He seemed to be laboring under the impression that I despised him and everyone and everything here. Nothing I did or said would apparently dissuade him of this belief. I somehow had to show him that I considered this place my home, and that I would do my best here.

How could this be accomplished?

For now, I simply had to be sure to make no serious mistakes—that might anger Jarrod—while I figured out how to make some sort of peace with Kai. Once that happened, I hoped he would support me . . . that he would be on my side.

Though this seemed a dim hope, there was little choice but to press onward.

"Thank you," I told Sebastian. "I can speak to the cooks myself."

He shrugged.

Turning, I left the main hall and asked Betty directions to the kitchen. She was helpful enough and pointed down a passage leading west.

As I reached the end of the passage, I walked through the open archway into the kitchen, and there I found three women among the ovens and pots and pans. The eldest was quietly kneading bread on a table.

The other two women were barely past twenty, and they sat at a smaller, second table laughing and chatting with each other over mugs of steaming tea and plates of scrambled eggs with strawberries on the side.

The woman making bread saw me first and froze. Then the other two looked up. One of them was strikingly pretty with black hair, pale skin, and a smatter of freckles. The other one was somewhat stocky with reddish hair.

The pretty one nearly sneered at me as she took in my dress. The mild regret I'd felt upon greeting Betty and Matilda was nothing in comparison to what I felt now. I should have donned my yellow muslin gown and had Miriam pile up my hair.

"What do you want?" the pretty girl asked rudely.

"Lavonia!" the older woman gasped. "And Cora. This must be your new lady."

Lavonia's manner made me anxious. I was being tested. My mother would have dismissed the girl on the spot, but I was uncertain. Again, what were the breadth and limits of my power?

Instead of calling her on impertinent manner, I turned to the gentle elder woman making bread.

"What is your name?"

"Ester, my lady."

I nodded. "Ester, will that bread you're making be baked by midday?"

"Yes, my lady."

I spoke only to her. "When it's baked, could you please prepare trays with slices of fresh bread with butter, bowls of strawberries, boiled eggs, and several pots of tea? I'd like this carried up to the hall for any of the men who come in to eat."

"Yes, my lady."

"If they want anything, they'll send for it," Lavonia said.

I ignored her and continued speaking to Ester. "If there is ham in the larder for dinner tonight, I'd like you to serve ham with whatever vegetables are available. I'll have decanters sent in, and I'd like two decanters of red wine drawn from the casks." I paused. "I'll send Betty and Matilda right at dusk this evening."

"Yes, my lady."

I finally looked at Lavonia. "I trust you will be of help with this if you wish to keep your place in this house."

"Is that a threat?" Her face twisted with anger. "Lord Jarrod will hear of this!"

My stomach clenched, but I only nodded to her once as I swept from the room.

* * * *

By evening, I took a short break from my work to run upstairs and let Miriam lace me into a silk gown and pile up my hair. I wore the diamond pendant.

When I came back down, I looked the part of lady of the house.

Upon reaching the main hall, I heard masculine voices and walked in to find Jarrod, Rolf, Sebastian, and Kai all there. Jarrod and Rolf were both looking about the place in surprise at its transformation.

They seemed especially interested in the tapestries. I still didn't know what to make of Rolf. At first, he'd been openly stunned and angry when I hadn't chosen him, but I soon had a feeling that he loved Kai and didn't begrudge his youngest brother. After that, he'd been civil to me if not friendly.

"Dinner will be served shortly," I said from the archway.

All four men turned as I walked in. Kai took in my dress and hair, and though he glowered, he never stopped following me with his eyes.

"You approve of the changes?" I asked Jarrod.

He glanced at the properly set table and the nearest tapestry. "I do."

At that moment, Betty and Matilda came in carrying trays of sliced ham, roasted potatoes, peas, and two decanters of wine.

"Shall we sit down?" I suggested.

Jarrod shook his head as if amused. "I approve indeed." Then he looked to Kai. "Now I want a grandson."

Kai glanced away.

* * * *

That night, Miriam dressed me for bed and lingered in my room until I sent her off. I would have preferred her to stay, but I knew that wouldn't do.

I wondered if Kai would come, and I feared that he would come.

Time slipped past toward the mid of night.

He didn't come, and my fear shifted.

My husband didn't want me and cared nothing for me. Where would this lead?

What a foolish choice I'd made.

Chapter 15

As the weeks passed, I struggled to try and become the Lady of Volodane Hall.

With some regret, I retired my comfortable old blue wool and was not seen in it again. I had a part to play now, and if I wished to survive, I needed to look that part.

Almost before I knew it, I began to understand the rhythms of daily life here—at least to a point. Jarrod and Rolf were often out overseeing the land or running drills with the guards. Kai spent much of his time in training with a sword. Sebastian spent his time playing cards with the off-duty guards. Sometimes, he talked to me.

I knew I should be careful of seeming too partial to Sebastian, but he was the only one who spent any time with me, and he made me feel less alone. Whenever I was in the same room with Kai, he would follow me with his eyes, but he rarely spoke.

I wondered how much the rest of the household knew of the state of things between us.

To my fear and shame, this was partially answered one day when I'd gone outside to gather some lavender from the herb garden. I wanted to dry it and make a few sachets for my wardrobe. I was on my knees, cutting stems when I heard the sound of the back door opening and Jarrod walked outside, swiveling his head left and right. Looking straight ahead, he spotted me and strode over. As he wore a determined expression on his face, my stomach began to sink. He was looking for me. Had I done something wrong?

He reached me before I thought to stand, and this left me in an awkward position on my knees, being forced to look up at him from the ground.

"Why isn't Kai sleeping in your bed?" he demanded, asking the question as if the fault were entirely mine.

I could feel my face flushing. Who had told him this, and how could he speak of such things so openly?

Gathering my skirt, I stood with as much dignity as I could muster. "You'd have to ask him."

"I'm asking you."

Kai didn't like me and that was why he shunned my bed, but I had no intention of telling that to Jarrod. My position here was uncertain and precarious enough.

"I could not tell you," I managed to say. Beyond embarrassed, I tried to walk past him, to flee this conversation. "If you'll excuse me, I need to—"

His right hand shot out, and he grabbed my throat, his pointer finger and his thumb pressing into the soft area just below my jaw line. The pain was startling.

"Listen to me," he said. "Kai's like any young man. He's had his share of housemaids and village girls, so there's nothing wrong with him. I want a grandson, and I want one soon. You're pretty enough even if you are cold as ice. You get him into your bed, girl, do you hear me?"

He tightened his grip, and I winced, willing to say anything to make him stop. "Yes!"

After studying my face for a long moment, he let me go. "Get it done," he said.

Then he walked away with me watching after him in despair.

How could I possibly do what he asked?

* * * *

Pressing onward, with no idea how to change Kai's feelings toward me, I continued focusing on putting the keep in order.

I did my best with the house servants. Betty and Matilda were good workers and showed me due respect. I had no trouble with Ester either, but Lavonia and Cora both balked at the changes my arrival had wrought. They didn't like suddenly being expected to put out proper meals, especially my idea of an acceptable dinner.

I worried that Ester was doing too much of the work, and I wanted to dismiss Lavonia—who I saw as the main troublemaker—but I still feared making any sort of mistake or overstepping my bounds.

As things stood, if I did anything wrong and Jarrod blamed me, Kai wouldn't lift a finger on my behalf, and now I worried Jarrod might begin placing his desire for a grandson over his value of my family name and connections.

I wished desperately that my mother had taught me more about running a household.

Then . . . a few days later, Jarrod sought me out to tell me he'd arranged for a formal dinner, the first hosted here in many years. This was part of his plan to bring his family up in the world. He didn't mention his demands from out in the herb garden, but in regards to this upcoming dinner, I had no illusions about his expectations of me.

"Who's coming?" I asked.

"Lord Allemond Monvílle, his wife, and his brother. Their lands border our southern line, and I'm trying to buy a section of forest covered in oak. The timber alone is worth the purchase. Do you know him?"

"Yes."

"Good. Try to remember what dishes he likes, and what kind of wine. He's only coming to look down his nose at me."

I suspected Jarrod was probably right.

The household burst into activity. Matilda began cleaning madly. Miriam worked hard to create a gown for me. With Betty's help, I started sewing clothes for the men. Throwing caution to the wind, I even accepted Sebastian's help planning a menu, as he was particular about food and knew more of what might be available here in the north that we could serve.

We decided upon a first course of salmon with a white sauce.

All seemed to be in hand until mid-morning of the day of the dinner when Jarrod and Kai walked into the main hall where I was busy attempting to make some centerpieces from wildflowers. Kai appeared more quietly angry than usual.

"Is everything ready?" Jarrod asked. His voice had an edge.

I turned to face him. "Yes, I think so."

"It better be," he warned. "I want the Monvílles impressed by what they find here."

I wasn't certain anything would impress Lord Allemond, but I could at least make sure nothing went wrong. The salmon had just been delivered, and four large fish were in cold storage in the cellars.

Thinking on this, I was caught unawares when Jarrod said, "And you know I'll expect your help with this land deal. I want your best efforts."

As realization hit me, I couldn't draw breath. My father had told him. Then my shock began to fade. Of course, Father told him. How better to sweeten the deal? I had so much hoped to leave that part of my life behind.

The disappointment was crushing. Still, there was nothing for it now. Jarrod knew, and he'd use my ability every chance he had.

With a soft sigh, I was about to ask him whom he preferred me to focus on when Kai broke in.

"I don't see why we have to suffer through this at all."

Forgetting about me, Jarrod turned on him. "Don't you? Well, then it's a good thing you're not the eldest! If we're to gain Rolf a seat on the council, we have to match them tit for tat, and we can't have them looking down on us."

That was his goal? To gain Rolf a seat on the Council of Nobles? He was dreaming. New members were voted in by sitting members, and none of those men would ever vote for a Volodane.

Jarrod wasn't finished. He pointed at me. "That's where she comes in. Look at this place. Tablecloths. Tapestries. Porcelain dishes. Flowers on the table. Tonight, she'll help make us look like one of them, and that'll throw Allemond off his game. I'll secure this deal and show him who we are."

I kept silent. He'd only referenced my help with appearances.

Perhaps he didn't know about my ability. Perhaps my father hadn't wanted him to know. Had I been about to give myself away needlessly?

"I'm not saying I don't like the changes here," Kai answered. "I'm only saying we shouldn't have to play up to the likes of the Monvílles to gain Rolf a seat on the council. We shouldn't have to play up to anyone."

"Then you're a fool," Jarrod answered. "And that girl is wasted on you. She should have married Rolf."

Kai's body went tense, and I feared he might be about to say something he'd regret.

"Might I be excused?" I asked to draw Jarrod's attention. "I need to make sure your new clothing has been properly ironed."

"Mmmmm?" he asked absently. "Oh, yes. Off with you."

* * * *

As soon as Jarrod gave me leave, I fled from the hall and hurried down the passage toward the stairs to the tower. I wanted a few moments in my room. Kai didn't know it, but he'd done me a service by interrupting before I'd given myself away. Had Jarrod learned the truth, I'd have spent the remainder of his life reading anyone he doubted or wished to spy upon. From now on, I would guard my secret.

I made it only halfway to the entrance to the tower when Betty came trotting behind me. "My lady."

I stopped. "Yes?"

"Lavonia is asking for you in the kitchen. She says the fish has gone bad."

"Gone bad?"

"That's what she says, my lady."

To my surprise, Lavonia had actually volunteered to prepare and bake the salmon, leaving Ester free to focus on the sauces and other courses. But the salmon was to be the first, and therefore most important, course. I'd paid well for fish caught that very morning, and I'd checked them myself upon delivery.

Poor Betty appeared distraught.

"Don't worry," I told her. "I'll go and see about it now. I'm sure she's just being overcautious."

I wasn't sure of any such thing, but I turned around and headed west toward the kitchen. Upon arriving, I found it a busy place.

"Betty says there is a problem with the fish?" I asked, stepping through the archway.

Lavonia turned with her usual poorly hidden sneer. "They're spoilt. We can't use them."

Everyone stopped working and listened to us.

I shook my head. "That seems unlikely. I checked them myself upon delivery. Those fish were caught this morning."

"They're down in the cellar, in the coolest room," Lavonia said. "You want to come down with me to check them?"

Her eyes had narrowed and something in her voice caught my attention. My encounter with Jarrod and Kai had only reinforced my determination to leave a part of myself behind, to live a new life without invading the minds of others.

My father had also trained me to never read anyone without his express instructions. Doing so on my own would be the worst breach of rules imaginable. But this was a new world and I was living under new rules.

I couldn't be blamed for any mistakes with this dinner tonight. Even the thought terrified me. What would Jarrod do if every detail weren't perfect?

And in this moment, I had little doubt that Lavonia was up to something. Reaching out, I let my own thoughts sink into hers.

A flash of hatred hit me like a wall. She hated me with a passion. Her life had been easy before my arrival, and she saw me as the reason her life had changed for the worse. Then I saw an image, a plan of her leading me alone to check the fish. They would be the same fresh salmon I'd already checked.

But days ago, she'd bought four salmon from the son of a fishmonger, and she'd let them spoil in the sun. I saw an image in her mind of her preparing and sending out the spoiled salmon for tonight's dinner, and then in the aftermath, claiming she had warned me in front of all the kitchen staff, and that she'd shown me the spoiled fish, and I had insisted she serve it anyway.

She was going to ruin Jarrod's dinner party and blame me.

I pulled from her thoughts, frightened and yet uncertain what to do. To dismiss her, I would need proof, and even then, I may need one of the lords of the house to back me up.

"I'm sure the salmon are fine," I said. "I checked them myself. Please feel free to prepare them later."

She shrugged. "As you like."

Turning, I left the kitchen and headed for the front of the keep as a plan formed. I'd go to the barracks and find Sebastian. He was usually there this time of day playing cards. I'd show him the spoiled salmon out back of the hen house, and he would help me.

With purpose, I made my way out to the courtyard and across to the barracks. I'd never been here inside before, but the doors were open.

Stepping in, I found myself in a large room and then stopped at the sight awaiting me.

Tables had been pushed up against the walls, and about ten of the guards were watching two men in a sparring match. One of the men was a handsome young guard named Daveed. I only knew his name because he was a close friend of Sebastian.

The other man was Kai.

Daveed and Kai both used heavy wooden swords, as if playing a game, and indeed they did appear to be enjoying themselves. Kai was happy. Daveed swung at him over and over again, and Kai's body moved like water as he avoided being struck every time. Some of the guards were laughing at how easy he made this look.

I stood mesmerized, watching his grace and natural skill. Finally, he whirled like lighting and struck back, catching Daveed across the shoulder and knocking him sideways.

In that moment, Kai spotted me in the doorway, and he straightened. Unfortunately, Daveed didn't see me and thrust hard with his wooden sword, hitting Kai in the back and making him stumble forward.

I gasped, and all the men turned.

Sebastian was nowhere in sight.

"Oh, sorry," Daveed apologized to Kai.

As Kai caught his breath, he appeared confused regarding my presence here. "Megan?"

That was the first time he'd ever said my name.

My plan altered quickly. "Could you please help me with something?"

"Now?"

"Please."

After a brief hesitation, he tossed the wooden sword to a guard and came to join me. I didn't wait and hurried around the side of the keep toward the back, where the hen house and gardens were kept.

"Where are we going?" Kai asked.

It seemed so odd to be speaking with him like this, but I answered, "You'll see."

I led the way to the back of the hen house, right to where I'd seen the salmon in Lavonia's thoughts.

There they were, spoiling in the sun.

Pointing down, I said, "I've been worried Lavonia might be up to something to ruin your father's dinner, and I found these. I fear she intends to substitute them for the fresh ones I had delivered this morning."

His eyes widened. "What? Why?"

"So she could blame me. She's unhappy with some of the changes since my arrival. A short while ago, she called me in to ask me to inspect the salmon stored in the cellars. She did this in front of everyone there. Afterward, I came out here to look around, and I found these."

This last part was a weak explanation for my find, but he didn't notice.

"Did you dismiss her?" he asked.

"I have no proof. I wasn't certain what to do, so I went to find you."

"Wait here," he said.

With that, he walked through the garden and vanished inside through the back door. A few moments later, he came out again with Cora and led her through the garden.

"What is it you wish me to help you with, my lord?" Cora asked, sounding nervous.

Then she saw me.

Kai pointed down at the fish. "Did Lavonia put these here? Does she mean to serve them tonight?"

Cora's face went pale. "Oh . . ."

His mouth opened slightly. Until then, I'm not sure he'd believed me. "She did?"

Stricken, she didn't answer him.

He stepped closer. "Cora, tell me. This is important."

But he didn't sound threatening, and I got the feeling these two knew each other fairly well. They were about the same age.

"Oh . . . Kai, I'm so sorry," she said, using his given name. "I should have said something. I know I should have!"

"But why would she do this?"

Without speaking, Cora glanced at me with a guilty expression.

He shook his head in disbelief. "Inside," he ordered us both, and then he strode back toward the door.

We followed him to the kitchen. Ester was at a table rolling crusts for tarts. As we entered, Lavonia saw us coming.

"Lavonia, you're dismissed," Kai said. "You'll get a month's wages, but I want you out the front gates within the hour."

She was startled, even frightened for an instant, her gaze moving to Cora and back to him. Then her expression shifted back to its normal state of challenge. "You can't dismiss me. I'll go to your father."

"Is that what you want?" he asked. "Shall we go see him now? Should I show him those fish behind the hen house and tell him the story Cora told me? He'll do more than dismiss you."

In truth, Cora hadn't said much. I had. But his words silenced Lavonia as the weight her of situation began to sink in.

Kai turned to Ester. "I want her gone within the hour. You'll have to make due tonight without her."

A flash of relief crossed Ester's eyes. "Yes, my lord."

He nodded, glanced at me, and motioned to the doorway with his head. Then he walked from the kitchen and started up the passage toward the great hall. I followed. About halfway there, he stopped. We were alone.

"Why did you come to me with this?" he asked. "Why didn't you question Cora and dismiss Lavonia yourself?"

"Could I have dismissed her myself?"

"Of course. Why didn't you?"

The past weeks of fear and uncertainty and feeling completely unprotected all weighed down upon me and rushed back up. "Because I have no idea what I'm allowed to do!" I cried, not caring if anyone else heard. "And I'm afraid of doing something wrong! What would happen if I displeased your father? You dislike me so much you wouldn't care if he tossed me out the gates."

Kai stared down at me. Then he blinked several times.

"I don't dislike you," he said finally. He seemed on the verge of saying something else but shook his head. "Deal with the household staff as you see fit. My father couldn't care less what you do so long as everything runs smoothly. I thought you understood that."

Turning, he strode away, walking too quickly for me to follow.

But my feet felt stuck to the floor anyway. If I had full control of the staff, my world had just shifted—for the better. Even more, I kept hearing his words . . .

I don't dislike you.

* * * *

That evening, I headed for the dining hall at precisely the right moment.

Tonight, my hair hung loose with several strands in the front over my forehead and pinned up with a small jeweled clip. I wore kohl at the corners of my eyes and beet juice on my lips. My gown was burgundy silk with a v-neckline.

Stopping at the entrance to the hall, I looked in to take stock of what awaited me. All four Volodanes were there, wearing the new clothing Betty and I had made for them. Kai looked especially fine in a sleeveless black tunic.

The hall was clean and properly arranged. There were white cloths on the table along with porcelain plates, silver cutlery, and pewter goblets. The centerpieces added color.

My gaze drifted to the guests: Lord Allemond, his wife Rosamund, and his brother, Phillipe. Several of the Volodane guards stood discreetly near the walls, along with several of the Monvílles'.

With a deep breath, I stepped forward and entered the hall.

Allemond was the first one to see me, followed shortly by everyone else, but I couldn't help a stab of satisfaction at the flicker of uncertainty that passed over his face. "Megan?"

I smiled and held out one hand—as my mother would have done. "My lord. How lovely to see you."

Kai stared at me as well, taking in the sight of my v-neck dress and my hair.

Lady Rosamund showed nothing besides false pleasure, kissing my cheeks. "How nice it is to see you looking so . . . well, so soon after your marriage to the youngest of the Volodanes. We'd heard nothing of it at all until it was over."

This was a carefully worded barb about my hurried marriage and to suggest there had been speculation over the reasons, and of why I'd been passed off to the youngest of the three sons.

I pretended not to understand and beamed back at her. "Thank you. I am settling well into my new home."

Phillipe Monvílle leaned over and kissed my hand. "My dear," he said, although he'd never taken notice of me before.

Kai's body went stiff at the sight, and I worried he might ruin the dinner party. But he remained in place, and the moment passed.

"Shall we all sit and enjoy some wine before dinner?" I asked.

This was the signal for everyone to be seated. Wine was always served before dinner at these gatherings. Jarrod took his cue from me and sat at the head of the table. Normally, a hostess would alternate the men and women.

"The seating won't be proper," I said, smiling at Rosamund. "We are too outnumbered by the men and must do our best."

At this, her brow furrowed slightly, as if my easy countenance concerned her. "Yes, quite."

On the inside, I felt anything but calm. We all sat, and Lord Allemond examined the porcelain dishes and pewter goblets. He frowned at their fine quality and shifted in his chair.

It was clear that none of this was playing out as he'd expected.

Betty and Matilda poured wine from the best cask my parents had sent.

Not long after, the fish course arrived.

I was so nervous that I wasn't certain how much I could eat, but I tasted the salmon. It was perfect. Lord Allemond tasted it as well. He'd not expected the food to be perfect.

Glancing down the table, I could see Jarrod enjoying his guests' disappointment.

After that, as further courses were served, Sebastian took over the conversation. Neither Jarrod, Rolf, or Kai had anything to say to the Monvílles, but Sebastian was better at small talk and kept our guests entertained.

Kai appeared especially uncomfortable in the mix, and he looked over at me a good deal. I knew he didn't approve of this event—which he'd called "putting on a show."

He brightened only once when Phillipe spoke to him directly. "I'm sorry I didn't arrange any matches for entertainment here tonight. There wasn't time, but I've always been astonished watching you in the ring at Partheney."

I had no idea what he meant by "match" or "ring," but Kai actually smiled at him. "Thank you. Next time perhaps. We have plenty of room here."

Rolf entered the conversation to ask about their wheat crop.

By the time dessert arrived, nothing had gone wrong.

Then, just as we were finishing strawberry tarts with cream sauce, one of the Monvílle guards carried in a small harp. Watching this, Allemond frowned at his wife.

"Oh, my dear," she said, sounding strained. "I'd quite forgotten." She tried to smile. "It is a wedding gift. We've not heard Megan play in some time and hoped to impose upon her."

The Monvílles were then rewarded by the moment of discomfort on the part of the Volodanes. No one had told them I had often entertained my parents' guests with music.

Once again, the Monvílles had hoped to embarrass Jarrod, probably thinking that I would be too shattered to consider such a public display of myself.

Looking directly at Jarrod, I said, "Father, would you like me to play?"

I'd placed him back in control of the situation.

He nodded.

Standing, I went to the harp and settled myself, drawing upon the strings to test them. First, I played a lively, cheerful tune, and then I glanced over to see Kai staring at me.

When I finished, Phillipe called out, "Sing us a ballad. The one about the girl who drowns."

At this, Rolf and Kai glanced at each other in open surprise, as if uncertain this scene was playing out in their own hall.

When I began to sing, everyone fell silent. Even Betty and Matilda stopped moving. Though my voice would never fill a great room like this, I could carry a tune and hit the high notes with a pleasing sound.

Finishing the song, I allowed the final note to hang in the air. When I looked up, Kai still stared back at me, but I couldn't tell what he was thinking. Sebastian began to clap. The others joined him quickly.

"I think that might be enough music," Lady Rosamund said.

By way of answer, Jarrod stood. It was customary after dessert and entertainment for the guests to walk about a dining hall, sipping wine, looking at tapestries, and visiting with one another.

I also knew this was the time the men would conduct business. Jarrod, Rolf, Phillipe, and Allemond gathered by the hearth, standing as they spoke.

I had little interest in the land deal, so I walked about the hall with Lady Rosamund, discussing the tapestries. Sebastian came to join us, and Rosamund brightened at the sight of him, but this left Kai standing alone by table.

"Excuse me for a moment," I said to Lady Rosamund. She didn't appear displeased at being left with Sebastian.

I walked to Kai. His eyes were on me, as they so often were, but something was different now. Something had changed that afternoon when I'd had my outburst in the passage. He no longer seemed angry, only uncomfortable.

"Will you come join us?" I asked. "We're not discussing much of interest, but I do know the story of the tapestries. My grandmother told me."

The four tapestries depicted a trio of men hunting wolves in a series of forest scenes.

Wordlessly, Kai nodded and began to follow me. As we left the table, I heard Lord Allemond say, "My gamekeeper swears some of the trees have bark beetles. I haven't seen an issue, but with such rumors, it would be wise for both of us if you and Rolf come out and check for yourselves before money changes hands."

Jarrod answered. "The day after tomorrow?"

"Yes, I'm free that afternoon."

"All right then."

Kai and I joined Rosamund and Sebastian.

Pointing to the first tapestry, I began. "Many years ago, there was a winter so cold and harsh the deer began to die, and the wolves crept into villages, stealing small children when they could. Three men took it upon themselves to hunt the pack."

Rosamund appeared more interested in Sebastian than the story, but Kai listened closely.

We walked the hall from scene to scene, and I told the story of the hunters in the tapestries. Kai hung on my every word, sometimes looking at the rich images hanging on the walls.

Soon after, the party broke up, and I had Betty show our guests to their rooms.

After they left, Jarrod sized me up. "A good bargain indeed," he said.

Kai looked away as if embarrassed by his father.

* * * *

That night, in my room, once Miriam had left, I crawled beneath the covers and tried to sleep. I was tired and restless at the same time. I knew I should be glad the dinner had gone so well for Jarrod, but my mind kept going over the moments after we'd finished eating, when Kai had walked beside me, listening to the story I told.

For the first time, he'd seemed to almost welcome my company. Had I imagined this? Was he being polite for his father's sake?

I lay there in bed, trying to shut off my mind, but I couldn't.

Suddenly, I had to get up. I had to get out of this room and do something to help tire me enough that I might still my thoughts. I was in my nightgown, but by now, the rest of the household had gone to bed, so I put on my dressing gown and tied the sash around my waist.

Slipping from the room, I made my way down to the main floor. I decided to check the state of the hall and see that everything had been cleared away and readied for breakfast. I knew Betty and Matilda would have seen to this, but at least . . . it was something to do.

I needed to walk and think.

Passing through the archway of the hall, I was about to head for the table when I stopped cold.

Kai had pulled a chair up to the hearth and was sitting in front of it, alone, with one hand over his mouth. Either my sound or movement caught his attention because he glanced over and then stood up at the sight of me. He was still dressed in the same clothing, so I wondered if he'd even left the hall after dinner.

"Megan."

His eyes ran down my silk dressing gown. It was a soft shade of peach.

For a moment, I stood frozen, not sure what to do. But I couldn't very well walk back out, so I went to the hearth.

"I didn't mean to disturb you," I said. "I couldn't sleep."

He hadn't moved. "You aren't disturbing me." Neither of us spoke for the span of few breaths, and then he said, "My father was pleased with the dinner."

"I'm glad." Then I wondered if he wanted me gone, if he wanted to be alone, so I took a step backward. "Again, I'm sorry. I can see you want some peace."

As I started away, he said, "Wait." His voice sounded pained, almost panicked. "Do you want to go back to your room alone?" he asked. "Do you want to leave me here in peace?"

Why did he always have to be like this? He seemed to want something from me that I had no idea how to give. But deep inside, I knew this moment was critical, and in truth, the last thing I wanted was to go back to my room alone.

Looking him in the eyes, I answered, "No."

He closed the distance between us in one stride and caught the back of my head with his hand. The next thing I knew his mouth was pressing down on mine. He kissed me so hard it almost hurt. The act startled me so much my first instinct was to try and push him away, but that impulse passed.

He had me drawn up against himself, and I could feel the warmth of his body. The fierce pressure of his mouth changed when he opened it and slid his tongue between my teeth. I could feel his hunger and his urgency, and I found myself kissing him back.

He gasped and took hold of my head with both hands.

"Come upstairs with me," he whispered.

* * * *

The mid of night had passed before we were finally spent, and he still gripped me in his arms. Lying in my bed, we were both naked and sweat-soaked, and my mind reeled. No wonder my mother had told me nothing. How could she have explained?

How could anyone explain?

My lips were bruised, and my body was sore, but I wanted him to kiss me again. I wanted him to go on devouring me as he'd been doing for hours. I wanted to give back, as I'd been doing for hours.

How could I have known the joy and longing and need two people could feel for each other?

"I thought you didn't like me," I whispered in the dark.

"I thought you didn't want me."

I kissed his chest softly. "I want you."

He exhaled through his mouth and held me tighter.

Chapter 16

The next morning, I woke up in his arms with no idea what time it might be. I wondered if Miriam had been in, seen us, and slipped back out.

"Kai," I murmured. "We need to see the Monvilles off."

He opened his eyes and blinked at the sight of me, almost as if he couldn't believe I was there. Then he nodded. His clothes from the last night were in a wrinkled mess on the floor, and he pulled on his pants. "I'll meet you in the courtyard."

As he leaned over to kiss me, I hoped he wouldn't begin everything we'd done last night all over again because I wouldn't have the willpower to stop him. Thankfully, his own good sense prevailed, and after a quick kiss, he left my room.

Within moments, Miriam came and helped get me dressed. I could see she was dying to ask questions.

"A pleasant night, my lady?"

I couldn't help smiling. "Very pleasant."

She smiled back and said no more.

Once dressed, I went downstairs to learn from Betty that the Monvilles had already eaten breakfast and were making ready to leave. Hurrying to the courtyard, I found Jarrod, Rolf, Sebastian, and Kai all outside bidding the Monvilles farewell. Kai must have dressed quickly in his own room before coming down because he wore his usual long-sleeved wool shirt over his canvas pants.

"Do forgive me," I said to Lady Rosamund. "I fear I overslept."

"It's all right, my dear," she answered, her tone suggesting my behavior was anything but all right. "We didn't mind eating breakfast alone with no hostess."

I let her kiss my cheeks and watched her mount her horse. Oddly, I couldn't have cared less for her disapproval and found myself struggling to keep my eyes off Kai. Everything was different today. He loved me. He hadn't said it, but I knew.

Lord Allemond was surprisingly friendly to Jarrod and Rolf, complimenting Jarrod on the fine dinner.

Jarrod nodded as if such praise were expected.

"Tomorrow then?" Allemond asked.

"We'll meet you at the old hunting lodge in the north quarter," Jarrod answered.

"Good. I'm sure you'll find everything in order, but I think it's best you check for yourself."

With that, our guests rode out.

Only then did I allow myself to turn to Kai.

"I have a sparring session with Captain Marcel this morning," he said, "but we can do whatever you like this afternoon."

"Would you take me out riding on the land?"

I hadn't seen anything of the estate.

He nodded, seeming pleased by my request. Both Jarrod and Rolf were talking to each other and didn't hear this, but Sebastian did and raised an eyebrow at me. I ignored him and went back inside.

I was happy, already picturing myself riding beside Kai out on the land.

But first, I had to see to my own duties this morning and headed off to the kitchens for a task that would be expected of me, something my mother had always done the day after a banquet.

Along the way, I passed Betty and stopped her briefly. "Would you please find Miriam and send her to the kitchen?"

"Yes, my lady."

As I entered the kitchen, Ester smiled. "Was the meal last night to Lord Jarrod's liking?"

"It was perfect. Thank you so much." I looked at the other girls, including Cora. "And thank you. I know you all worked hard."

Cora had been watching me nervously, but she nodded at my words. I was glad of this, as it made me think she wanted to keep her position and that perhaps without Lavonia's influence, she might work out well.

Turning back to Ester, I asked, "So, how much food is left? How many of us will be needed to carry it down?"

She looked back at me in puzzlement. "Carry it down?"

"Yes, after a banquet, don't you take the leftovers down to the village for the poor?"

I realized that the Volodanes seldom held what might be considered a banquet, but surely they observed this custom over the winter holiday feasting.

"Oh, no, my lady," she answered, shaking her head. "The master wouldn't like that at all." She paused. "Did you ask Lord Kai?"

I hadn't, but yesterday, he'd given me complete control over the kitchen. Surely Jarrod wouldn't begrudge the poorest of the villagers a few leftovers? He'd wanted a proper lady of the keep. That was one reason he'd brought me here. It was my duty to follow through on what was expected of the mistress of a household like this one.

I thought on Kai's words to me.

Deal with the household staff as you see fit. My father couldn't care less what you do so long as everything runs smoothly.

"Pack up the leftovers. We're taking them down," I instructed. "Cora, you'll come with us." Once I'd given the order, Ester ceased her concerns and launched in. We packed up large baskets of sliced beef, cold chicken, fruit, tarts, and bread. We were nearly ready when Miriam walked in. Without even asking, she knew what was happening, as she and I had often accompanied my mother in the past. She began to help with the packing.

Part of my thoughts were still on the impending afternoon ride with Kai, but there was plenty of time for Ester, Cora, Miriam, and me to get down to the village, distribute the food, and then make it back before the midday meal.

Soon, we had eight baskets ready to go, and we each carried two.

The day was warm, so we decided to forgo our cloaks as we walked to the front gates with our burdens. I felt in charge for the first time since my arrival. Kai had given me a free hand, and I intended to use it.

Sebastian's friend, Daveed, was on duty at the gate. At the sight of him, Cora blushed a little. Daveed was quite striking with tan skin, blond hair, and nearly clear blue eyes.

He'd always been polite to me, and so I smiled at him. "Could you open the gate for us?"

Glancing at the baskets, he faltered in some confusion. "My lady?" He didn't make a move to open the gate. I believed it took two men anyway, as a heavy bar, the width of a tree trunk, had been positioned inside of iron brackets, and this had to be slid back for the gate to open.

I hoped he was not about to challenge me.

"We're bringing food to the village," I said as imperiously as I could.

Alarmed, his eyes scanned the courtyard, most likely for one of the Volodanes. "Have you asked Lord Jarrod or Kai for permission?"

"I don't need permission to leave my own home and walk into the village. Please do as I ask."

In theory, I had authority over him, and he knew it. Still concerned, he called to another guard, "Brandon! Come help me with the bar and then take my place on duty." He looked back to me. "I'll need to come with you. Lord Jarrod would have me hanged if I let you walk down there without a guard."

While I found this rather impertinent on his part, it also sounded sensible. My mother had always been quite safe in our home village with only a small gaggle of maids—and me—but I'd never been to Volodane Village and had only seen it briefly at dusk the night I arrived here.

"Very well," I answered.

Both men strained to slide the bar back, and the gate swung open.

The five of us passed through, and it closed behind us. I heard Brandon calling out for assistance, and a moment later, I heard the bar grinding back. Apparently, the Volodanes took no chances with their gate, even in broad daylight.

"Onward," I said, trying to sound cheerful.

Neither Ester, Cora, nor Daveed appeared cheerful, and I couldn't help wondering why, but Daveed reached out for one of my baskets.

"Let me," he said.

Since the baskets were heavy and I was the smallest of the women, I let him carry one of mine. Even though I'd been tired and damp the night I arrived, I remembered that the village wasn't far. Our party took a path down a hill, over one rise, and then down again.

The village came into view, and we closed the distance.

Dwellings spread out all around us. There were about fifty circular wattle and daub huts with thatched roofs, a few shops, a smithy, and a sturdy log dwelling that probably served as a common house. But in the daylight, I could see holes in many roofs and decay in the shops and dwellings.

At the sight of us, the nearest people began slipping away. The few I saw clearly were thin and dressed in rags.

Daveed set down his basket and kept so close to me I almost asked him to step away. I noticed his right hand hovering over the hilt of his sword.

"Do not draw that blade," I said. "I hardly think we're in danger from anyone here."

"Probably not," he answered, "but desperate people can be . . ." He didn't finish the sentence.

Miriam hadn't expressed any trepidation over our task until now, but she looked around at the state of the place in open dismay. "My lady," she said. "Perhaps he is right. We could simply leave the food?"

An old woman with a wrinkled face came from between two dwellings and stopped in surprise at the sight of us.

She made to leave again quickly, but I called out, "Please don't go. We've brought food."

Turning, she dropped her eyes to my basket.

"Could you bring any people in need to the common house?" I asked. This seemed a rather foolish statement since everyone here appeared to be in need. What could have happened to bring them so low? Why wasn't Jarrod doing anything to help?

The old woman slowly came up to me and looked down into my basket. "Are those strawberry tarts?" Her voice was stronger than I expected.

"Yes, we brought quite a few."

People began appearing again, slipping out from dwellings or between buildings, staring at our baskets. To my shame, I was glad for Daveed's presence. Then I chastised myself. These people deserved my help and pity, not my fear or judgment.

But then . . . as villagers began drawing closer, a different type of uncomfortable wave passed through me, something I couldn't stop. In addition to focusing on a single person and reading thoughts, I also had an unfortunate tendency to absorb strong emotions or sensations if enough people around me experienced the same feelings. Right now, all I could feel was fear, hunger, and despair.

I was determined to finish my task here.

"I am the new lady of the hall," I said, letting my voice carry. "Where I come from, after any sort of banquet or feast, we share the spoils with our people."

No one responded. All eyes were still on the baskets. The aura of despair leeched into me and became almost overwhelming. I fought it.

"Let us go to the common house," I said. "Where we can set up properly." Looking down at the old woman beside me, I asked, "Can you help keep order?"

"Yes."

"What is your name?"

"Opal." Then she called out, "Follow your lady."

Cora and Ester both appeared somewhat anxious, but we led the way to the common house.

Once inside, I oversaw the unpacking. "Beef over on that table and chicken over there. Tarts here, and bread last. We should have brought more bread."

No one ran at us or grabbed at the food. They stepped forward when their turn came and took what was offered. The hunger I felt from these people went deep. Daveed was wrong. They were beyond desperation. They had given up hope. The despair passed through me, sinking deeper and deeper inside me, until I found it difficult not to begin weeping.

I couldn't stop the flow of sensation or push it away.

Soon, I was struggling to breathe without effort. I'd never seen people in such a condition. I'd never felt such misery.

And still, I would not leave.

Opal helped to organize families, so that each family took a portion. Daveed appeared to forget about his sword, and he worked the bread table. I passed out portions of chicken. People shuffled through to accept what we'd brought. I saw a young mother of about eighteen with small boy. His arms were like twigs.

The despair inside me made it difficult to think.

All I could see was years ahead of suffering and hunger. The common room grew hazy, and my eyes were wet.

"My lady?" Miriam asked. "Are you well?"

I couldn't answer.

When all the food had been dolled out, the villagers began to leave. I'd been here too long. I had absorbed too much.

The room began to spin, and the floor rushed up.

Miriam called out, "Daveed!"

That was the last thing I remembered.

* * * *

When my eyes opened again, I had no idea where I was, but I seemed to be lying on a bed, and there were people rushing around me.

"Get that cold cloth!" Miriam called. "Where is Lord Kai?"

"Cora's fetching him," Ester answered.

I was in my room. Miriam and Ester were both with me.

Then I remembered where I'd just been, and all the despair of the village sank deeper inside me. I sobbed once.

"My lady," Miriam cried.

The door slammed open. "Where is she?" It was Kai's voice. A pause followed. "What happened to her?"

The next thing I knew, he was on the bed beside me, lifting me up against his chest.

"Megan."

I couldn't stop weeping and gripped his shirt. "They're so hungry," I whispered. "So sad. You have to help them."

"Who?"

The voices around me grew muted. I heard Kai making demands of Miriam, and then I heard him say, "The village? She went down to the village? Who let her out the gate?"

No one answered, and then he said, "We need to bring her out of this. Ester, have a bathtub brought in here and order buckets of heated water."

Again, the sounds grew hazy, but I heard activity and more people. Then I heard water splashing . . . and splashing.

"Get out," Kai ordered.

"But my lord . . ." Miriam said.

"Now!"

The sound of feet followed and the door closed. Kai stripped off my dress and my shift. He lifted me as if I weighed nothing, and the next thing I knew, he lowered me into warm water, almost hot. He splashed handfuls on my face, and I choked once or twice.

"Megan, can you hear me?"

My head began to clear. "Kai?"

Using his hands, he rubbed my arms hard.

My head cleared even more. "Stop," I whispered.

He stopped. His face was near to mine. I remembered everything from the moment I'd set off for the village until the floor had rushed up. Looking around, I saw that I was in my room.

"How did I get here?"

"I don't know," he answered tightly. "I don't know what happened. You were in the village? Why would you go there?"

Tears ran from my eyes again. "To bring them food from last night's dinner. They're so starved, Kai, so hopeless. I could feel it."

He grabbed a spare blanket off the bed and then lifted me out of the tub. "Try to stand." After wrapping me in the blanket, he whisked me off my feet again and went to the bed. This time, he sat with his back against the headboard and held me.

"Who let you out the gate?"

Something in his voice gave me pause, and I didn't answer the question. The overwhelming emotions of sorrow were fading, and exhaustion came in to take their place. I closed my eyes.

"I'm tired," I whispered.

* * * *

When I awoke again later, he was still sitting with his back against the headboard holding me. I sat up.

"Do you feel better?" he asked.

I didn't exactly feel better, but I was myself again. How long had I been sleeping? "What time is it?"

"Around mid-afternoon."

The ramifications of what I'd put him through began to sink in, and I expected him to start questioning me again. He didn't.

"Will you be all right resting on your own for a while?" he asked. "I need to go downstairs and see about a few things."

Embarrassed, I pulled away and lay down on the pillow. "Of course. I'm so sorry. I've never fainted in my life."

He didn't answer. Instead, he left the bed and walked to the door. "Rest."

Then he was gone.

I was still naked, but I was dry now and allowed myself to curl inside the blankets for a while, trying to make sense of the order of events. I remembered nothing from the moment I'd fainted to when I'd re-awakened. What had happened in between?

I'd get no answers in here.

Still feeling drained, I forced myself out of bed and found a clean shift and a gown that laced up the front. Not bothering to brush my hair, I left my room and made my way down the stairs.

When I reached the main passage, I heard Kai shouting in the great hall.

"Who opened the gate?"

He sounded so angry. Quickly but quietly, I went to one side of the archway and peered in. I didn't want him to see me. I wasn't up to facing his anger.

Inside, the hall, I saw Kai, Sebastian, Captain Marcel, Daveed, and several other of the house guards. Jarrod and Rolf weren't there. Captain Marcel looked uncomfortable, shifting weight between his feet as if this were the last place in the world he wanted to be.

"Who?" Kai repeated.

Daveed was pale. "I did, my lord, and I accompanied them down into the village."

I drew in a sharp breath as Kai strode over. I thought he might be about to spit out harsh words—on my account—but I was stunned when he drew back his fist and punched Daveed in the face hard enough to knock him off his feet.

"Kai!" Sebastian yelled, running forward and grabbing his younger brother, pinning Kai's arms to his sides. "Stop!"

Daveed was picking himself up off the floor, shaking his head to clear it.

"Stop this now," Sebastian said, still holding Kai. "From what I understand, Megan fainted down there, and Daveed was the one who carried her back up." He looked to Daveed. "Why did you open the gate?"

"She ordered it," Daveed answered. Blood flowed out the side of his mouth, and he wiped it with the back of one hand. "I didn't know if I could refuse."

"I was fifty feet away in the barn!" Kai shouted. "Could you not have come and asked me?" Then he tried to throw Sebastian off. "Let go."

Sebastian let go, but Kai seemed more in control now.

"Listen to me," he said to all the guards present. "No one is ever to open the gate for Lady Megan without my permission. Anyone who does will find himself out of work and looking elsewhere to sell his sword. Is that understood?"

"Yes, my lord," the men said in unison.

"Dismissed."

As the guards started for the archway, like a coward, I fled a short way down the passage and stepped into an open storage room to hide. I was embarrassed that Daveed had suffered on my account, and I wasn't ready to see him yet. Earlier today, I'd had no idea what result my actions would bring. I'd only wanted to follow a tradition.

As the footsteps of the men moved past me down the passage though, I began pondering other things. First, I owed a thanks to Daveed if he'd carried me all the way from the village to the keep . . . and he may have lost some teeth for his trouble.

Second, did Kai mean what he'd said? Was I only to ever be allowed out of the courtyard with his permission?

* * * *

That night at dinner, I wasn't sure what to expect. Would Jarrod and Rolf have heard of the day's events? Would I need to defend my actions? They'd been out on the land all day, checking fields for the impending harvest.

Nothing was said as we gathered, and I began to think they hadn't heard.

Kai was quiet and hadn't said much to me since the afternoon, and I wondered what he was thinking.

Sebastian was the last one to join us, and he poured himself a large goblet of wine upon sitting down.

"Pleasant day?" he asked Rolf sarcastically.

Those two didn't care for each other, but I had no idea why. I think perhaps they were simply very different people.

Rolf didn't bother to answer.

Only when Betty and Matilda came in carrying trays of food for our dinner did Jarrod frown. The women were serving ham and cheese pie.

"Where's the beef from last night?" he asked Betty. "Have some of that brought in."

I braced myself. "She can't. I took it down to the village this morning."

"You what?"

"And the chicken and the tarts," I added. "It is tradition. Among the noble families, after a feast or a banquet, the lady of the house is to take all leftovers to the nearest village and share them with the poor. I didn't realize your family didn't observe this custom."

"You gave it all the villagers?" he asked, incredulous.

"I only thought to follow noble customs. I should have asked you first."

He shook his head and turned to Kai. "And what did you do when learned of this?"

Kai's body was tense, and I knew he wanted this conversation to end. To my relief, Sebastian answered. "He punched one of the guards and threatened to dismiss any man who ever let her out the gate again."

At that, Jarrod laughed. "Good boy," he said to Kai.

Did he know how condescending he sounded?

Then he looked down at his dinner. Thankfully, he was fond of ham and cheese pie, and nothing more was said of my adventure.

* * * *

Later that night, right after Miriam finished dressing me for bed, Kai walked into the room, and I couldn't read his face.

I sent Miriam out.

It was too soon for me to question my husband about the order he'd given the guards. Picking that battle now would most likely only make things worse.

"I'm sorry for any trouble I caused today," I said instantly. "I only meant to follow a tradition my mother taught me."

"What made you faint?" he asked. "The condition of the villagers? Did the sight of them unsettle you so much?"

I couldn't tell him the truth. A part of me wanted to, but I feared where that might lead, and I was determined to keep some secrets to myself.

"I don't know," I answered. "But something must be done to help them."

He held up one hand. "That is my father and Rolf's domain. We can't interfere."

"But surely—"

"Megan!" he cut me off and sank down onto the bed. "Not now."

He looked weary, and I remembered how he'd tended to me earlier, bringing me back to myself and then holding me. I had no wish to trouble him further tonight.

Walking over, I stood in front of him. When he was sitting, I could look him in the eyes. I placed both my hands on the sides of his face, and he breathed in softly.

"Do you want me?" he whispered.

It struck me then that Kai only felt desire for women who equally wanted him. I wondered if all men were like that, but I doubted so.

Leaning in, I touched my mouth to his by way of answer.

Instantly, he took hold of my arms and pulled me down onto the bed beneath him. His mouth pressed down on my mine as it had last night, and his tongue entered my mouth with the same urgency. I could feel his strength and his weight.

I forgot everything else.

I wanted his hands on me. I wanted his mouth on me. Right now nothing else mattered.

Chapter 17

The following morning, Jarrod and Rolf prepared to ride out. Apparently, the night before last, at the dinner, they'd settled on a plan to meet Lord Allemond to inspect some trees in regards to the upcoming land deal. I remembered hearing them speak of something in this regard.

Kai, Sebastian, and I walked out to the courtyard with them. Ten of our guards were already mounted and waiting. Daveed was among them, sporting a bruise on his jaw.

Wearing their chain armor and swords, Jarrod and Rolf looked every inch the hardened men I thought them to be.

Jarrod swung up onto his horse, and I stood below him.

"Should we wait dinner for you or should I just have Ester keep something warm?" I asked.

"We're meeting in the north sector of his lands," he answered. "If we're not home by dinner, go ahead and eat."

I nodded and stepped back, but as I turned, I saw Sebastian standing beside Daveed's horse. He had one hand on the horse's shoulder, and Daveed was leaning down so they could speak without being overheard.

There was nothing unusual about this. I'd often seen Sebastian and Daveed in close conversation. I knew they were good friends. Yet now, something about the position of his hand caught my attention. It was so close to Daveed's leg, and I was struck by the feeling that Sebastian wanted to touch him.

I'd never noticed such things before, but Kai had awakened something in me. I knew how it felt to stand beside him and long to touch him. Every time I thought of what he and I had done with each other in the night, I longed to vanish with him into some private corner where no one could see us.

I recognized this same emotion on Sebastian's face. Then I shook the impression off. Young lords didn't feel such things for their house guards. I was becoming fanciful.

Finally, Sebastian stepped away. "I'll see you tonight," he said.

Rolf was watching them too.

Jarrod wheeled his horse and the entire contingent cantered toward the gate.

Kai, Sebastian, and I stood in the courtyard until they were out of sight.

"What shall we do with our day?" Sebastian asked. "How about a game of cards?"

I smiled. "You two play. I was lax yesterday, and I need to make sure Betty and Matilda have seen to cleaning the guest rooms."

* * * *

Not long past dusk, I met Sebastian and Kai in the great hall.

"Your father said we should go ahead and eat if they hadn't returned yet, so I've ordered dinner be brought in."

Sebastian smiled. "Dinner without Father and Rolf? What a treat."

The three of us sat down at the table. Betty carried a tray with baked trout and greens.

"Is there bread?" Kai asked.

"Yes, my lord. I'll fetch you some."

She had just turned away when a loud crashing sounded from somewhere at the front of the keep. It sounded as if the front doors had been opened hard and fast enough to slam against the walls.

"Sebastian!"

I knew the voice. It was Daveed. He was nearly screaming.

Kai bolted first, with Sebastian running after. I ran after them, down the passage for the front doors. We reached the open doors to find Daveed on his knees panting for breath. His head was bleeding from a wound, but he saw us coming.

"Kai . . ." he choked out. "Your father . . . get your father."

Kai ran past him as Sebastian skidded to a stop and dropped to his knees. "Daveed."

I hurried after Kai, thinking to find the contingent in the courtyard and learn what had happened. Only one lathered horse stood waiting, with Jarrod draped over its back. Other guards from the barracks were running out by now.

Kai got to Jarrod first. "Father!"

Reaching up, he struggled to lift Jarrod's prone form off the horse. Once he'd done this, he dropped down while holding his father in his arms. Jarrod was unconscious, his skin was nearly white, and there was an ugly slash across his stomach.

As the other guards reached us, several knelt to see if they could help Kai with Jarrod.

Captain Marcel swung his head left and right. "Where's Lord Rolf? Where are the rest of our men?"

"Get Lord Jarrod inside and into a bed," I said.

Kai's face had turned nearly as white as his father's. "Captain, take him. Do as your lady says and get him inside." He jumped up and ran back to the open doorway. "Daveed, where's Rolf?"

"I'm so sorry," Daveed said in open anguish. "He's gone. We were ambushed."

"Gone?" Sebastian repeated.

Several men came up behind us carrying Jarrod. I went with them to the tower and then up to Jarrod's room.

"Lay him on the bed," I said.

Jarrod's wound was still bleeding. Had it penetrated his stomach though, he'd already be dead.

"Send for water," I ordered Captain Marcel.

Kai, Sebastian, and Daveed entered the room.

"Sebastian, help me with this armor," I asked.

As he moved to assist me, Kai looked down at us.

"Daveed," he said. "What did you mean about Rolf? Where is he?"

Daveed wouldn't look at anyone, and he began speaking quietly. "Dead, back where he fell. Right as we rode up to the lodge to meet Lord Allemond, men came out of the trees . . . maybe thirty of them. We were outnumbered. They struck Rolf down first."

He went on to say that Jarrod had been injured, but not fallen off his horse. Daveed had jumped onto the horse and ridden fast before he could be stopped.

"I left everyone else behind," he said, his voice edged with pain and self-recrimination.

The room fell silent again, but now Kai was shaking.

"You did the right thing," I said to Daveed. "What else could you do? Had you not tried to save Lord Jarrod, you'd both be dead."

Daveed raised his eyes to me, but I'd only spoken the truth.

"It was Allemond?" Kai demanded. "He planned this?"

Daveed nodded. "Yes, he must have."

"Then he's dead! Captain, prepare the men! All of them. We'll attack tonight and burn Monville Hall to the ground."

"No," Sebastian broke in. "Captain, stand down. We can't attack the Monville estate. That place is a fortress, and with a wall high enough for archers."

"We can't sit here and do nothing!" Kai shouted. "They killed Rolf!"

Sebastian grabbed his shoulders. "I didn't say we'd do nothing."

Kai jerked away, lost in grief, but I suspected Sebastian was right. An open attack would only further injure the Volodanes.

Standing, I hurried to Kai. "I'll write to my father and tell him everything. When the council learns of this, Allemond will be punished."

Sebastian joined us. "Good. Kai, listen to her. She's right, and I won't allow any of our men to be killed in a futile attempt."

As he said this, I realized that with Rolf gone and Jarrod incapacitated, Sebastian was in charge of the keep.

I turned back toward Jarrod, whose eyes were still closed. "Everything else can wait. Is there a physician within riding distance?"

"Not that I know of," Sebastian answered.

"There's Abigail," Kai said, his voice still shaking. "I can ride and get her."

"No," Sebastian said flatly. "He wouldn't want that."

"Who's Abigail?" I asked.

"A wise woman from the village just beyond our own," Kai answered. "She's a skilled healer."

"She's a witch," Sebastian said, "and Father wouldn't want her touching him."

His words surprised me. At this point, we had to try anything.

"I'm going to see what's taking so long with the water," I said. "We need to clean the wound. Kai, would you come with me?"

He looked so defeated that for a moment, I wasn't sure he'd heard me. Then he followed me out into the passage. Once we were alone, I gripped his shirtsleeve.

"Is this Abigail a true healer?" I asked.

"Yes, I've seen her at work."

"How far away is she?"

His eyes settled on my face, and I had his full attention. "Two villages to the east, but the distance isn't far."

"Then ride and get her. Bring her here."

"Sebastian said no."

"He's wrong. If we don't do something, try something, your father will die."

As the youngest member of the Volodanes, perhaps Kai had lived so long under the shadow of doing as he was ordered that it had never occurred to him to disobey an order from his father or one of his brothers.

But now, as my words sank in, he nodded. "I'll hurry."

Then he was running down the passage for the stairs. Betty bustled past him, carrying a basin of warm water. She and I entered the room, and I set about cleaning Jarrod's wound.

Sebastian stood behind me, watching for a while, and then he looked around. "Where's Kai?"

"I sent him after Abigail."

"What?"

His tone held an edge of threat I'd never heard, but then again, I'd never crossed him before.

"We must try something. Kai cannot lose his brother and his father in the same night, and I know you don't want your father to die."

A flicker passed across his eyes, and I shivered. Did he wish for his father's death?

"I'll not let her bleed him further or use any leeches," he said.

I didn't answer. If she were a woman to employ such methods, Kai never would have suggested her name. He never would have ridden to fetch her.

"Daveed," I said. "Go and find Miriam and have her tend to your head. Then you should rest."

Sebastian nodded to him, and he went out. Shortly after this, Sebastian cleared the room of everyone but himself and me. Jarrod hadn't even twitched. His chest barely rising and falling was the only indication that he still lived.

"I'm sorry about Rolf," I said softly.

"I wish I could be," Sebastian answered.

Were they really so estranged that he couldn't even mourn his dead brother? It wouldn't be so for Kai. He had loved Rolf.

Time ticked by, and finally, I heard hurried footsteps out in the passage.

Kai ran in. "I've brought Abigail. We must let her try."

Someone entered behind him. She was not at all what I'd expected. In my mind, I'd pictured a crone, an old wise woman. But Abigail was perhaps thirty. She wore a faded red gown, and her thick brown hair hung loose down her back. She carried a bag in her hands.

I stood. "Thank you so much for coming. Will you come look at his wound?" I pitched my voice to show her the respect a healer deserved, and she came to join me.

Sebastian tensed, but glanced at Kai and said nothing.

Leaning down, Abigail spoke only to me as she probed Jarrod's wound. "The blade missed any organs, my lady, but we must stop the bleeding. He's lost so much already."

"How can we seal it?"

She opened her bag and removed several items. "I have thin fishing line and a small needle. I'll need to sew him up."

Looking up to Sebastian, I begged, "Please."

Emotions warred across his face. "And what if her tender ministrations kill him?"

Kai strode over. "He's more likely to die if we do nothing! Let her try."

With a sharp exhale, Sebastian stepped away.

I nodded to Abigail, and she began to work, threading the needle and starting at the left side of Jarrod's wound. She sewed carefully and slowly, and the process took some time. We were well into the night by the time she finished.

After tying off the thread, she drew a bottle from her bag. "I'll need a clean rag."

"What is that?" Sebastian asked.

Again, she spoke to me. "It's a mixture of ground garlic and ginger in vinegar. It must be applied to the wound three times a day to stave off infection."

I felt some of my tension easing. Kai had been right to ride out for this woman.

"Thank you," I said, grasping her hand. "We'll see that you are well paid." For the first time since seeing Jarrod in the courtyard, I began to hope that Kai would not lose his father. I brought a clean rag and Abigail showed me how to apply the mixture.

"Now, all we can do is wait," she said.

"Can you stay the night?" I asked. "We can arrange a guest room."

"Yes."

"What about you, Megan?" Kai said. "You must be tired."

"No, I'll sit with him."

He pulled a chair over near the bed and sat. "Me too."

"Oh, for the sake of the gods," Sebastian said, sighing and sinking down on the end of the bed. "Then I suppose it's a family vigil."

I hoped this was a front on his part, and that he was more worried about Jarrod than he let on.

* * * *

In the early hours of the morning, while Kai slept in his chair and Sebastian dozed at the end of the bed, Jarrod's eyes fluttered open, and he looked at me sitting beside him.

"Try not to move," I whispered. "You're badly hurt."

He watched me in confusion at first, and then I saw some cognition coming back into his face. He tried to speak and failed and tried again.

"Where's Rolf?" he got out.

I grasped his hand. "I'm so sorry."

* * * *

The following few days were difficult for us all.

Jarrod suffered from his wound while dealing with loss on several fronts. He had valued Rolf as a son and a companion. Those two had overseen the land and the harvests and made great plans for the future together.

With Rolf gone in an instant, what would become of Jarrod's plans?

His injury kept him in bed. I sat with him, fed him, and tended his wound.

Kai was angry and mourning and hungry for revenge. Sometimes, I felt that he was simply waiting for Jarrod to heal enough to announce a plan for vengeance upon Allemond Monvíle.

Sebastian seemed to struggle with both his obvious lack of mourning and his mixed feelings over his father's recovery. I understood him the least. He rarely came into Jarrod's room.

But on the second day, Kai was with me as I tried feeding his father some broth.

"I need to get out and check the west fields," Jarrod said, pushing away the spoon. "Make sure the men there are looking after the wheat and barley."

"Father, you can barely sit up," Kai argued. "You cannot leave that bed."

"The men need to know we're watching!"

"I'll ride out," Kai said.

"You?"

"Isn't Geraldo the leader of the nearest west village? He knows me, and I can make sure he knows I'm watching."

Jarrod leaned back and nodded slowly as if this idea had not occurred to him. "Good. Don't tell him what's happened. Just tell him you'll be helping to oversee the harvest this year."

"All right."

Kai leaned down and brushed my cheek with his lips before he left.

As the door closed behind him, I turned to Jarrod. "You need to stay calm and not move around so much or you'll tear your stitches."

"I'm not a child."

"No one is calling you a child. Now eat some of this broth."

That night near dinnertime, I went downstairs while he was resting and asked Betty to bring in our meal, but only Sebastian awaited me in the hall.

"Where's Kai?" he asked.

"Probably not back yet. I've gone ahead and told Betty to bring dinner."

"Back from where?"

At that moment, Kai strode in. He was dusty and slightly sunburned, but he also looked less angry than I'd seen him since Rolf's death.

"Where have you been?" Sebastian asked.

"Out in the west fields, but I think the wheat and barley are both in good shape. No signs of disease at all."

Sebastian went still. "Father sent you into the fields?"

"Well, he can't go himself."

A moment of silence followed, and then Betty entered carrying a large tray with a plate of roasted rabbit and potatoes. The three of us moved toward the table. Sebastian seemed troubled, possibly more than troubled, but I couldn't see why.

As we sat, he said, "I thought if Father didn't recover well enough to resume his duties, we might hire a land manager to take over for Rolf."

"A land manager?" Kai echoed, sounding appalled. "You know Father would never agree to that. We look after what's ours."

"And you will take Rolf's place collecting taxes?" Sebastian challenged.

Kai breathed in through his mouth. "If I have to."

"Could we not leave this for now?" I said, hoping to ease the tension. "Your father might make a full recovery, and then he can decide how he'll wish to proceed. Right now, the loss of Rolf is too fresh for any decisions."

Kai looked at me and nodded, but the rest of dinner was a strained affair.

I didn't know why Sebastian was so against Kai taking Rolf's place. If he wanted to be the one taking charge, riding the land, overseeing the crops, why he did not just say so? Kai had a generous heart and would gladly have shared those duties, even taken second place to his older brother. But Sebastian appeared to want no part in these tasks.

He simply didn't want Kai doing them either.

* * * *

Whether Sebastian liked it or not, Kai rode out every day. Sebastian never once offered to accompany him. At night, in bed, Kai would tell me of his adventures, of the people he met and the flocks or crops he checked.

"You sound as if you like the work?" I asked.

"I do. It makes me feel useful, and I like being out on the land, connecting with our people. I want to talk to Father about lowering taxes this year, maybe cutting them in half. We don't need the money, and our people need more of a chance to thrive."

"You're a good man."

By day, I sat with Jarrod. I wouldn't let him out of bed, but before long, he was able to sit up without tearing his stitches. When he was bored enough to begin snapping at me and finding fault with my every move, I brought in a deck of cards and Kai's chess set. We played for hours.

I'd brought some books from home, and I tried reading to him, but much of what I'd brought was history or philosophy, and he had little patience with either.

On the afternoon of the sixth day, I sat in a chair beside the bed, working on some embroidery as he slept.

"What is that?" he asked.

Raising my eyes, I saw that he was awake. The cloth in my hands was tightly held inside a small wooden frame, and I held it up for him to see. I was nearly done with a section of pink and yellow roses. "It's a pillow cover."

To my surprise, his expression softened. "I never thought to see a lady working on a such a dainty task in this house."

I hesitated. For so long, I'd wanted to ask about Kai's mother, but something had held me back. "Did your wife not embroider?" I asked carefully.

"Bridget?" He laughed and then winced. "She'd have thrown that out the window or used it to start a fire."

Setting my embroidery in my lap, I perked up with interest. "She didn't care to sew? What was she like?"

"She cared nothing for sewing or playing harps or reading history books or any such niceties. She was a big woman with thick wrists and strong shoulders, looked just like Rolf with long hair. She bowed to no one and argued with every word I said." His voice caught.

"You loved her."

"I did."

Again, I hesitated. "How did she die?"

"When Kai was born. I couldn't believe it at first. She birthed Rolf and Sebastian so easy they both nearly dropped out onto the floor. But Kai was turned rump down, and the midwife couldn't turn him proper. Bridget strained all night, and he finally came, she was torn something fierce. She died before dawn."

His eyes were far away, remembering a painful time in the past.

"Poor Bridget," I said. "And poor Kai, to grow up never having known his mother."

"Aye." Jarrod nodded and looked at me. "He feels things more deeply than the other two, takes after my own mother."

It seemed so odd to be talking like this with Jarrod. I had no idea he understood Kai so well.

"In his mind though," he went on, "I think Kai sees his mother as someone like you, small with fine manners who'd blow away in a strong wind."

"He would have loved her for exactly who she was."

"Aye," he said again. To my further surprise, he patted my hand. "You're a good girl. I was worried at first, but you've done well by Kai, given him more faith in himself, and you fit in here. The gods know how, but you do."

I was so moved by this I had no response. These were the first kind words I'd had from him.

His eyelids fluttered.

I stood. "You rest, and I'm going to get you some tea."

* * * *

The next day—day seven—he could no longer be kept in bed. Right after breakfast, he yelled at me to help him up.

"I can't support your weight," I answered. "You don't *move*, and I'll be right back."

After running downstairs, I caught Kai before he'd ridden out, and he helped his father down to the great hall so Jarrod could at least sit downstairs and have some company besides mine.

The first thing he did was order Betty to bring him "some real food," and she scrambled off.

A few of the guards came in to play cards with him, and this was a relief to me. He needed something to do. I'd watched his wound carefully, and it was knitting. I didn't think it would do him any harm to have a change of scene so long as he didn't try to stand on his own.

Sebastian watched all this with a cold expression. "So he's up and about, is he?"

"To a degree," I answered. "I may need you to help me get him back upstairs later."

"If he'll let me."

"Of course, he'll let you. Sebastian, sometimes, I don't know what you're thinking."

At that he flashed a smile. "And a good thing too."

For the following week, Jarrod grew a little stronger each day, to the point where he didn't need me every moment.

His period of convalescence continued to solidify some changes in the family dynamics. The guards began coming to Kai for instructions, and I had full control of the household, including the budget. I hired a laundry woman from the village, who was glad for the work.

One day, Kai surprised me by coming home for lunch and saying, "I still owe you an afternoon ride."

He was right. With everything that had happened, I'd been so needed at the keep, we never had gone out for the ride we'd planned. That seemed a long time ago now.

"What about your father?" I asked.

"He'll be fine. Betty and Miriam can look after him."

Excitement took hold. He had a horse saddled for me, and we rode out the gates. The day was fine, and the sun shone down. Kai took me south to the apple orchards. I could see his pride in the neat long rows of trees and the ripening fruit. For the first time, I felt the breadth of being a part of this estate, and I realized how small my world had become back at the keep.

"I should like to do this more," I said. "Perhaps I can come with you some days to meet the people who work the land?"

A part of me wondered how he would respond.

But he nodded instantly. "Of course. I'd like that too. I promise that many of our people live better than the ones in Volodane Village. I should like you to meet them."

In that moment, I loved him more than ever before. He wanted me to be a true part of his world.

A few days later, Jarrod began walking on his own. But this brought a different set of troubles. Now that he was healing, he reached a period of fresh mourning for Rolf.

At dinner one night, Kai asked, "Will we do anything to take revenge?"

I'd written to my father on the matter, but received no answer as of yet.

"Not openly," Jarrod answered. "I don't think we can." He was dour that evening. "There's a gathering in Partheney at the end of summer, and I'd hoped to bring Rolf, but now . . . now, we'll have to wait."

"What for what?" Sebastian asked.

Jarrod glanced at Kai, but said nothing. The mere motion of his eyes made me nervous. In his plans for the family's future, did he think to replace Rolf with Kai as a political figure? I wasn't sure Kai would agree.

The next day, a letter arrived for me. I hoped it was from my father—with an answer regarding actions being taken against Allemond Monville—but I didn't recognize the handwriting. I broke the seal and read:

My Dear Megan,

While I'd only recently heard of your marriage, I just this week learned of the death of your new brother. I send my deepest condolences. Allemond Monville is devastated by the tragedy, and he is still uncertain how the dispute broke out between his men and the Volodanes'.

Please take this invitation in the spirit with which it is meant.

Lord Henri and I are having a house gathering the week after next. I know you are in mourning, but Volodane Hall might seem a lonely place right now for you, Kai, Lord Jarrod, and Sebastian. Please do come and join us if you feel you can be comforted by companionship.

With warm regards,

Violette Cornett

I read the letter several times. Clearly, even after Rolf's death, the Cornetts believed the Volodane star might be on the rise. Violette was a friend of my parents, but she did not know me well enough to express such concern.

I wasn't sure how to interpret the invitation or some of the implied subtext.

Finally, I took it to Jarrod.

He read it and looked up. "So Monville is passing off the attack as a mysterious 'dispute' breaking out amongst our guards . . . with Rolf somehow caught in the middle?"

"It would seem so."

He shook his head angrily and read the note again. "How many nobles will attend this gathering?"

"Probably a good number."

"Then we should accept. Kai needs to take his place among them, to become familiar with them. It's a start."

"And Sebastian too."

His eyes were shifting back and forth as he thought. "Mmmmm? He can be useful at times, but he pleases himself and no one else. Most of the time, he's no good to me."

I thought this an unfair assessment of his now eldest son, but I said nothing.

"What if the Monvilles are there?" I asked.

"What of it?"

"Kai will attack Allemond on sight. You know he will."

Jarrod frowned as if this had never occurred to him. "I'll speak to him."

Chapter 18

The next week was a blur of activity as Miriam and I spent hours each day sewing new clothes for everyone, and I made packing lists.

Jarrod continued healing, but he walked slightly bent and ran out of breath quickly. I knew this both frustrated and worried him. What if he was never the same? I think he'd always taken his strength and health for granted. He nearly had a fit when he saw the gifts I'd had loaded into a wagon: casks of wine, fine tea, and early apples from the Volodane orchard.

"It's expected," I explained. "We can't arrive empty-handed."

Finally, the day of our departure arrived.

The Cornetts' estate was to the east of ours. We left in the morning with the expectation of arriving that same evening. Kai was unhappy at having been forced into this visit—thankfully, his ire was aimed at his father and not me—but his protests were more silent than verbal.

Sebastian relished the idea.

At my insistence, Jarrod rode up on the wagon's bench beside the driver, but he didn't argue much. I knew he'd never last the day on a horse.

Kai rode with the guards, and I rode beside Miriam, with Sebastian directly behind us. As Jarrod had gauged, we arrived in the early evening.

Even in the fading light, I could see the Cornetts' manor was large and exquisite, with a white-painted stucco façade and a stylish black front door. At the sight of it, Kai shifted uncomfortably in his saddle. He hated being put on display and forced to make small talk with nobles.

Upon dismounting, we were met by several servants and shown inside the manor. A tall woman in a starched white apron approached us in the entryway.

"My lord and lady and the other guests are dressing for dinner. I'll show you to your rooms." She paused and looked to me. "Is it acceptable for you and Lord Kai to share?"

"Yes. Thank you."

After this, we were shown to our various rooms where we changed into evening attire. Then we were shown back downstairs.

As we walked toward the back of the manor, I saw a large archway leading to a great dining chamber, and my stomach clenched. I could only make guesses as why we'd been invited, and I had little idea what awaited us.

Tonight, I wore a red velvet gown and Helena's diamond pendant.

As I entered the dining hall on Kai's arm, numerous heads turned. I judged there to be about forty people and focused my attention entirely on the smiling woman walking toward me.

"Megan, my dear," Lady Violette said, kissing both my cheeks.

She was beautiful, tiny and pale with black hair.

Her warm welcome felt sincere. I almost believed Violette was glad to see me and that we'd been friends before tonight.

She turned to Jarrod. "Please accept our sympathies for your loss."

He nodded as if unsure how to respond.

"I do hope you know you are among friends here," she went on. "Lord Henri and I should have invited you to visit long before now. It took Megan's marriage to your Kai to jog us into action, and I apologize."

"You needn't apologize," Sebastian answered. "We've not invited you to visit us either."

Taking in the sight of him, she smiled coyly and said, "Goodness, where have you been hiding?"

"As a tragic prisoner in our keep." He smiled back.

I could see right away that those two were kindred spirits. She took his arm and led him into the room. We followed.

Holding Kai's arm, I could feel his tension. The next few moments were a blur of greetings or introductions. I knew most everyone by name and face. My parents were not in attendance.

I couldn't help scanning the room to see everyone who'd been invited.

Lord Henri saw us and came over. He greeted Jarrod first and then turned to Kai. "So glad you're here. Did you bring your sword?"

"Yes."

These two actually seemed to know each other. As they fell into conversation, I decided to use the moment to slip over to Violette, where she was chatting away with Sebastian.

"Are the Monvilles here?" I asked her quietly.

She shook her head. "No, my dear. It's the oddest thing too. Lady Rosamund was the one who prompted me to invite you . . . of course I should have thought to do so on my own. I could tell she's fond of you and that she felt such pain over Rolf's death. They'd planned to be here, and then two days ago, I received a note with their excuses. Lord Allemond feels he cannot spare the time with the pending harvest. I've never known him to be so concerned so early in the season."

I nodded and glanced at Sebastian. He appeared to be absorbing Violette's words as well. Lady Rosamund had arranged for our invitation, and then the Monvilles decided to stay away? Did they fear reprisal? If so, why would Rosamund have us invited in the first place? It made no sense.

Looking over, I saw that Lord Henri had abandoned Kai and Jarrod, so I hurried back.

A few moments later, I introduced them both to Viscount Bretagne and his son, Richard. From memory, I believed these two men were less proud than some of the others, and my instincts were not wrong. Soon all four men were engaged in conversation—even Kai.

Lord Henri called us to dinner, and I was glad to sit and eat.

I was tired from the long day's ride and nearly winced when Lady Violette announced dancing after dinner. But it turned out to be a blessing, as I learned my husband rather enjoyed dancing, and the two of us were able to pass the rest of the evening in no one's company but our own, lost in the music and each other on the dance floor.

Finally, people began to drift away, and I felt it late enough to say our good nights.

With great relief, I finally found myself in bed beneath a down comforter and wrapped in Kai's arms.

"Was the night so awful?" I asked.

"No, but if Father seeks to place me on the Council of Nobles, he has a disappointment coming."

"Has he said anything to you?"

"He doesn't have to. I can see his mind working."

"What will you do if he asks?"

"I'll tell him no. I'd do almost anything for him. I'd die for him, but I've no mind for ruling matters of state. That was Rolf. I'm happy to spend the rest of my life riding our own lands, married to you, and raising our children. That's all I want."

This was the first time I'd heard him speak of children. Closing my eyes, I saw us in the apple orchard as a family, with a girl and a boy playing beside us. Still, this happy image faded when I thought on how Jarrod would react to Kai's refusal. The crisis was coming, and Kai would have to weather it as best he could.

"Lord Henri has organized some matches for tomorrow," Kai said. "And when he asked me, I told him I'd fight."

All other thoughts left my head. I sat up.

"Matches? Fighting?"

"You know. It won't be anything like a full tournament. Just a few matches for sport."

I stared at him.

"Megan," he said. "You do know what a tournament is?"

"Yes, of course, but men get injured in tournaments, even killed. What have you agreed to?"

I was terrified, and to my consternation, he pulled me back down against his chest. "It's nothing. Lord Henri just wants a few matches for amusement's sake, so his guests can make bets. We'll probably fight to only second or third blood, and no one's managed to cut me in years."

I tried to get my head around this. Matches for amusement? So that Lord Henri's guests could place bets?

"You'll be in no danger?"

"None at all."

My worry seemed to affect him in a more amorous way, and he tilted my head back so he could kiss my mouth.

I began kissing him back and forgot all about tomorrow.

* * * *

Everyone slept until midday and then spent time dressing, and in the mid-afternoon we gathered in the dining hall for a casual buffet-styled meal. As the afternoon waned, Henri Cornett walked to the archway and announced, "Shall we go below and watch a few matches?"

Kai looked down at me. "It's time."

No matter how much he had assured me last night, I didn't want him to do this, and yet he appeared to be looking forward to the afternoon's events.

I tried to smile at him.

Then I was swept along with Jarrod and Sebastian and the rest of the crowd. Within moments, I found myself in a stairwell leading downward. At the bottom of the stairs, I stepped out into a large underground chamber with no windows. Torches in brackets on the walls provided flickering light.

Rows of benches had been built in a circle all around the room, and standing on the top bench, I looked down into a pit on the floor below, about forty paces in circumference.

"An arena," Sebastian explained.

Kai left us, and I didn't see where he went, but Sebastian and Jarrod stepped downward over the benches to find a place nearer the front.

I followed, and we took our seats with me in the middle.

All around us, people began finding seats, chattering to each other. "Who's up first?" Sebastian asked.

"I didn't ask," Jarrod answered, "but they'll save Kai for the end."

There was a door at the back of the pit area below. That door opened and two men emerged. One of them was young Richard Bretagne and the other was a stranger, a stocky man in a leather hauberk.

Both carried swords.

"Who's the other man?" I whispered to Sebastian.

"Probably a mercenary," he answered. "Henri must have hired a few men for the day."

Standing, Lord Henri called, "Second blood!"

I didn't like this and wished the Cornetts had chosen some other form of entertainment.

Seeing my discomfort, Sebastian leaned closer. "Don't be worried. They'll only spar with each other, and no one aims for the face. The first man to strike a second cut on his opponent wins."

I nodded. "Kai told me some of this last night."

"Wait until you see him. He started competing at sixteen, and he's never lost a match."

He called out to Lord Henri. "Two silver pieces on Richard."

"Done," Henri called back.

Others around us began calling bets.

Not long after, the bout began. Richard was slender but quick. His opponent was larger, stronger, and a little slower. Richard made the first cut, but his opponent made the next two.

The small crowd cheered. It seemed most people had bet on Richard's opponent.

"Second blood!" Henri called.

Down in the pit, Richard smiled at his opponent, and the two men shook hands. This did help me to relax. It made the event feel more like a game.

Several matches followed, all between one of the nobles and a paid fighter or soldier Henri had hired. Each fight was similar to Richard's with a display of footwork and circling and swinging. One of the nobles won and then two of the mercenaries, but each match ended with the shaking of hands.

Sebastian lost at least five silvers. Jarrod never placed a bet.

Finally, I heard a few loud cheers and looked down to see Kai coming out the door and taking his place in the pit for the final match.

People in the crowd were pleased. It seemed quite a few of them had already seen Kai fight.

"No one will bet against him," Sebastian said in my ear. "This one is just for show."

Still, I couldn't help being nervous, and then I looked at Kai's opponent. He was tall with long arms. His head was shaved and beads of sweat ran down his temples. It wasn't warm down here. There was a sheen across his face, and his eyes were glazed. He gripped the hilt of his sword tightly.

"Something's wrong," I whispered to Jarrod. "You need to stop this."

He glanced down at me. "Quiet."

My anxiety began to grow as the two men on the floor began circling each other. This mercenary was different from the others.

"Please," I begged Sebastian. "We need to stop this."

"Don't fuss," he whispered back. "Kai will be fine."

He was wrong. So was Jarrod.

Kai was in danger. I knew it with every breath I took, but there was only one avenue open to me, and I had hoped never to use it again. After my one reading of Lavonia, I'd wanted so much to leave that part of my life behind.

As if to entertain the crowd, Kai flipped his sword once and caught it. People applauded and cheered.

Sweat ran down the mercenary's face, and I had no choice, not if I was to protect my husband. Focusing all my strength, I reached out for Kai's opponent's thoughts, and a wall of desperation hit me.

His thoughts and emotions rushed and swirled in my mind.

He was an ex-soldier who'd married, had children, and tried his hand at farming. A bad crop had forced him to borrow money at high interest. Another poor year had left him in dire straights. He and his family were about to be turned from their home to starve. Allemond Monville had offered to pay the entire debt and interest if he would kill Kai in the ring. This man had killed before, many times, and he'd agreed.

He believed he'd probably signed his own death warrant as well, but at least he would save his family.

I jerked away from his mind with only one thought. He was going to kill Kai.

In a flash, Kai moved fluidly inside this opponent's guard and nicked the man's shoulder.

The crowd cheered.

Without an instant's hesitation, I leaped from my seat and jumped down into the area with my skirts flying. People behind me gasped.

Neither of the men fighting saw me. They were too focused on each other.

As Kai continued moving past the man and was turning back, the mercenary abandoned all rules of the match and swung for Kai's face, slicing his cheek open. Unprepared for this, Kai stumbled, and the man swung downward, cutting through the back of his right knee.

"No!" Sebastian cried, jumping to his feet.

Kai fell backwards onto the floor of the pit. The man gripped the hilt of his sword with both hands just as I reached them. Throwing my body over Kai's, I held up one hand in instinctive defense and looked up to the mercenary.

At the sight of me, he froze.

Then his expression hardened and he raised the blade higher, ready to bring it down through us both. But it was too late. Guards had poured from the lower door, and one of the Cornetts' men reached us first. He rammed a knife into the side of the man's throat.

For a just a second, I thought I saw a flash of guilt pass across this guard's features, but then Sebastian reached me and dropped to his knees, and all of my attention turned to Kai.

His face was bleeding, and so was his leg. He writhed in pain.

"Help!" Sebastian shouted at Lord Henri. "We need help."

* * * *

The Cornetts were patrons to a physician who lived nearby, and Henri sent for him before we'd even moved Kai out of the arena. Watching my husband, as he was carried to our guest room, was one of the most difficult things I'd ever lived through. I believed Kai to have a high pain threshold, and he was in agony.

Upon, arriving, the physician took one look at him and pulled out a bottle of poppy syrup. He made Kai drink enough of it to put him to sleep. Then Kai's wounds had been dressed. The slash on his face would probably leave a scar, but no one was concerned with that.

Our fears were for his leg, and the physician could tell us little. He struck me as competent but not gentle or comforting.

"The main thing you need to guard against is infection," he said. "If it becomes infected, it will have to come off."

Jarrod looked as if he were about to be ill. "And if it doesn't?"

"Only time will tell how much use it will be," the physician said bluntly. "There are no bones broken, but the cut is deep and across the back of his knee. It might heal enough for him to put weight on it, but even if, he'll most likely always have a limp, and his days of sparring with swords are over."

Jarrod closed his eyes.

Not long after that, Lord Henri cleared the room to give us some peace. As he himself left, he said, "I will get to the bottom of this. You can be assured."

Then Jarrod, Sebastian, and I stood around Kai where he lay.

"What made you jump down into the ring?" Sebastian asked me. He must have been waiting to ask me this.

I couldn't tell him the truth. If Jarrod learned my secret, he'd be determined to exploit it.

"Something was wrong," I answered. "I could see it in that man's face. He was sweating, and I nearly needed a shawl."

"And that was enough to send you running in front of all those people? If you'd been wrong, you would have embarrassed Kai almost beyond forgiveness. You know how proud he is."

I looked away.

Sebastian sighed. "I'm sorry. You saved his life."

"But she didn't save his leg," Jarrod said bitterly.

For him, that was all that mattered right now. Kai was his last hope, and now Kai had been maimed.

"We still don't know what happened," Sebastian said, "Why would some mercenary try to kill Kai? I assume he was hired? But that blasted guard had to go and kill the only person who might have been able to give us answers."

By now, I'd had some time to think, to try and piece things together. I knew Allemond had hired the man—or perhaps coerced was a better term. It seemed the Monvílles had arranged for our invitation and then originally planned to attend the gathering. Perhaps Allemond had second-guessed this in the end and decided that after Rolf's recent death, another attack on the Volodanes might put him in the path of blame? If he weren't here, no one would think to blame him.

I thought on the fleeting guilt in the expression of the Cornett guard who'd killed Kai's attacker. Had Allemond arranged to pay him a sum he couldn't refuse? For Sebastian was right. If the mercenary had lived, he would have been tortured until he talked. Now, he was silenced forever.

"Who'd hire someone to kill Kai?" Jarrod asked. "Cornett?"

"No." Sebastian shook his head. "His outrage is genuine. I can tell the difference. That's what bothers me. I looked all around at faces and everyone was stunned."

At this, I saw a possible opportunity to at least give a warning. "Lady Rosamund asked for our invitation to this gathering, and the only noble who's ever made a move to harm us is Allemond Monvílle."

Jarrod's eyes met mine. "I've been thinking the same thing. We've no proof, but this could have been arranged."

I knew it had been.

We were all quiet for a while, and then Sebastian asked, "Father, once we get home, do you want me to handle it my way?"

Jarrod nodded.

"You'll have to give me a free hand."

Jarrod nodded again.

I had no idea what this meant.

* * * *

Near midnight, Sebastian ordered me to go to his guest room and sleep for a few hours. He promised to sit with Kai and come fetch me if my husband woke up.

Exhausted, I fell asleep, and light outside the window was just appearing when I opened my eyes. I'd remained dressed, so I rushed from the bed and hurried the few doors down the passage to the room I'd been sharing with Kai.

When I entered, Sebastian was sitting by the bed, leaning in, and talking to Kai, who was awake. Sebastian's face was troubled, and his voice was intense.

"Don't say that! It's not true."

Kai's face was hard and angry as he stared up at the ceiling.

As I entered, Sebastian stood. "Here's Megan. Maybe she can talk some sense into you."

Without another word, he swept of the room. Feeling cautious, uncertain what I'd walked into, I went to the chair and sat down, grasping Kai's hand. He didn't grasp back, nor did he take his eyes off the ceiling.

"Sebastian says the physician doesn't even know if I'll ever be able to put weight on my leg," he said.

"No, he said that time will tell."

"Same thing. I may not walk again."

He sounded as angry as the day I'd met him, almost like a stranger to me now, who'd come to know the other side of him.

"And you may," I said.

"He also told me you jumped down into the area, ran in, and threw yourself over me?"

He didn't remember? Maybe he'd been in too much shock and pain.

"Yes."

"You should have saved yourself the trouble. Then I'd be dead, and you'd be free. Now you're saddled with a cripple."

"Kai!" I couldn't help the exclamation. "How can you say that?"

"Because it's true."

My heart was breaking at his pain, and there was nothing I could say to help him.

"Get out, Megan," he ordered. "Send in a maid to nurse me if you must, but I can't have you in here."

"Kai . . .?"

"Out."

* * * *

We remained at the Cornetts for three days, and then Jarrod decided it was safe to take Kai home in the wagon. He had to be carried down on a door, and I knew how much the shame of this hurt him. He hadn't said another word to me.

Upon arriving home, we settled him in his room on the third floor of the tower.

"Betty can look after me," he said, lying in his bed and once more looking up at the ceiling.

"No, she will not," I answered. "I will."

"I don't want you in here."

"Well, that's unfortunate because you have no say in the matter."

Being home again gave me strength. There was nothing he could say or do there that would send me away. I fed him, nursed him, and changed his dressing, and made certain there was no sign of infection in his wound.

It closed up and began to heal.

Unlike when I was nursing Jarrod, Sebastian was eager to help with Kai, and this made things easier. After a week, he got Kai up on his feet and had him limp around the room, putting some weight on the leg.

At first, Kai was resentful of this to the point that I wanted to slap him, but the second time they tried it, he actually put some weight down. I could tell it hurt, but the leg held.

After this, he was encouraged and worked harder.

The next day, Sebastian came to me and said, "I'm leaving, and I may not be back until tomorrow."

Nonplussed, I asked, "Where are you going?" I didn't want him to leave. Not now.

He smiled. "Tell you when I get back." Leaning down, he kissed the side of my face. "Kai needs you. Just stay in the room with him."

Sebastian never expressed physical affection to me, and this worried me more than anything else.

That day, I had Kai lean on me as he practiced walking. He was doing better.

"Good," I said, trying not to struggle beneath his weight.

He didn't answer. He still wasn't speaking to me much, and at times, I struggled to remain patient with him. It was difficult to believe he was still angry with me for having saved his life, but this was the front he insisted upon showing.

I walked him around the room until he began growing tired, and then I led him back toward the bed. As he was getting settled, a knock sounded on the door.

"My lord?" a familiar voice said. "My lady?"

"Come in," I called.

The door opened and Daveed walked inside carrying a set of wooden crutches. "My father was a carpenter, and I've been working on these."

For the first time since his injury, Kai's face lit up. "Let me try them."

He was already tired, but I wasn't about to stop him. Daveed got him up and helped him arrange the crutches under his arms. Within moments, Kai was swinging himself around the room with no help.

"If you like," I said, "we could have a bedroom made up for you downstairs. That way, you'd have the run of the main floor, even the courtyard."

Though nothing really made him happy anymore, this idea appealed to him—enough that he let Daveed half carry him down the stairs. I had a room made up for him near the great hall, and Kai's world became a little wider.

That night, when dinnertime arrived, he swung into the hall on his crutches and Jarrod watched him coming.

"How's the leg?" Jarrod asked.

He'd been less helpful these past days, but I knew he was suffering inside. His own wound prevented him from being of much physical assistance, and he was hardly the type to give comfort or encouragement. He'd lost his eldest son, and now his youngest son's mobility was in question.

"I don't know," Kai answered honestly. "The pain is lessening. And thanks to Daveed, I can get around on my own." He looked around. "Where's Sebastian?"

"Gone out."

Jarrod didn't elaborate, but I had a feeling he knew exactly where Sebastian had gone. I couldn't help wondering. Sebastian rarely left the grounds of the keep.

We ate dinner, and Kai played a few games of chess with his father while I worked on some sewing. The evening felt almost normal, so much so that when Kai took up his crutches and announced he was going to bed, I walked with him to the room I'd had made up.

At the door, I touched his arm. "Should I stay? I'd like to."

The tone of my voice made my meaning clear. We'd not slept in the same bed since that first night at the Cornetts.

He turned away. "No. I'm . . . I'm better off sleeping alone."

After going inside, he closed the door. Standing outside, facing it, I wanted to weep. I'd felt alone at times in my life, but never this alone.

Had I lost him?

* * * *

The next day, Sebastian arrived home shortly following lunch. Kai had just gone to his room to rest.

As Sebastian walked into the great hall, I ordered food brought for him.

"Where were you?" I asked.

"Paying a call on Rosamund Monvílle," he answered. "The Monvílles were quite hospitable considering my unannounced arrival. They specifically asked after Kai. Wasn't that considerate of them?"

I nearly gasped and was glad Kai wasn't here. "The Monvílles?"

Jarrod looked Sebastian up and down. "Is it done?"

"Not yet, but soon."

"What do you mean?" Jarrod demanded. "What did you do?"

Sebastian shrugged. "Met a pretty kitchen maid and spent some time with the food stores."

Jarrod was quiet for a moment. "I hope you know what you're doing."

I wanted to know what was happening, but something in both their faces kept me from asking.

Later that afternoon, Kai went out into the courtyard on his crutches. I went out to watch over him, but the guards were glad to see him, and this made me step back. He didn't seem remotely embarrassed to be seen on his crutches. The only thing he couldn't stand was to be seen requiring help from anyone.

I was grateful to Daveed.

Over the next few days, this gratitude increased as I realized how important it was that Kai spend time outside with the guards. Captain Marcel had some influence over my young husband and had helped to train him in techniques with the sword.

"Use the crutches," the captain said, "but put some weight on that leg when you can. You'll need to strengthen it slowly."

He made it sound as if Kai was facing an injury like any other, something that needed only time and effort to heal. I think this did more for Kai's spirits than anything else. He began to work harder at his own recovery.

Two weeks following Sebastian's visit to the Monvílles, Captain Marcel came into the great hall as we were eating dinner. As he would never do this without a good reason, we fell silent.

"What's wrong?" Jarrod asked.

"Forgive me, my lord, but I've just heard some news, and I felt it couldn't wait."

We all looked at him with a mix of expectation and trepidation.

"Allemond Monvílle is dead," the captain said.

"Dead?" Kai repeated. "How do you know this?"

"A friend of mine . . . from my days in the king's army stopped by Monvílle Hall yesterday seeking work. He was refused, but while there, he learned that Lord Monvílle has been dead nearly two weeks, poisoned."

"Poisoned?" Jarrod echoed.

"Yes. Apparently, there was a cask of fine wine in the kitchen. It was his favorite though Lady Rosamund did not care for it. No one else was allowed to drink from his special stores. Someone laced the cask with hemlock. A kitchen maid was . . . questioned, but as of yet, no culprit has been named."

Jarrod glanced at Sebastian, who'd been silent during this exchange.

"Go on back to the barracks," Jarrod told Marcel.

The captain hesitated. "My lord?"

"What?"

"My friend . . . the man with the news, is still seeking work. May I hire him?"

"Yes," Jarrod said absently. "Give him a place here."

"Thank you."

As Captain Marcel left, Kai shook his head. "Poisoned. Someone cheated us of ever taking revenge."

"Did they?" Sebastian said, taking a bite of roast chicken. "Perhaps they did us all a favor."

Looking at him, I suddenly felt cold.

* * * *

Midsummer passed into late summer, and Kai reached a point where he could walk without his crutches. His limp was pronounced, and he had to keep much of his weight on his left leg. This created an awkward stride for him as he could only place weight on the right foot for a few seconds while quickly moving the left one forward.

But he was walking.

The slash on his face was little more than a red line now, and it would eventually turn into a white scar, but it didn't bother him. Captain Marcel once said it made him look battle-scarred. Kai almost smiled. I was ever grateful to the captain.

Though Kai was self-conscious about his limp, I think he could have come to terms with it had his father not watched him so carefully for improvement. At times, Jarrod winced when he saw Kai come into a room with his odd, step-drag-step manner of walking. This hurt Kai's confidence as much as Captain Marcel helped it.

Relations between my husband and myself had not improved. He was civil but nothing more.

One day, as the harvest was about to begin, he had a horse saddled, and he rode out the gate. I watched him go.

Up on the horse, he was capable of gripping with both knees and no one would even be aware of this injury.

Poor Jarrod was not so fortunate. As of yet, he still couldn't ride without causing pain to his abdomen. Up on a horse, he needed the muscles in his stomach, and they'd not healed properly.

When Kai came home that night, Jarrod and I were in the great hall by ourselves. Hearing the familiar sound of Kai's footsteps, I turned to see him come through the archway. Something was different. I could see it right away. He looked almost . . . happy. In addition to his need to be seen as utterly independent, he was a person who also needed an occupation. He needed to be useful. I loved that about him.

He'd spent the day out on the land, overseeing the workers and the impending harvest, and this alone had washed a way a good deal of his internal pain and self-doubt.

I smiled at him, and to my joy, he smiled back.

Then as he kept coming toward us on his step-drag-step-drag-step, his eyes turned to Jarrod and the color drained from his face.

Jarrod didn't smile nor watch Kai with pride. His expression was tight and strained.

"You rode out?" he asked, though we both knew he had.

"Yes," Kai answered uncertainly. "The wheat is ready to thresh."

"Did you stay on your horse?"

"No, not all the time. I needed to speak with some of the workers."

"So they saw you . . . like that?"

Kai's already pale face turned ashen, and I wanted to strike Jarrod. All of Kai's happiness was gone. He would have been grateful for the success of his day, with a promise of the future he'd wanted as a lord of the Volodane lands. But his father would never see him as anything but a limping cripple.

Nothing I did, nothing Captain Marcel did, could change this.

Early in Kai's recovery, an idea had come to me, but he'd been doing so well on his own I had not voiced my thoughts. Now, I realized that if I wished to save my husband, two things had to happen. First, I needed to get him away from his father, and second, I needed to help him heal his leg.

"My lord," I said, turning to Jarrod. "I have remembered something I wished to share with you."

His eyes were still on Kai. "Mmmmmm?"

"My mother has a cousin who lives on the west coast, near Avingion. I call him my uncle even though he is not. He and his wife own a line of fishing vessels, and my sister and I often spent time in the summers with their family."

Annoyed, Jarrod glanced at me. "And?"

"I remember an event where a first mate of one of the ships was badly injured by a whaling hook that cut into the back of his leg. The sand along that stretch of beach is deep, and once the wound was healed, my uncle had this man walk and walk in the sand to strengthen the leg. It worked."

Now, I had his full attention.

"What?" he asked, and then I could see him thinking. "That *could* work. If I send a fast horseman with a message ahead of you, would they welcome you on few days' notice?"

"Yes."

Kai limped closer, mortification turning to anger. "I can't go to the west coast. The crops are about to come in."

Jarrod motioned to his leg. "Fixing that is more important. If need be, I can take a wagon out to oversee the harvest and give Captain Marcel instructions for places I can't go."

"No. I'm not going to the coast."

"You'll go where I tell you."

"Into banishment until I can walk without a limp?"

"You're no good to me like that! What will the other nobles say when you come into a room dragging your leg like a cripple?"

Kai went silent. His father had not given up the dream of placing at least one son on the Council of Nobles. Worse, he was ashamed of Kai, embarrassed by him.

I felt ill. Yes, it seemed that I would be allowed to take Kai away from here, take him to the coast, but at what price? My husband's glare moved to me as if I were the cause of his banishment.

Chapter 19

Two days later, Kai and I left for Avingion. We took a small retinue of guards, but I left Miriam at home. I wanted as few people from the hall as possible. If Kai was to come back to himself, he needed a complete change of scene.

He didn't say a word to me for the entire journey, and we slept in separate rooms at inns along the way.

Jarrod had sent a rider ahead with a message to my uncle and aunt, informing them of our pending arrival, and in spite of Kai's anger, I couldn't help looking forward to the visit. My mother's cousin, Andre Calais, and his wife, Margaret, had been an important part of my childhood. They weren't really my parents' *type* of people, and my mother sometimes showed reticence in claiming Uncle Andre as kin. But Andre and Margaret had often invited Helena and me to visit during the months when my parents preferred to travel alone, and so they took advantage of the opportunity. Also, my uncle was well off financially and had been known to loan my father money without ever asking to be paid back.

None of this mattered to me. I'd loved spending time in the summers with them, sailing with Uncle Andre, running on the beaches, mending fishing nets, and looking for starfish. Helena spent much of her time in the kitchen with Aunt Margaret, enjoying the close companionship of a mother figure. The Calais family dynamics could not have been more different from our own.

As Kai and I and our guards rode up to their home, near dusk, a familiar sense of peace washed over me. The family lived in a large, six-bedroom stone cottage on the beach. It was whitewashed with weatherworn shutters, but to me, as a child, it had been the most welcoming place in the world.

Waves broke against the shore, and six long docks stretched out into the water. My uncle and aunt owned a small fleet of fishing vessels. Uncle Andre rented out most of the boats to other fishermen, but his favorite was a two-masted vessel called the *Iris*, and he was her captain.

Beside me, Kai looked all around, at the docks and back to the large cottage, but I couldn't tell what he was thinking.

The front door burst open, and a middle-aged woman came hurrying toward us. She was thin and small-boned, with a long braid of dark hair hanging down her back.

"Megan!"

I nearly jumped off my horse. "Aunt Margaret."

She clasped me in her arms. "I'm so sorry about Helena's death. We've only just learned of it and of your marriage. Your mother was remiss in writing to us. But we were glad to get your new father's message and hear that you were coming."

Looking up expectantly at Kai, she said, "You are most welcome here." He nodded stiffly.

She didn't appear to notice his cold reply. "Come inside both of you. Our men will see to your guards and your horses."

Just then, a man came out of the house. "Megan, my girl."

I couldn't help it. I ran to him, and he lifted me off the ground.

Uncle Andre had always struck me as larger-than-life. He had broad shoulders, weathered skin, and thick silver hair. He possessed a kind soul, but when he gave an order, people listened.

Kai was off his horse now, and he came toward us on his step-drag-step-drag-step stride. His expression was challenging, as if daring Uncle Andre to mention it.

Instead, Andre assessed him from his feet to his head.

"So, this is your young man," he said. "I hope he's good to you."

"He is," I assured. "Always."

Kai made no response, and Aunt Margaret ushered us inside the house. Within moments, we were surrounded. Andre and Margaret had three children who I'd always called my cousins. All three were grown now, with children of their own, and two of these cousins lived farther down the coast. However, my cousin, Emily, and her husband, Kieran, and their two children all lived with my aunt and uncle.

"Emily!" I cried, embracing her.

Everyone seemed to be babbling at once—all except for Kai. I knew he was probably overwhelmed in the moment but would grow accustomed to the bustle and noise.

"I've steamed a pile of crabs for our supper," Aunt Margaret said, "and made buttermilk biscuits. Megan, would you like a cup of wine? Kai, do you prefer tea or ale?"

My husband stood watching all of this without comment. By way of answer, he asked, "Is my room ready?"

Margaret blinked. "Yes . . . come this way. We only have one guest room at present, but it's on the ground floor, so you shouldn't have trouble."

I wondered how much Jarrod had told them in his letter. She seemed comfortable speaking to Kai about his limitations.

"Can you just direct me?" he asked.

"Of course, down this passage, second door on the right."

"Thank you. I won't take any dinner. Good night."

With that, he left the room, with me staring after him. I knew he was angry, but I'd expected him to at least eat dinner.

My uncle patted me on the shoulder. "Not to worry. He's proud. That's a good thing. I'll have him up early tomorrow, and we'll see how he does."

I had no idea what this last part meant, but I was ready to accept Andre's help. So far, I hadn't done well helping Kai on my own.

* * * *

After a quick supper, I went to join Kai in our room.

Whether he liked it or not, we'd have to share a room—and a bed—here. Upon slipping inside the door, I found him already in bed with his face to the wall. As I'd brought only dresses that laced up the front, I struggled out of my traveling gown and laid it over a chair. Instead of seeking a nightgown, I decided to sleep in my shift.

Then I crawled in beside him.

When I touched his back, he didn't respond.

"I'm sorry you're unhappy," I whispered.

I didn't expect him to answer, but he said, "I've been sent from my home, by my father, at your bidding. What did you expect?"

Sighing softly, I had no answer.

* * * *

The next morning, a loud knocking sounded on our door.

Without invitation, the door opened.

"Breakfast!" Uncle Andre called in. "We need to be on the *Iris* by dawn."

Kai sat up. "What?"

"Get dressed or we'll be late," Andre ordered him.

"I'm not going anywhere."

"Yes, you are. No one lives here for free. We all work. Megan will help tend the nets, and you'll help haul in the catch. Now, on your feet."

"No."

Andre didn't move. "You'll be on that boat with the rest of us, or I'll throw you out, write to your father, and tell him you were too lazy to pull your own weight."

He closed the door.

Kai was breathing hard. I hurried out of bed and grabbed a gown from a travel chest—my old blue wool. Within moments, I was dressed and out the door, leaving Kai to think a moment on his own.

As I hurried to the kitchen, I called, "Emily, can you braid my hair while I eat?"

Not long after, I heard a drag-step-drag-step coming toward us, and Kai entered the kitchen wearing his canvas pants and wool shirt.

"Good morning," my aunt said brightly, handing him a plate of scrambled eggs and toasted bread. "Eat up."

As Kai had had almost nothing the day before, I knew him well enough to know he'd be starving—and he liked scrambled eggs and toasted bread. I got him a mug of tea.

He ate.

After that, Uncle Andre, Kieran, Emily, Kai, and I headed down for the docks. Aunt Margaret stayed home with the children.

A saltwater breeze blew off the ocean, and I took in the air with pleasure. As we reached the *Iris*, I scrambled up the short plank from the dock leading to the deck. Kai came more slowly behind me, but he had no trouble.

"You ever been on a ship, lad?" Uncle Andre asked him.

"No," Kai answered. "I've only been to the coast when we visited Partheney so I could enter in the tournaments."

"You've fought in the Partheney tournaments?"

Kai nodded.

I found this line of conversation sad, but it was the most Kai had said in days, so I didn't discourage it.

Two sailors had been prepping the *Iris*, and we were ready to sail. Uncle Andre called it a boat, but it was really more of a small ship. As the vessel drifted from the dock, I wondered if Kai would become seasick. I was never troubled, and I liked being out on the water.

Emily's husband, Kieran, motioned to Kai. "Up here."

I'd only met him a few times. He was a slender, quiet man, but I knew enough to know that he made Emily happy. Kai joined him at the bow as the *Iris* picked up speed, and in spite of everything, I could see Kai's interest, his fascination with the sight of the prow cutting through the rushing waves.

Then Uncle Andre called to them, "You two, come grab this net."

A long, thick net had been laid out on the starboard side. Sections of it were attached to the rail.

Another pile of nets waited near the aftcastle, where one of the sailors was steering. Emily and I would spend our day going through those, checking for any breaks and mending them for when they would be needed.

Looking somewhat puzzled but not reticent, Kai came back to join Andre. "What do I do?"

"This is a drift net. Grab that end. We're going heave it over, let it run along the side of the ship for a while and then haul it back in."

Kai was openly interested now, and the sight made my heart race. Turning away, I focused on my own task.

The day began to slip past.

When Kai, Kieran, and Andre hauled in the net, the deck came alive with wriggling fish, and the men set to sorting them, throwing back what couldn't be sold or used. From the corner of my eye, I watched. Kai caught on quickly.

"Good," Uncle Andre said, nodding.

For lunch, Emily broke out a large basket Margaret had sent. We ate sliced apples and some delicious fried cakes made from cornmeal and cheese. Kai ate four of them, all the while asking Kieran and my uncle questions about the fishing process.

No one noticed his limp, and so neither did he.

Hope rose inside me.

In the afternoon, we headed back toward shore and made dock. Uncle Andre held back a large halibut, but turned the rest of our haul over to his sailors to sell to the fishmongers in Avingion.

As we started up the beach, Uncle Andre turned to Kai. "Try sinking your whole weight onto that leg in the sand. I had a first mate who'd taken a cut like yours, and he used the sand to heal himself."

I felt myself tense. This was the first time anyone had mentioned Kai's injury quite *that* bluntly. But Andre sounded a good deal like Captain Marcel, and Kai was not offended.

"How?" he asked. "Like this?"

Stepping forward, he placed his right foot firmly into the sand, shifting his weight as his foot sank slightly.

"Yes, good," Andre said. "Now, try to step as normally as you can with the left."

Kai tried to take a step. It was awkward, but the softness of the sand helped to ground his right leg, and I could see that the movement didn't pain him much.

"Keep that up," Andre said. "The leg will strengthen."

We arrived at the cottage, and the children ran out to greet us. Aunt Margaret came on their heels, taking the halibut from her husband. She kissed him. "How did things go?"

"Well," Andre answered. "Young Kai is a born fisherman."

For dinner, Margaret rolled pieces of the halibut in an egg batter and fried them in a cast iron pan. We had raspberries from the garden and roasted potatoes as well. Kai ate like man who'd put in a hard day's work, and he no longer seemed to mind the constant chatter all around him.

Later, once the dishes were done, we gathered in a sitting room for what the family called "story hour," where they took turns entertaining each other by telling stories. Aunt Margaret was the best at this, and she told a tale of a handsome lieutenant besotted with a haughty girl who spurned him. He befriended her handmaiden, with the hopes of learning secrets to win the haughty girl's heart . . . and ended up falling in love with the handmaiden.

As Margaret told this story, Kai leaned forward in his chair, and I remembered how much he'd liked hearing my story of the wolf hunters in the tapestries.

As Margaret finished, Kai looked about the room in a kind of wonder, and I realized he'd never known anything like this. His mother died the night he was born, and he'd grown up with a cold father and two brothers at each other's throats. He'd never known a loving family who enjoyed eating together and gathering like this in a parlor.

Not long after dark, Andre pronounced it to be bedtime.

I headed off to the guest room I shared with Kai, and a few moments later, he came inside and closed the door.

Had we only arrived last night?

Perhaps pressing my luck, I said, "I suggested bringing you here because I thought it would help. I never meant for you to feel as if you were being sent away."

"I know that."

Did he? If he'd known, why had he blamed me?

Unlacing my dress, I slipped out of it and stood there in my shift. He turned away, went to the bed, sat, and pulled off his boots. Lying down fully clothed, he started to roll over with his face to the wall again.

Going to him, I took his arm and tried to gently pull him toward me.

"Kai," I whispered, leaning in and touching my mouth to his.

Grabbing my shoulders, he held me away. "No," he said. "I won't have your pity."

"Pity?"

"You don't want me. How could you? You saved my life, so now you're saddled with me, but I won't ever ask anything more."

My long weeks of patience came to an end.

"Do you plan to make us spend the rest of our lives like this?" My voice was loud enough to be heard outside the room, and I didn't care. "To go on punishing both of us? You think I don't want you? I ache for you! I can barely stand to be in the room without touching you."

I took hold of his face, and he didn't push me away. His eyes were searching mine, and I leaned down, kissing him again. "I ache for you," I whispered.

To my wild relief, his hand was on the back of my head, and I felt the once-familiar pressure of his mouth on mine, almost hard enough to hurt but not quite.

He pushed me down beneath himself, and I reveled in the welcome feel of his weight and the careful strength in his hands.

"Kai."

* * * *

The days flowed past, one into the next. We spent most days on the water aboard the *Iris*. Sometimes, the men would take smaller boats and fish with long poles.

In the late afternoons, Kai and I walked the beach, so he could put more weight on his leg in the soft but heavy sand. Emily and Kieran often came with us, and occasionally, Uncle Andre.

One day, Kieran asked how the injury had happened, and Kai told him. Both Kieran and Emily's eyes widened at the story. Kai lived in a very different world from their own.

But after several weeks of this, I began to notice a marked improvement in his limp.

One morning, I woke up to realize we'd been living in the cottage for over a month, and autumn was setting in. When Kai arose to get dressed, he walked from our bed to his travel chest, and I barely noticed him favoring his right leg.

There was a chill in the air. Summer had ended.

After breakfast, as we all stepped outside, Uncle Andre smelled the breeze. "Everyone should bring coats today. The weather may turn."

Emily and I ran back inside to get all the coats.

That day, I think Uncle Andre simply wanted to be out on the sea. He told us not to bother with the nets and to enjoy the coming autumn.

Then he got out the largest fishing pole I'd ever seen. It was as thick as my wrist and sported a reel. When he stood by the rail and cast out the baited line, the pole stretched well out over the water. The line was almost as thick as twine

"This cooler weather is good for Scarlet-Fish to rise," he explained.

"Scarlet-Fish?" Kai asked.

"Great fish as long as a man, with red scales. I only caught one once, and he managed to pull the pole out of my hands."

"Are they a delicacy?"

"Gods no." Uncle Andre laughed. "Their flesh tastes like ash, but there are more than a few nobles and rich merchants willing to pay a small fortune to mount one on a wall."

Listening to this, I tried not to show disapproval. To me, it seemed a waste to kill such a creature only to use it as a wall decoration.

"What should I do today?" Kai asked.

Clearly, Uncle Andre was feeling lazy. "Go to the prow or the aftcastle with your wife and feel the wind in your face."

With a wry smile, Kai led me up to the aftcastle. Kieran was at the wheel. We joined him up there, and I stood in front of Kai. He wrapped his arms around me, and we both tilted our heads back to feel the sea wind in our faces as my uncle had suggested.

I'd never loved anyone as I loved Kai, and in that moment, there was no place in the world I would rather have been. The morning passed swiftly, and just before midday the sky began to darken.

Kieran looked up. "Andre?"

My uncle looked up as well. "Turn us about."

I knew he probably feared a storm coming, and it would be wise to head back in.

Watching Kieran turned the wheel, I wasn't paying attention to anything going on down below until I heard Uncle Andre call out, "Whoa!"

With no idea to whom he was speaking, I looked down to see him gripping his pole with all his might. A great flash of red leaped up out of the water and dove back down.

Andre was jerked against the rail, hanging onto the pole with both hands, knuckles turning white.

"Kai!" he shouted.

Without hesitation, Kai jumped off the aftcastle and landed on both feet. His right leg held him as firmly as his left when he landed, and he ran the few steps to Andre, reaching forward and grabbing the pole up above Andre's hands.

Both men heaved backward, and the muscles in Kai's arms strained against his wool shirt. Andre let Kai hold the brunt of the fight while he wildly cranked the wheel until he could reel no more.

The great fish in the water leaped up again. I'd never seen anything so bright red. It was worthy of its name.

Kai and Andre heaved again. Then Andre cranked the reel.

"Don't let it go!" Kieran called from the aftcastle.

I wasn't fully aware how long this went on, but everyone forgot about lunch. Andre and Kai alternated between heaving and reeling . . . heaving and reeling, until at last the Scarlet-Fish was directly below the rail in the water. The two sailors came running and positioned themselves one on each side of pole. They cast a net down and used it to pull the great fish over the rail.

I watched it flopping on the deck, gasping until it went still. Its crimson scales were bright in the dark day. It was a beautiful creature, longer than a man, with a ridged fin down its back. Again, I regretted that it had died only to become a trophy.

Panting, Kai dropped to his knees.

Andre dropped beside him. "If you can do that, lad, you can do anything."

At the look that washed over Kai's face, I forgot the fish. Kai believed Andre. So did I.

* * * *

That night in bed, Kai held me tightly and buried his face in the top of my hair. He'd been a little troubled all evening, and I wasn't sure why.

"What's wrong?" I asked. "Are you unhappy here?"

"No. You were right to bring us to this place, to these people. I've never known a life like this."

I understood him well enough to guess what he was thinking. "But you miss home?"

He nodded. "This is a good life, a good home. But it's someone else's life and someone else's home."

"Should I write to your father? Ask if we can come back?"

"I think so."

* * * *

The next day, we stayed at the cottage. Andre and Kieran had taken the Scarlet-Fish to be preserved somehow, so that it could be sold to a buyer who would mount it on a wall.

Kai and I walked the beach even though we didn't need to. He would always have a slight limp, but it was almost unnoticeable now.

We were just heading back when I looked ahead and saw a tall, familiar form walking toward us. Almost as if summoned, Jarrod Volodane had appeared. He stopped and watched us coming.

"Father," Kai said.

They'd not parted well, but Jarrod had come after us. Perhaps a month with no company besides Sebastian's had taken a toll.

"You're better," Jarrod said.

"Yes."

Knowing the strain needed to be broken, I hurried forward and grasp Jarrod's hand. "It's good to see you. We were just speaking of coming home."

"Were you?"

He sounded almost desperate. Had he been lonely?

But Kai wasn't ready to give in yet. He wanted to go home, but it seemed he wanted this on his own terms.

"Father, if we come with you now, you need to understand one thing. I will never, ever seek a seat on the Council of Nobles. That was Rolf, not me. I want no other life than to be your son and Megan's husband. I want to ride our lands and raise my children and never leave home except perhaps to come here on holiday. Can you accept that?"

I expected Jarrod to sag with disappointment, but he didn't. Maybe he'd known all along?

"Just come home," he said. "Both of you."

Chapter 20

After a barrage of thanks and good-byes and promises to return, we packed up and headed north. Jarrod rode a horse now, but it appeared he did so from pure pride as I could see his discomfort. He also walked slightly bent over, and I suspected he might never be the same.

My thoughts kept drifting to another matter though. Instead of riding a horse, I'd ask if I could sit on the wagon bench with the guard who was driving. I cited my preference for comfort, and Kai didn't find this odd.

However, my reasons were my own. I had a secret and didn't wish to tell him just yet.

The journey passed swiftly, and I was surprised when my heart lifted at the sight of Volodane Hall up on the rise ahead of us.

"Home," I said.

For better or worse, this decaying keep had become my home, and the men who lived there had become my family.

Once inside the courtyard, we left our horses and luggage to the guards, entered the keep, and made our way to the great hall. From the archway, I saw three people inside. Miriam was sitting quietly, working on some sewing. Sebastian and Daveed sat near her, playing a game of cards. There was a large pitcher and two wine goblets on the table.

"Miriam," I said.

Looking up, she broke into a smile and ran to me. I embraced her, thinking on how much she had been missed.

As Kai walked in, Sebastian watched. Kai's limp was barely there.

"Look at you," Sebastian said, closing the distance between them and clasping Kai in his arms.

"You're here," Kai said, patting his back. "I'd thought you'd be off to Rennes by now."

I wasn't sure what that meant, but the air suddenly felt thick with tension as Sebastian looked to Jarrod.

"Father felt it best that I stay," Sebastian answered, sounding bitter, with his words somewhat slurred.

"Are you drunk again?" Jarrod asked him.

"And I am glad to see you," Sebastian continued, still speaking to Kai as if Jarrod wasn't there. "But now that you're home, I hope to take my leave first thing in the morning."

Though I wasn't certain what was happening, Kai seemed to understand and turned to his father. "May Sebastian set off for his holiday to Rennes tomorrow?"

Jarrod's expression flattened. "Holiday? From what?"

Daveed kept his eyes on the floor.

Sebastian wasn't looking well. He was thin and pale with dark circles under his eyes, and Jarrod had just suggested he'd been drinking too much. Before leaving for the coast, I'd not given much thought to how these two would fare for a month or more here at the keep on their own, with no other company for dinner.

Perhaps I should have.

Whatever had happened, it had sent Jarrod running to fetch Kai and me home, and it seemed to have pushed Sebastian into an unhappy state.

"May I go?" Sebastian asked tightly, this time speaking to his father.

Jarrod stepped closer to him. "Off to Rennes, to drink and spend my money and do whatever you please. What have you done this year to warrant a holiday? You've done nothing!"

"Lady Rosamund Monville might not agree. I suspect she rather appreciates being a widow."

With his face going red, Jarrod stepped even closer. "When are you going start doing your part around here? Start seeing to the lands and crops like your brother."

"Do my part?" Sebastian exploded. "You want me riding out collecting taxes for you? That was Rolf's favorite pastime, being your bullyboy! Now you're trying to put Kai in his place, and he has such a good heart he'll do anything you ask. But I won't! I'm not your errand boy, and tomorrow, I'm leaving for Rennes."

Kai looked stricken at the things his father and brother were shouting at each other. I had a feeling this eruption may have been building the entire time we were away, and our return had ignited it.

Sebastian strode from the hall. Daveed got up quietly and followed.

"Father," Kai said. "Should I go after him?"

Jarrod ran a hand over his face. "Let him go."

Miriam reached out and grasped my fingers. "Are you hungry, my lady? I could have Ester put some supper together?"

"Yes, thank you."

Once she left, the three of us remaining stood in awkward silence. I could say nothing to heal the growing wound between Jarrod and Sebastian, nor could I put Kai at peace in this regard. Yet, I wanted to do something to make them both feel better.

I decided it was time.

"Before we eat," I said. "I have some happy news to share."

Kai was still shaken but turned to me. I wasn't sure Jarrod had heard the words.

"We're going to have a new addition next spring," I added, touching my stomach.

For the span of the few breaths, neither of them spoke.

Then Kai was at my side, looking down at my hand. "Is that why you wouldn't ride on the way home?"

I smiled at him.

"A grandson?" Jarrod finally spoke, and his expression altered to joy. He came to join us. "In the spring?"

"Or a granddaughter," I corrected.

"It'll be a boy," he said with great confidence. "The Volodanes breed sons."

Soon after, dinner came in and we sat down, speaking together of which room might make the best nursery, and Kai could barely contain his excitement.

Jarrod's painful argument with Sebastian seemed forgotten.

* * * *

That night, I was grateful to sleep in my own bed—with Kai beside me.

Exhausted from the journey, the family quarrel, and my revelation of news, we both fell asleep quickly, with my head on his arm.

I dreamed first of the sea, of riding high on the waves on Andre's boat, but this shifted to a vision of running and playing in the apple orchards here on Volodane lands. A little girl and a little boy chased me, all of us laughing as we ran.

The shouts of laughter shifted to angry shouting, and the shouts grew louder.

I sat up. Kai sat up beside me.

The shouting came from down the passage, two voices.

"Unnatural!" one came. "I knew it! Spawned from some darkness, not from me!"

Somehow, I was out of bed first, and I didn't bother throwing a dressing robe over my nightgown. I ran out the bedroom door with Kai behind me, wearing nothing but his underdrawers. I raced down the passage.

At the curve of the passage, outside of Sebastian's bedroom, I saw Jarrod. His features were twisted in rage.

"Unnatural!" he shouted.

Sebastian stood before him, seemingly naked but for a blanket wrapped around his waist and a dagger in his right hand. Looking beyond him, I saw Daveed inside the room, near the rumpled bed covers, naked too except for a pair of pants he held in front of himself. I didn't understand what was happening.

"And how would you know?" Sebastian challenged his father. "How would you know anything at all about me?"

Jarrod jerked a dagger from a sheath on his forearm. "I'll see you dead!"

But Sebastian's blade was at the ready, and I knew if anyone died here, it would be Jarrod.

"No!" I cried, running forward, between them, and trying to hold off Sebastian.

"Megan!" Kai yelled from behind me.

After that, things happened almost too quickly to follow. At the sight of me, Sebastian hesitated in his strike, but Jarrod couldn't stop himself from his rush forward and knocked me into Sebastian, who caught me.

The next thing I knew, Kai had a hold of his father, pinning Jarrod's arms to his sides, and shouting. "Father, stop! Sebastian, you stay there!"

Then he looked inside the room, probably still trying to reason out what was happening, and he saw Daveed. Something flickered across his face, and he held his father more tightly.

I pushed Sebastian backwards, and he let me.

"Close the door," I said quietly.

His dark eyes lowered to mine, and he reached out for the door, closing it with Kai, Jarrod, and me outside in the passage.

"Unnatural," Jarrod whispered.

"Don't say that," Kai answered. "Don't ever say that."

* * * *

Somehow, we got Jarrod to bed and decided to leave facing the aftermath in the morning.

Once back with Kai in my room, I tried to make sense of what I'd seen. "Does Sebastian love Daveed as you love me?" I asked.

"Yes."

I didn't know such things were possible. No one had ever told me.

"Does it make you think of less of him?" Kai asked.

I thought on that and shook my head. "Why should it? It's no business of ours who Sebastian chooses to love."

Kai pulled me into his arms. "I fear Father feels quite differently."

* * * *

The next morning, just as we were stirring, a soft knock sounded on our door. "Kai?" a voice asked from the other side.

After quickly pulling on his pants, Kai hurried to the door and opened it, letting Sebastian inside.

"Are you all right?" Kai asked.

Sebastian laughed without humor. "I've no idea how to answer that question."

I climbed from the bed and donned my dressing robe.

Watching me, he said, "You seem to have a penchant for saving my father."

I didn't answer.

He turned back to Kai. "I can't face him, not now, not ever. I can't stand to have him looking at me as if I have leprosy. You know I won't be able to stand it."

Kai wavered. "I know."

"I don't know what to do. I can't stay here, and my income depends on Father's grand generosity."

Kai seemed on the edge of suggesting something, but he asked, "Are you sure you and Father cannot find a way to live together?"

"And how would that work now? He'll dismiss Daveed before breakfast." His voice broke.

Kai sighed. "I was thinking about something last night. What if I talk him into giving you the house in Rennes, with a yearly stipend?"

"What? He'd never do that."

"He might. I hate to say this out loud... but I think he might want you gone as badly as you want to leave."

Sebastian's expression flickered between hope and pain. "You'd do that for me? You'd ask him."

Kai nodded. His eyes showed nothing but sorrow.

* * * *

Two days later, Sebastian and Daveed rode out for Rennes.

Kai had made all the arrangements with Jarrod himself. Sebastian was to own the house outright with a yearly stipend large enough to cover paying for servants and expenses.

It hurt Kai to see his brother ride off, but this was the best that could be managed, and we both knew it.

The family living at the hall now consisted of Jarrod, Kai, and me.

Kai took up his duties riding out over our lands, and sometimes, Jarrod went with him. As the months passed, and Jarrod's dependency on Kai grew stronger, Kai began expressing a voice of his own.

He managed to get his father to agree to cut back on taxes and to allow all the people living on Volodane lands to fish the streams freely, hunt game, and set snares.

I was proud of my husband.

One day, in midwinter, he asked me, "Are you happy?"

"Yes."

"Is there anything I could ever do for you?"

I had been waiting for this. "There is one thing."

"Name it."

"Lift your order that I'm not allowed to pass through the gate without your permission. No, don't look at me like that. I assure you that out of consideration, I would not leave without telling you my destination, but it troubles me that I *can't* leave without your orders to the guards. Do you understand?"

For a moment, I thought he might refuse, but then he nodded. "I'll lift the order."

That had been the only thing I wished.

The following spring, I gave birth to baby girl. Jarrod went into a sulk, but Kai was thrilled. We named her Bridget.

Soon after, I found Jarrod in the nursery, humming her a lullaby, and I didn't interrupt. I suspected he might be a better grandfather than a father.

Two years later, I had a boy. We named him Rolf.

As soon as Rolf could walk, we took both children to the apple orchard. I let them chase me around the trees, laughing, as Kai looked on. I saw peace and pride in his eyes.

I had my family, and I had love.

Chapter 21

The world around me vanished, and I found myself standing in the storage room of my parents' manor, staring into the three-tiered mirror.

I dropped to my knees.

Now, there were three reflections of the dark-haired woman as she gazed out at me from all three panels.

In a flash, I was hit by the full memories of all three lives I'd lived out with each brother . . . Rolf . . . Sebastian . . . Kai.

"Which one?" the woman asked. "Choose."

She wanted me to give an answer right now?

Struggling to take in breath, my mind raced. If I chose Rolf, Kai would die. If I chose Sebastian, Rolf and Jarrod would both die. If I chose Kai, Rolf would still die.

"Wait!" I cried. "Once I choose, will I still remember what I've seen?"

If so, I could alter events.

The woman shook her head. "The mirror offers a gift to you, not to others. You must make this choice for your own sake, and your sake alone. Once you have chosen, all the memories you have seen will be gone."

I closed my eyes in pain. I would remember nothing. I could save no one.

"Choose for yourself," she said. "This is a gift. Which of the paths do you most desire?"

Soon enough, even without her prompting, I would have to make a choice.

On my knees, I let the images from the mirror wash over me.

Rolf . . . he was so much more than he let most people see. With him, I would have deep respect. I would be valued. He would give me confidence and a belief in myself. I'd have power and influence over matters of state, and I could use this to help the people of our nation.

These things mattered to me.

Sebastian . . . with him I would know a much-needed feeling of safety and intimacy at first. I would depend on him and love him. This would dissolve into loneliness, sorrow, and self-doubt, but at the end of such pain, I'd receive a great gift: independence. I'd be able to live my life exactly as I pleased, with a home and money of my own. My thoughts flowed over the life that I'd carve out for myself, answering to no one. How long had I dreamed of this?

This mattered to me.

Kai . . . moody, prickly, passionate, unpredictable Kai. Life with him would often move between the heights of joy and the depths of despair. It would be messy and confusing and satisfying. Even here, in this cold storage room, I could still feel the pressure of his mouth on mine and the urgency of his touch. With him, I would have my children, my own family.

These things mattered to me.

In the end, the choice was really not so difficult, not as it had seemed at first.

"Kai."

The woman nodded. "The third choice."

The air before me wavered and the mirror vanished.

* * * *

Startled, I found myself on the floor of the storage room where I'd taken refuge. How long had I been in here? Had I fallen asleep?

Quickly, I rose, fearful that my mother would come looking for me at any moment, and I hurried from the storage room back to our dining hall, dreading what awaited me.

As I walked back in, I saw my mother conversing with Sebastian while my father spoke with Jarrod and Rolf.

Kai stood off by himself, uncomfortable and awkward, his long hair hiding half his face.

Suddenly I knew. Something inside me spoke his name, and just like that, I made up my mind.

"Kai," I whispered.

Read on for a preview of the next Dark Glass novel from *New York Times* bestselling author Barb Hendee...

A CHOICE OF CROWNS

Olivia Geroux knew her king was reluctant to marry her, whatever the negotiations had arranged. But she never expected to find handsome, arrogant King Rowan obsessed with his stepsister instead. Before she can determine what course to take, she overhears her greatest ally plotting to murder the princess. Olivia must act quickly—and live with whatever chaos results.

As the assassin hunts his prey, a magic mirror appears to show Olivia the three paths that open before her:

~ If she hesitates only a moment, the princess will die—and she will become queen.

~ If she calls for help, she will gain great power—but she must also thrust away her own happiness.

~ If she runs to stop the murder herself, she will know love and contentment—but her whole country will suffer.

As she lives out each path, her wits and courage will be tested as she fights to protect her people, her friends, and her heart. And deciding which to follow will be far from easy.

A CHOICE OF CROWNS

New York Times bestselling author Barb Hendee reveals a world of ruthless desire, courtly intrigue, and compassion as one woman shapes the fate of a nation.

Available in February 2018

Chapter 1

I've heard it said the most important moments in one's life pass more swiftly than others. Perhaps it's true.

I only know that all my senses were on alert as soon as my father sent for me, asking me to come to his private rooms. At the age of eighteen, I'd never once been invited to his rooms. In the past several weeks, he'd been closeted away much of his time, sending and receiving messages, but I had no idea what this was about—as he didn't see fit to share such intelligence with me.

Now . . . he wanted to see me, in his rooms?

I could hardly refuse, nor in fact did I want to. I was curious.

Gathering my long green skirt, I nodded curtly to the servant who'd delivered the message and made my way to the base of the east tower of our family keep. I knew exactly where his rooms were located, even if I never been inside.

Upon arriving, I stood with my back straight and knocked on the door. "Father? You sent for me."

"Come," he said from the other side.

With my hand shaking only slightly, I opened the door. Inside, I found a somewhat austere main room that appeared to be a study, with a large desk and chair. There were tapestries of forest scenes on the walls, and an interior door led to a bedroom.

My father, Hugh Géroux, sat behind his desk working on what appeared to be a letter, but he stood as I entered. In his early fifties, he still cut a striking figure, with a smooth-shaven face, dark peppered hair, and dark eyes.

"Olivia," he said, as if meeting me for the first time.

We didn't know each other well, as I was the fifth and youngest of his children. I had two older brothers and two older sisters, and my father had used all four of them carefully to enhance his own wealth and prestige. My mother died of a fever when I was only seven, so my father raised us alone in a manner that was both distant and overbearing at the same time.

My family, the line of Géroux, was among the old nobility of the kingdom. While past famines and civil wars had destroyed several of the ancient families, ours survived. We were survivors. My father respected strength and nothing else.

His eyes moved dispassionately from my feet to my face, as if assessing me.

I knew only too well what he saw. I was tall for a woman. He was tall, and I could almost look him directly in the eyes. Unfortunately, the current fashion for women was petite and fragile. My hair was long and thick, but it was a shade of burnished red, and again, red hair was not currently in fashion.

Still, I'd been raised to remain sharply aware of everything going on around me, and it was no secret that most men found me desirable. My face had often been called pretty, with clear skin and slanted eyes of green.

I looked best in green velvet.

Though I was not vain, I had also been raised to understand that survival was based on value, and at some point, I'd be given a chance to prove myself valuable.

Had that chance finally come?

"You'll need to pack tonight," he said. "You leave for Partheney in the morning."

In spite of my careful awareness of self-control, I nearly gasped. "Partheney?"

This was the king's city. My family's lands were in the in the southeast corner of the kingdom. Partheney was in the northwest, near the coast of the sea. I had never been there.

"You're to marry King Rowan," my father said flatly. "His mother, the dowager queen, and I have arranged it."

I stood still as his words began to sink in, but I still couldn't quite follow what he was trying to convey. "King Rowan . . . the dowager queen . . . is this why you've been receiving so many messages?"

His eyes flashed, and I dropped my gaze, cursing myself.

Father did not brook questions from his children. He expected only two things from us: strength and obedience. But the slight shaking in my hands grew to a tremble. Had I heard him correctly? I was to marry the king?

Stepping around the desk, he approached me. "Do you know anything of the rumors surrounding King Rowan?"

Unfortunately I did, hence the reason my hands trembled. Even here, in the isolated southeast, rumors still reached us. In his late twenties, Rowan de Blaise was a young king and had held the throne for only two years.

But over those two years, four betrothals with foreign princesses had been arranged via proxy. Envoys had been sent to Partheney to finalize negotiations. In all four cases, when the envoys arrived, Rowan refused to even see them. He'd sent them away.

"I know some of the stories," I answered my father. "I know betrothals have been arranged, and he's sent the envoys packing."

"Yes." My father nodded. "His mother, the dowager, was the one who arranged the betrothals. She is anxious to see him married and founding a line of heirs."

"Why will he not marry?"

My father waved one hand in the air. "That is of no matter. What matters is the dowager has decided to stop seeking a foreign princess and marry him into one of our own noble families. She's wise and has chosen the line of Géroux. We'll be linked to royalty, and I'll be the grandfather of kings."

The truth of all this hit me, and my hands ceased trembling.

I would be queen.

Clearly there were obstacles, but I allowed my initial worries to vanish and let my mind flow. Father expected complete success from himself and would expect nothing less of me. This thought made me brave.

"If Rowan has refused to even see the envoys," I began, "what makes you and the dowager think he will agree to entertain negotiations this time?"

My question was bold, but instead of growing angry, Father only looked at me as if I were simple—which I was not.

"Because as I said, you will leave in the morning," he answered. "I'm not sending envoys. I have no faith in envoys. I'm sending you. You'll go to the castle, meet the king, and handle negotiations yourself. You are a daughter of the Gérouxs. He cannot turn you away."

"You'll not come with me?"

"No. That was my first instinct, but the dowager believes it best if the king is given no choice in facing you directly. It will force him to be . . . polite." His expression darkened. "And you will not fail to secure him. Do you understand? You will not fail."

I met his eyes without flinching.

"I understand."

* * * *

Dinner that night was both strained and exciting. We sat in elegant clothes around a long table while our servants poured wine.

I allowed Father to deliver the news to my siblings—after the first course had been served. Silence followed for a long moment.

Inwardly, I triumphed at my sisters' mouths falling open.

"Olivia?" Margareta asked. "To marry King Rowan?"

She herself was married to a minor baron who'd not only forgone a dowry but also paid a fortune for the privilege of the marriage—in land. My father had long wanted a forty-square-league territory at the bottom of our own lands that boasted fine vineyards. Margareta was a shrewish woman who didn't care for her husband, but she'd married him all the same, as father had ordered it. Unfortunately, her husband soon grew tired of her and began bringing his mistresses to live at the family manor.

Margareta now spent much of here time here, citing that Father "needed her." He did not need her, but he didn't mind her presence so long she played the dutiful wife and gave the baron no reason to demand his land back.

Raising a goblet to his mouth, Father offered her measured stare. "Why not Olivia?"

"Because . . . because . . ." interrupted my other sister, Eleanor, "she is so young."

Eighteen was hardly considered young for noblewoman. I'd had female cousins married off as early as sixteen.

But—I shamefully admit—with some glee, I knew this news would come as a particular blow to Eleanor. At the age of twenty, she was engaged to marry a silver merchant. Father had arranged it. The man had no title, but his family was obscenely wealthy. Over the past months, Eleanor had been boasting to Margareta and me about the upcoming luxuries she would enjoy for the rest of her life.

As she stared daggers at me across the table, I could see the quiet fury in her face, and her thoughts were so open.

Why her and not me?

Both my sisters had inherited our father's dark hair and our mother's small size. They were considered fashionable and beautiful. I had inherited our mother's coloring and our father's height.

My brother George—the eldest—had also inherited our father's coloring. He swallowed a bite of roast beef. "Do you think Olivia can manage this?" George would inherit our lands and my father's title. He was calm and calculated, all mental gears and wheels and little heart. "I've met Rowan twice, and he struck me as rather intractable."

Father nodded. "She'll manage."

This turn in the conversation caused both my sisters' faces to light up.

"I've heard King Rowan prefers men," Margareta said, not bothering to hide her spite. "That may prove challenging."

I shrugged, speaking for the first time. "He'll still need to marry. The people expect it. The nobles expect it."

Her brown eyes flashed hatred at my cavalier reaction.

Eleanor leaned forward. "I've heard he's so possessive of his throne that he won't share it with anyone, not even a queen."

"That's not true," George answered without an ounce of passion. "He works well with the council of nobles. He's no tyrant. So long as Olivia makes no mistakes, she'll secure him. She'll have the support of the council and the dowager queen. They all want to see him wed. Olivia just needs to act wisely."

As these words left his mouth, a fraction of my confidence wavered. He and my father would both view any failure here as *my* failure, that *I* had made mistakes. Without meaning to, my gaze shifted to the empty chair at the table. This had belonged to my other brother, Henri. Of all my siblings, he might have been the only one to show me support, to perhaps offer comfort. But he wasn't here. Father had wanted him to rise high in the military, and he expressed a preference to study the arts of healing abroad. They'd argued.

In a cold rage, my father had purchased him a lieutenant's commission in the far north, in the cold, along the border, and sent him away. Henri hated the cold, but Father believed in punishing any act he viewed as dissent.

I could not forget this.

I could never forget this.

"She will succeed," Father said.

I nodded. "Of course."

Eleanor's jealous anger glowed off her face, but I met her eyes evenly. I couldn't wait to be queen and force her to kneel and kiss my skirts.

* * * *

The following morning, as the sun crested the horizon, I stood in the courtyard of our keep watching my trunks being packed into a wagon. I'd packed everything that mattered to me, as I had no plans to return.

No one from my family was present to see me off, but I hadn't expected anyone to rise early. There was no love lost between any of us, and it was pointless to pretend otherwise.

"We're almost ready, my lady," said Captain Reynaud, the head of my family's guard. He was in his late forties, of medium height and a solid build. His beard had gone gray, but his hair was still brown. He wore a wool shirt, chain armor, and the forest green tabard of the house of Géroux. He was loyal and steady, and I trusted him with my safety.

Father assigned him and nine other guards to escort me to Partheney. Captain Reynaud had made the journey several times with my father or George, and he knew the best routes for each time of the year. Thankfully, we were now in early summer and the roads should be dry.

I watched two of the men tying down my final trunk.

Another guard led my horse, Meesha, from the stable. She was a lovely creature of dappled gray. I'd decided that I would prefer to ride than to sit on the wagon's bench.

Walking over, I reached out to take her reins, and then I stroked her nose. The guard walked away to check the lashings on the back of the wagon.

"We have quite a journey ahead," I whispered to Meesha.

Yes, a long journey with an uncertain ending. I'd stayed up late in the night, talking to my brother, George, as I oversaw the packing of my belongings. Though he and I had seldom had reason to speak outside of the dinner table, he'd been only too willing to help prepare me.

Linking our family to royalty would open doors for him.

Still, he'd told me little that I hadn't known before. Father expected us all to be well informed.

George didn't know any more than anyone else as to why the young king was so reluctant to marry. A man in his position should have a legitimate child in the cradle by now. But Rowan's path to our throne had been unusual. When he was a boy, his father had been king of a small territory off our eastern border, known as the kingdom of Tircelan. His father died, leaving the queen, Genève, and their son, Rowan, at the mercy of a pack of ambitious nobles all vying for power.

Our own king, Eduard, was a widower with a small daughter named Ashton. Upon hearing of the death of the neighboring king, he rode to Tircelan to personally offer any needed assistance—as he feared possible upheaval or civil war so close to his own border.

But upon meeting Genève, Eduard fell in love. They married, and Tircelan was absorbed into our own much larger kingdom. Any initial resistance was stamped out quickly. This all occurred when Rowan was twelve and Ashton was two. Not long after, King Eduard formally adopted Rowan as his son.

Over the next fifteen years, the blended royal family became admired and loved by the people. Eduard was a good king, respected by the noble families for his attention to securing our borders while not over-taxing the commoners.

Then one night at dinner, he grabbed at his chest and died.

By right of blood and birth, Ashton should have taken the crown, but she was only seventeen—and a woman—and our council of twelve noblemen held a vote to crown Rowan as king. This vote passed unanimously. There was some surprise among the common people, but Rowan and Ashton had long been viewed as brother and sister . . . and he was the elder brother.

He was crowned without incident two years ago.

Now, he needed a queen. He needed to secure the line with heirs.

I had no intention of letting this chance slip through my fingers, not for any reason. No matter the obstacles, I would overcome them.

Footsteps sounded behind me, and I blinked at the sight of my father walking across the courtyard. Had he come to see me off? To kiss me good-bye?

The absurdity of either thought almost made me laugh.

What did he want?

Stopping a few paces away, he studied me again. This morning, I wore a gray cloak over a simple traveling gown. Even in summer, the nights and mornings could be cool.

"Daughter," he said.

"Yes, Father?" I responded dutifully.

"Lord Arullian has asked for your hand again."

Of all the things he might have said, this was not one I might have expected. Lord Arullian was a corrupt earl in his late fifties—rumored to be sadistic. He'd already had three wives. Two of them died under suspicious circumstances, and the last one killed herself by drinking poison.

Watching my father carefully, I said nothing.

"It would sadden me to see you in his hands," Father went on, "but the connection would be good for the family. Should you come home in failure, I see little choice but to accept his offer."

Though the morning was not overly cool, I shivered.

His threat was clear. I would succeed or he would make me suffer as Arullian's next wife.

"Yes, Father," I answered. "But I won't fail. The next time you see me will be to attend my wedding to King Rowan."

He smiled. "Of course. I have no doubt."

"We're all set, my lord," Captain Reynaud called. "Is Lady Olivia ready to leave?"

Stepping toward me, my father reached out. I took his hand, put my foot in the stirrup, and let him help me settle into Meesha's saddle. I could not remember him ever having touched me before.

"Good-bye, daughter," he said.

"Good-bye."

I looked around the courtyard at the keep. I would not miss this place. I hoped to never see it again.

My new home was the castle in Partheney.

ABOUT THE AUTHOR

Barb Hendee is the *New York Times* bestselling author of The Mist-Torn Witches series. She is the co-author (with husband J.C.) of the Noble Dead Saga. She holds a master's degree in composition/rhetoric from the University of Idaho and currently teaches writing for Umpqua Community College. She and J.C. live in a quirky two-level townhouse just south of Portland, Oregon.

Printed in the United States
by Baker & Taylor Publisher Services